# THE SEER

# Fatal Charm

## LINDA JOY SINGLETON

Llewellyn Publications
Woodbury, Minnesota

FIRST EDITION
First printing, 2007

Format by Steffani Sawyer
Cover design and illustration by Lisa Novak
Llewellyn is a registered trademark of Llewellyn Worldwide, Ltd.

**Library of Congress Cataloging-in-Publication Data**
Singleton, Linda Joy.
  Fatal charm / Linda Joy Singleton.—1st ed.
    p. cm.—(The seer ; 5)
  ISBN: 978-0-7387-1153-9
  [1. Psychic ability--Fiction. 2. Supernatural--Fiction. 3. Familyproblems--Fiction.]  I. Title.
  PZ7.S6177Fat 2007  [Fic]--dc22
                                        2007010672

Llewellyn Publications
A Division of Llewellyn Worldwide, Ltd.
2143 Wooddale Drive, Dept. 978-0-7387-1153-9
Woodbury, MN 55125-2989, U.S.A.
www.llewellyn.com

Printed in the United States of America

## To Write to the Author

If you wish to contact the author or would like more information about this book, please write to the author in care of Llewellyn Worldwide and we will forward your request. Both the author and publisher appreciate hearing from you and learning of your enjoyment of this book and how it has helped you. Llewellyn Worldwide cannot guarantee that every letter written to the author can be answered, but all will be forwarded. Please write to:

Linda Joy Singleton
⅍ Llewellyn Worldwide
2143 Wooddale Drive, Dept. 0-7387-1153-95
Woodbury, Minnesota 55125-2989, U.S.A.

Please enclose a self-addressed stamped envelope for reply, or $1.00 to cover costs. If outside U.S.A., enclose international postal reply coupon.

Many of Llewellyn's authors have websites with additional information and resources. For more information, please visit our website at www.llewellyn.com.

To Felicia Velasquez
for sharing her astral travels with me.

To Cassandra Whetstone for critique advice.

To Taylor and my cousins Courtney and Kadie.

And to all my wonderful fans
who asked for this book.

*Part One*

*Homecoming*

# 1

Is it wrong to hate someone simply because they were born? I wondered this as I spied on the thief who had stolen more than my face.

The gloomy gray morning suited my overcast mood. I'd gotten up early, skipping breakfast so that my empty stomach now growled at me. I hadn't wanted to drive here, yet felt drawn to this house like a fly to sticky paper.

I had to see the red-haired girl again. I'd never

spoken to her and knew little more than her name: Jade. I'd tried tuning into her psychically, but my roller-coaster emotions were short-circuiting my sixth sense, and I got nothing.

The logical part of my brain knew the girl hadn't done anything wrong, yet I hated her anyway and wanted to hurt her as deeply as she'd hurt me. She was my enemy—the half-sister secret my father had hidden until yesterday.

Slouched low in a dark jacket with my blond hair hidden beneath a cap, I peered out my car window at the yellow house fronted by an oversized brick planter. There were no flowers in the planter, only dead-looking weeds, and morning mist glistened each worn brick with dew, as if the house wept bloody tears.

I'd parked inconspicuously under the overgrown vines of a willow and hoped no one would notice one more car in a neighborhood jam-packed with vehicles on the curbs, driveways, and even lawns. I mean, there were five cars crammed in the yellow house's driveway.

Did one of them belong to Jade?

Leaning closer to my car window, I glimpsed her through sheer curtains as she moved in what I guessed was a living room. Golden light from a lamp sparked her red hair so it seemed to be on fire. She cupped a phone to her ear while gesturing with her free hand. I couldn't see her face from this distance, but her body language oozed drama, and I wondered what she was saying. Even more, I wondered if she was talking to him.

Our father.

It had been accidental—me finding out.

While Dad was driving me home (after a disturbing day that included betrayal, violence, and the police), his cell phone rang. I could tell by the furtive way Dad whispered and glanced over at me that something weird was going on, so I pretended to be asleep. But all pretence ended when Dad detoured to this house where he was greeted by a girl about my age and a woman I guessed was her mother. Except for the girl's red hair, she looked shockingly like me. But I was even more shocked when she wrapped her arms around my father and called him "Daddy!"

My first thought was that the girl had mistaken my father for someone else.

But I'd been the one mistaken.

About my father.

Afterwards, Dad drove me to a nearly deserted coffeehouse and we faced each other across a table.

Hurt and anger brewed with my hot tea, leaving a bad taste.

"Don't look at me that way, Sabine. Let me explain. Please," my father had said in a quiet, pained voice that would usually sway me.

But I was stone, sipping hot bitterness.

Still I couldn't help but listen as he talked.

He explained that he'd met Crystal at the casino where she worked as a dealer before he married my mother. Crystal was beautiful, wild, and unpredictable, unlike the proper, pedigreed girls he usually dated. He thought he was in love and asked her to marry him. They were engaged for only a few weeks when she jilted him for a wealthy older man. Dad was heartbroken, but got over her quickly and went on to marry my mother. I was born a year later.

He hadn't even known Crystal had a child, not until her husband died four years ago, owing so many creditors that his wife and daughter were bankrupt. That's when Crystal sought out my father and introduced him to thirteen-year-old Jade: his eldest daughter.

"Jade's resemblance to you left no doubt she was mine." My father sighed deeply, his hands folded around the coffee cup as if clinging to a life preserver. "She's missed out on so much. I couldn't make up for the lost years, but since then I've done my best to be a supportive father."

"But what about us?" I asked softly. "Your real family?"

"You haven't lacked for anything."

"Except you."

He closed his eyes as if I was the sun and looking too closely would steal his sight. And he said nothing. This lawyer father I'd idolized my whole life and who could sway a jury with skilled eloquence offered no words in his own defense, only slumped his shoulders with the grim acceptance of my guilty verdict.

A waitress came over with a coffeepot, refilled Dad's cup, and asked me if I wanted more tea. I shook my head, my gaze fixed on Dad, not looking up. When she turned to the next table, I asked softly, "Does Mom know?"

"No. And I'd prefer it remained that way."

"You want me to lie for you?"

"I hope you'll respect my privacy."

"What do you know about respect?" My hands tightened around my teacup, and I was tempted to fling more than words in his face. I thought how his face lit up when he described "wild and unpredictable" Crystal. Add to that the growing tension between my parents and all the nights Dad was "working late."

Ohmygod! This was about more than Dad discovering another daughter. He'd fallen in love with Crystal again and was cheating on my mother. It all made sense. The next step would be divorce—which would rip apart my family. My younger sisters, Amy and Ashley, would be devastated.

"This hasn't been easy," Dad said gravely. "It's complicated, torn between all the people you love. You wouldn't understand."

Why did adults always say that? As if they knew everything and thought that being young meant being stupid. But Dad was wrong—I understood more than he knew. He wasn't the only one with secrets.

I'd been keeping a big one from Josh—my sexy and sweet boyfriend who trusted me. Josh had been unavailable a lot lately so we hadn't been together much. Maybe we were growing apart. I wasn't sure, but unless we broke up, it wasn't right for me to lust after another guy. Yet that's how I'd been feeling about Dominic (the handyman/apprentice employed by my grandmother Nona) since we'd been working together to find a remedy for Nona's illness. Even worse—in a fireworks life-or-death moment, I'd kissed Dominic and enjoyed it. Now I couldn't stop thinking about him.

How could I judge my father when I was just as guilty?

So I agreed to keep Dad's secret. Not to protect him, but to protect my ten-year-old twin sisters who deserved more, and even for Mom who had her faults but was still my mother and I didn't want her hurt.

But I won't be like you, Dad, I thought with resolve. No more lying to Josh and lusting after someone else. I will make it work with Josh. I will forget all about Dominic.

So what was I doing spying in this rundown neighborhood where weeds thrived more than grass, miles from my parents' upscale home? Did I want to find out more about Jade? Was I jealous of this half-sister who seemed to be getting more than half of my father's attention? Did I want revenge or to get to know her? Or maybe I was here to prove to myself that she didn't matter; that my family was still intact and everything was fine with my world.

Shadows stirred in the living room and a man walked toward Jade. But he didn't stop and she didn't put aside her cell. Then the front door opened and the man stepped out of the house.

For a second I thought I was going to catch my own father sneaking out after spending the night with his girlfriend. But that wasn't possible. Dad's car had still been in the driveway when I'd left over an hour ago. Besides, this man was much older than my father; heavy-set, gray-haired, and wearing awful tweed slacks with a mustard yellow, long-sleeved shirt. If my best friend Penny-Love were here, she'd want to shoot him for fashion crimes.

Tweed Man glanced around surreptitiously and I wondered if he sensed me watching. Quickly, I ducked down low. I cautiously peeked out the window again. The man kept his head low, as if he was hiding something, as he crossed the lawn to a midsize burgundy pickup.

Who was he?

I leaned forward for a better look until my nose bumped against the glass.

As Tweed Man turned to open his car door, silver flashed off a round object hanging out of his back pocket. At first glance, it looked like a silver bracelet dangling from a chain. But realization struck, and I gave a soft gasp.

Handcuffs.

# 2

Within a few hours my life took a swift turn in a new direction, so there was no time to wonder about my new half-sister, her mother, or the man with the handcuffs.

After spying, I came back home to find my family stuck in a weird time warp. Dad flipped blueberry pancakes while Mom squeezed oranges and my younger sisters sat at the dining room table. Ashley, AKA Miz Drama Diva, belted out a new song she'd composed while Amy, Miz Book Butterfly, had her nose in one of the vintage mystery series she collected.

This cozy family scene was surreal, as if I'd stepped into a sitcom where everyone smiled too much and the laughter was faked. It was like floating out of my body and watching from a distance, except my feet remained solidly on the ground.

"The chef's specialty today is blueberry pancakes. Would you like a stack?" Dad asked with a wave of a spatula at me. The deep lines on his face yesterday were gone and he looked happier than I'd seen him in a long time.

"Of course she does. Who can resist the chef's specialty?" Mom said in a teasing tone. Orange juice dribbled down her hand as she turned to smile at me. "Sabine, get a plate and sit with your sisters. Where have you been so early?"

"No where special. I just felt like driving." That sounded lame, but my mother didn't probe deeper. So I quickly averted further questions by grabbing a plate and holding it out to the "chef."

I scooted a chair beside Amy who didn't even look up from her book, so all I could see was the top of her dark head and a purple dust jacket on a book titled *Hoof Beats on the Turnpike*. Ashley, on the other hand, was in constant motion and only read under protest for school assignments. My sisters may look alike—tall, slender, with dark lashes contrasting sky blue eyes and long, wavy black hair—but lately they strived to be different. Not that Mom noticed—she still bought them double everything and overloaded their schedules with music classes and modeling gigs. Amy was less than enthusiastic, but Ashley's eyes sparkled with Hollywood stars.

"Want to hear my new song?" Ashley jumped up from her chair, spinning a pirouette in lavender slippers. "I woke up with the melody in my head and the words came real fast. What do you think of my title—'Crushed By You'? It's all about this girl who crushes on her brother's best friend. I think it's my best yet."

I nodded and listened while she sang a bluesy song that sounded too mature for a ten-year-old, but then Ashley was full of surprises—like my entire morning. I still felt seriously confused...but relieved, too. Dad and Mom were acting strange, stealing touches and ogling each other with flirty looks. I had the feeling they'd done some serious talking last night and reached an understanding.

Maybe my family would be okay.

Dad obviously kept his promise about talking to Mom about my moving out. I didn't know what he said to convince her, but it worked. That evening my mother took me aside and told me she'd decided I should move back to Sheridan Valley.

"We'll all miss you terribly, but my mother's health is fragile and she needs you more than we do," Mom said as if this was all her idea. I kept a straight face and just nodded, like I was making a supreme sacrifice. But inside I was jumping over the moon for joy.

The next day I had a déjà vu moment.

My suitcases were packed and I was moving out.

Mom waited downstairs, ready to drive me to Sheridan Valley.

I felt a strange displacement of time, as if my life had rewound seven months to the traumatic day I'd been forced to leave school because my premonition that football jock Kip Hurst would die on prom night had come true. I was shunned, labeled a "witch," and sent to live with my grandmother.

But what should have been a punishment turned out to be a blessing. I loved living with Nona, who totally got me because she was psychic, too. I enrolled at Sheridan High and hid the fact that I saw ghosts and regularly had conversations with my spirit guide Opal. I worked hard to be normal and fit in with my new best friend Penny-Love and her cool friends. I even hooked up with deliciously hot Josh DeMarco.

Things were going great (well, except for some freaky premonitions and hauntings, but no one I cared about died, so everything turned out okay). I loved my new life and would never have moved back to San Jose—until my mother summoned me. There was no arguing with The Maternal Dictator, so for the last few weeks I'd lived in San Jose, keeping up with homework through independent study, secretly waiting for my chance to return to Sheridan Valley.

My chance had come.

Only this time I wasn't being sent away in disgrace. My packed bags had no aura of shame. I was going back to the home of my heart—with Nona.

The two-hour drive was pleasant, with light conversation about things that didn't matter: Mom's ambitions for my sisters, her frustration over a rude member of her Women's Auxiliary Club, and her search for a new hair stylist since the regular girl quit. I found myself wondering if Mom had any clue about Dad's secrets.

Did she know that Dad almost married another woman? Did she know Dad might have been having an affair with this woman? Did she know I had a half-sister? And on the nights Dad claimed to work late, did she know Dad was seeing his other family? How could she not know? My strong, competent mother had to suspect something. Or maybe she did, but was afraid if she pushed Dad to choose between his families, she'd lose everything.

It was such a strange thing to feel sorry for my mother. Yet I did.

When we slowed into Lilac Lane and turned down the gravel driveway, overwhelming joy brought tears to my eyes. Everything looked so wonderfully the same, as if I'd never left and each blade of grass and graveled stone stood still in time. Nona's yellow, ranch-style house was peacefully nestled among shady trees, with a pasture, barn, livestock, and dense woods on the surrounding ten acres. The house needed painting, some of the fencing posts sagged with age, and the fields were wild and overgrown. But it was my own perfect paradise and I wouldn't change anything. No matter what, I was accepted here and loved.

As we neared the house, we were greeted by a strange sight—five girls standing in a row wearing red sweatpants and Sheridan Valley shirts and waving red and white pompons. My best friend Penelope Lovell (nicknamed Penny-Love) raised her arms and shouted, "Ready! Go!

"SABINE! SABINE! Who reigns supreme?" Penny-Love chanted, and the other girls echoed each word with a resounding yell. "Gimme an S! Gimme an A! Gimme a B-I-N-E! What's that spell?" They all jumped and waved their poms. "SABINE! WELCOME HOME!"

Catelyn and Jill sprang into back flips, while Kaitlyn sliced the air into splits and Penny-Love jumped so high that when she hit the ground, gravel spit up around her red tennis shoes.

I flung open the car door and rushed out.

"I'M BACK!" I squealed. Then I was hugging Penny-Love and the other members of the Sheridan Cheer Squad. We laughed and jumped and even cried a little.

There was Nona, too, wearing a long paisley skirt with butterfly pockets and a dark blue jacket, her gray-blond hair clipped back with a butterfly barrette. Perched beside her on the porch was my white cat with mismatched, blue-green eyes, Lilybelle. Even one of the cows leaned across the fence and mooed as if to shout out "welcome" along with the cheerleaders.

I felt a wonderful sense of homecoming.

Of course, a few special people were absent. Like my Goth friend, Thorn, who had her own psychic uniqueness but scorned society (especially cheerleaders); rebel-with-a-computer Manny, who was editor of the school newspaper; and of course, Josh and Dominic—the two guys causing a tug-of-war in my heart.

Mom and Nona went into the living room to talk and my friends helped me lug my suitcases upstairs. Once we were in my room, gossip maven Penny-Love couldn't wait to announce a "surprise."

"Guess who made this?" Grinning widely, she showed me a balloon twisted into a heart.

"Josh?" I nearly dropped the suitcase I'd just lugged up the stairs.

"Who else?"

Not a question I wanted to answer. I bit my lip and asked, "You saw Josh today?"

"Yeah. At school lunch break. He was rushed for some meeting, so he didn't say much. But he asked me to give this to you. Isn't it soooo romantic?" Penny-Love flounced onto a corner of my bed and hugged a pillow. She was so in love with everything romantic that she'd recently started working part-time for my grandmother's computer dating business, Soul-Mate Matches.

"Josh should give lessons to the losers I usually date," Kaitlyn said.

"You're so lucky," Jill added. "He's like the ultimate Mr. Romance."

"Yeah…lucky." I reached for the balloon. "Thanks."

"Careful not to pop it," Penny-Love cautioned. "It's fragile."

So is my relationship with Josh, I thought with irony.

I wasn't even sure what had gone wrong. Even when I had to move away, we kept in touch through emails and phone calls. But we never talked about us. His last email went on about this guy from his magician's club with the odd name of Grey and in my email I'd shared some of the lyrics from Amy's newest song. We kept everything surface without touching on serious issues between us, as if we were both afraid of what we'd uncover if we went too deep.

I ran my fingers over the rubbery balloon heart, wondering why this thoughtful gift made me sad. Josh could get any girl he wanted, yet he'd chosen me. I was lucky to have a guy who was both popular and a humanitarian, giving his time on weekends to entertain kids in hospitals. What girl wouldn't love a guy who put on a clown wig and red nose to make sick kids laugh? Only I wasn't sure what I felt…admiration, respect…but love?

If I loved Josh, why did I long to see Dominic?

Every day that passed without hearing from Dominic was a black hole on my calendar. He'd left last week to search for the final silver charm needed to locate the remedy to cure Nona's illness. To look at Nona, you'd never know she was critically ill. But her memory was slipping away, like sand in an hour glass, spilling out of time. When the disease reached its climax, she would lapse into a coma. But this wasn't something I could discuss in front of my mother or cheerleading friends.

"So what's been going on at school?" I asked my girlfriends, bending over to unzip my suitcase. "Any new hook ups or break ups or scandals?"

"Always!" Penny-Love giggled. "But first I want to know what's really going with you and your sexy magician."

"He's only an apprentice," I said, sidestepping the question.

Penny-Love wagged her red and white pompon

at me. "Since when did learning stage tricks take up so much time? Shame on him for standing you up so much."

"Is there trouble in magic-land?" Jill asked with her usual bluntness. She wasn't a gossip like Penny-Love, but she had a take-charge attitude that was so honest she could get away with being bossy without being a bitch.

"We're fine." I tried to act casual as I avoided the curious gazes, opened my suitcase, and began to put away my clothes. I slipped a silky black blouse on a coat hanger and hung it in the closet.

"Just fine?" Jill persisted. "Last time I asked you were 'absolutely fantastic.'"

"I'm absolutely fantastically fine," I lied.

"I don't buy that…oh, but I wish I could buy a cute outfit like this." Penny-Love had followed me to the closet and pointed at a feathery yellow skirt with a chiffon spaghetti-strap top.

I shook my head. "Yellow's not your color."

"I know." She tugged on one of her dark red curls. "I also know something's up with you and Josh. Or why would he ask me to tell you he was sorry?"

"He said that?" I frowned.

"Sorry for what?" Kaitlyn and Catelyn asked

in unison. Kooky Kaitlyn and Conservative Caitlyn were best friends and complete opposites, purposefully spelling their names differently and clashing with their fashion styles. Kaitlyn wore layers of vivid colors while Catelyn draped herself in sophisticated black. Yet they did so much together, they moved like echoes of each other.

Trapped under the piercing scrutiny of my friends, I was tempted to slam into my closet and hide my reddening face behind a door. I really hated answering personal questions. I mean, I hadn't even been home for twenty minutes and already my love life was under fire. If I said the wrong thing, it would be all over school before I ever returned tomorrow morning. Penny-Love may be my closest friend, but she made no excuses for her big mouth. In fact, she was proud to be the Queen of Sheridan High Buzz. And usually I enjoyed hearing her latest gossip—as long as it wasn't about me.

"Josh and I are better than ever," I insisted as I emptied socks, undies, and bras from my suitcase to the appropriate drawers. I wasn't a complete neat freak, but I did like things orderly.

Penny-Love arched her brow. "Even though

he stood you up repeatedly when you were living with your parents?"

"Long-distance relationships are hard. But I'm back so we'll go out more often."

"Pen, stop digging for dirt," Jill said with a wag of her finger. "Can't you tell Josh and Sabine are über-perfect together? What's up with you anyway? Jealous?"

"As if!" Penny-Love sniffed, pushing a red curl away from her eyes as she sat cross-legged on my carpet. "I have Jacques, the most incredible guy ever, rugged and strong, yet sensitive, too. He's my sweet artist and painting is only the beginning of his many talents. Let me tell you…"

Pushing aside my suitcase, I plopped on the carpet beside my best friend and leaned in to hear her very sexy retelling of her latest date with Jacques (whose real name was plain old Jack). She grinned proudly when she got to the part about Jacques asking to paint her nude. She was thinking of saying yes, but only if he brushed out all her freckles. Of course with P-L, I never knew how much was truth and exaggeration. But who cared? The focus was off my romantic confusion and it was great to be back with my friends. They might not know the secret me—the psychic freak with a direct line to dead people—but when I was with them I felt normal. And being "normal" was like taking a relaxing vacation from weird.

Unfortunately this vacation was about to end.

Soon I'd go on the weirdest trip of my life.

And witness a murder.

# 3

My girlfriends hurried off for a cheerleading meeting at Jill's, which I was invited to but declined because:

- A) I was only a mascot friend and not part of the squad.
- B) I had to finish unpacking.
- C) Total exhaustion.

When my mother told me she was heading back to San Jose, I offered to walk her to her car. Lilybelle trailed after us, pouncing down the porch steps and swatting at one of the chickens before returning to rub around my ankles.

Mom was quiet as we walked and I braced myself for an awkward scene. You just never knew when she would slip into Dictator Mode. But instead of the expected lecture warning me to avoid psychic "nonsense," Mom wrapped me in a hug and said she'd miss me. I didn't completely believe she meant this, but it was nice to hear. She even slipped me a few twenties, which I saw no reason to refuse and promptly tucked in my pocket.

Then it was just Nona and me.

My grandmother invited me to sit with her in the kitchen, so I pulled up one of the four mismatched chairs. Nona's kitchen was one-fourth the size of my mother's gleaming chrome and granite kitchen, with homey pine cabinets, floral designed linoleum, and a cozy dining nook with a mural of wild roses blossoming up one wall. The round wood table still had a pink stain from when I was six and accidentally spilled Nona's Desert Rose nail polish. My mother would have immediately thrown out a damaged table.

"Tea?" Nona asked with a lift of the kettle.

"Yes, please," I said, smiling. "Jasmine flower."

"Excellent choice."

I leaned forward slightly to watch the bubbling water spill into a reddish brew from a tea kettle shaped like a Victorian house. The porcelain kettle had been an anniversary gift from her second (or third?) husband, and was designed with a circlet of painted tarot cards. As I looked at the symbols, one seemed to throb and flash a secret message. The Hanged Man symbol that warned that things were not as they appeared to be.

I didn't want to think about warnings.

The floral tea was sweet—and being with my grandmother was even sweeter. She didn't have to say anything and neither did I. We shared something beyond understanding. Nona teased that our connection went back to long ago past lives when we'd been sisters and even spouses. Did I believe this? I wasn't sure, but whether I believed or not didn't really matter.

For a while, we sipped tea in comfortable silence.

Beneath the table, Lilybelle rubbed against my legs, her fluffy tail tickling me. I reached down to scratch behind her ears, which made her purr loudly. I'd missed my kitty and the other farm animals. My mother's decoration scheme didn't include messy pets, only a large aquarium with rare species of fish. But you couldn't cuddle a fish. And Lilybelle's purr rumbled like a kitty love song.

I smiled across a wisp of kettle steam at my grandmother, feeling truly at peace and grateful. Even more reassuring, Nona glowed with remarkable health, showing no signs of memory loss. I hoped her illness was in remission, and she wouldn't lose her way again while driving to the grocery store or misplace her keys in the refrigerator. Penny-Love had reassured me that my grandmother was handling business duties better than ever, but I hadn't quite believed it until now. Mega relief. Even Mom had noticed the improvement in Nona, although she still warned me to keep an eye on my grandmother.

"It's great to be back. Thanks," I told my grandmother, my spoon making a clinking sound as I stirred my tea.

"I'm the one who should offer thanks." She reached across the table to squeeze my hand. "It's been quiet and lonely without you. I've even missed finding your makeup all over the bathroom counter."

"I put my stuff away…well usually," I added. "Anyway, you couldn't have been that lonely with Penny-Love around."

"Penny? Oh yes…"

"She's been having a blast working for you. It's all she ever talks about in her emails, aside from Jacques. She's in love with the concept of love and signs everything; Penny-Love, Professional Love Assistant," I added chuckling over the title Pen had given herself.

"Love Assistant?" Nona repeated, sounding puzzled.

"Corny, I know, but it makes Pen happy. I'm just glad she's been around to help you. I felt bad enough leaving, but knowing Penny-Love and Dominic were here made it easier. Although I guess Dominic hasn't been around." I should have stopped there and reminded myself I had a boyfriend. But I was hungry for any news of Dominic and couldn't resist asking, "Have you heard from him?"

"Heard what?"

"How Dominic is doing." I kept my face blank, hiding the jump in my heart at Dominic's name. "Not that I care or anything. I'm just curious. Has he called?"

"The phone hasn't rung…at least I don't think…What did you ask?"

A mask slipped from her face to reveal terrifying truths. She had no idea what I was talking about. Nona had checked out and I was looking at a stranger; not my grandmother. Her eyes were ringed in dark circles and her fingers trembled as she held too tight to her tea cup. Wisps of her silver-blond hair dangled from her scarf as if she'd hastily bound it up without brushing. Her fingernails, which were usually manicured in glossy polish, were chipped and as pale as bone.

"Are you okay?" I asked many questions with these three words. Why aren't you taking better care of yourself? How is your memory? Have you lost important papers, missed appointments, neglected the animals? Can you remember what you did yesterday? Do you remember me?

"Of course I'm okay." My grandmother jutted out her chin defiantly. "Pour me more tea, will you?"

"But your cup is nearly full."

"It's cooled off and I can't abide cold tea." She held out her porcelain cup. "Be a dear and refill this for me."

"Sure, Nona." Calm words to hide turbulent fears. Something was definitely off here. But I took the cup and walked over to the sink.

With a flick of my hand, I dumped the tea and watched lavender-brown liquid swirl down the sink. A slight shuffling sound behind me made me look over my shoulder just in time to see Nona reaching into her butterfly skirt pocket. She withdrew a thick bundle of notes. She peered through reading glasses, flipping through the papers with focused concentration and murmuring under her breath.

As if she sensed me watching, she looked up—but I immediately glanced away. Still I could see her peripherally as she shoved the notes back into her pocket. I poured the tea, then strode back to the table and set the hot cup before her.

"Thank you, dear," she said, sounding almost cheerful.

"Careful, it's hot."

"That's the way I like it. And you're right about Penny-Love being a valuable 'Love Assistant.' She's a great help running Soul-Mate Matches. Although she doesn't know the matches aren't only made with computers—that my guides give me information from the other side. As for Dominic, I couldn't ask for a better handyman and apprentice. His ability to connect with animals is amazing."

She was repeating facts like an overachieving student trying to impress a teacher. My fears worsened, but I tried to act calm. "So where is Dominic?"

"Who can keep up with young people?" She waved away my question like an insignificant wisp of lint. "Why don't you go outside and look for him? He's around here somewhere."

No, he wasn't. Alarm bells rang and my gut twisted with worry. Dominic was in Nevada searching for the last charm needed to find the remedy for Nona's illness. He hadn't been here for several days.

"Nona, please tell me what's going on. Don't pretend with me."

"Pretend what?" she asked innocently.

"That everything is all right."

"I'm not pretending anything. What an absurd notion. And why are you looking at me like that?"

I held out my hand. "Show me those papers you have hidden."

"I don't know what you're talking about," she snapped, not meeting my gaze.

Instead of arguing, I lunged forward and reached into her butterfly pocket. Before she realized what was happening, I'd grabbed the clump of papers.

"Give those back!"

"No!" I jumped back.

"Those are my personal and private papers. You have no right to take them!"

"Stop it, Nona," I said, skimming the papers through tears.

Nona's notes. Important and minor details of her life scribbled down to help her remember: names of friends, clients, relatives, and even the farm animals. There were details about her business, meditation chants, and diagrams of the house and out-buildings. She listed bill payment dates, bank accounts, phone numbers, and an hour-by-hour schedule. She had fooled everyone.

"Nona, tell me the truth," I said sadly.

"Give me those notes!" she demanded.

When she reached out, I simply handed her the papers. But I'd already seen enough and was too miserable to argue. It was like watching all the beautiful colors fade from a glorious painting. Soon only a blank canvas would remain, and there was nothing I could do, except pray Dominic succeeded on his mission.

"So now you know," Nona said with defeat.

"Oh, Nona." I wiped dampness from my cheek. "How can I help?"

"Hold yourself together, Sabine. For the moment I have my wits, and I refuse to wallow in self-pity."

"You'd never wallow. You're the strongest woman I know. Keeping these notes was brilliant— you even fooled Mom."

"She was easy because she's afraid of change and saw what she wanted to see, as most people do. But I couldn't fool you. To be honest, I'm relieved. I don't think I'll be able to hold myself together much longer."

"You'll beat this illness. Dominic will get the last charm then we'll find the cure. I know it," I said, although in truth I knew nothing. My sixth sense tuned in great on other people's problems, but short-circuited my internal radar when problems were too close.

"My short-term memory is dreadful. I'm losing large chunks of each day. I'll suddenly find myself somewhere I don't remember going surrounded by strangers. My notes save me embarrassment, but soon I might forget they exist."

"I'll help you remember."

"But you can't watch me 24-7 and waiting for Dominic seems increasingly futile. So it's time to try something else," she said, pursing her lips with firm resolve.

"There is no other cure. You told me the story about our ancestor Agnes creating the remedy, then dying before she could tell anyone where it was hidden. Finding something that's been lost for over one hundred and fifty years won't be easy, but we'll do it. Too bad we can't just call Agnes on the phone and ask her where she hid it."

"Why not?"

"Um…she's been dead for over a century."

"A little detail like that can't stop us." Nona's face lit up. "I don't know why we didn't try this sooner."

"Try what?" I asked uneasily.

"Contacting Agnes personally. We'll hold a séance."

# 4

Nona spent the rest of the evening on the phone organizing a séance.

I was glad to see her proactive, but I was skeptical about séances. I'd tried to fake one with my sister Amy a few weeks ago that had been a disaster. Sure, it would be great to contact Agnes so she could just tell us where the remedy book was hidden. But what if a darker entity came through instead?

*Have faith*, I heard a voice in my head.

Immediately I got a strong mental picture of a regal smile, upswept black hair, and smooth tawny skin. Opal, my spirit guide, oozed with more attitude on the other side than most living people. I'd recently learned sad details of her earth-life hundreds of years ago and discovered a vulnerable human side to my spirit best friend. She'd loved, lost, and died so tragically she swore she'd never endure another earth-life. I didn't know why she'd chosen to be my guide, and when I asked she'd only say that it was one of the mysteries I'd find out someday.

"So will Nona get well?" I asked with thoughts and not words. Even though I was alone in my bedroom and couldn't be overheard, it felt strange to talk aloud to someone I could only see in my head.

*Your grandmother is vigorous and has resources that would amaze you.*

"Is that your usual confusing way of telling me not to worry?'

*In all of the existence of humans, worry has yet to achieve any concrete solutions except as to act as a catalyst of unpleasant physical maladies. You would do well to release yourself from restricting emotional gravity so as to discover what is truly of consequence.*

I sighed. "I have no idea what you just said."

Her sigh traveled across worlds.

*Humans are so frustrating. Didn't I speak clearly enough for your limited comprehension?*

"Spirit guides are way more frustrating. Can't you just tell me either yes, Nona will improve, or no, she won't?"

*Yes…I could tell you.*

"So is she going to get well?"

*Fore-knowledge is a multifaceted tool that can hinder free will and restrict the natural sequence of your journey.*

"What about my grandmother?" I mind-shouted. "Will we find the remedy in time? Is it a good idea to hold a séance?"

*Not necessarily good, but certainly intriguing. You never know what will happen or who will show up.*

"Will you be there?"

*Perhaps as a silent observer, but not in an active role.*

"Can't you just tell me what's going to happen? If I knew Nona was going to get better then I'd stop worrying."

*Worry, much like fear, can be conducive to taking action, and without such energy you could float off-course into an uncharted sea.*

"Didn't you just tell me that worrying was bad?"

*I cannot be held to task for your limited inter-pretations.*

"Just tell me something…anything!…so I know there's still hope."

*Hope is a constant bright star that glows within you and reaches out to embrace and nurture others.*

"I only care about Nona. How can I help her?"

*My dear Sabine, your very presence is of supreme benefit to your grandmother. You're on a path fraught with impending peril and will find surprising alliances on an unexpected journey.*

Impending peril? An unexpected journey? Surprising alliances?

Now I was seriously getting a headache. Did my "surprising alliance" have anything to do with the partnership I'd formed with Dominic? Would we find the missing remedy by working together? Well, I was up for the challenge. I'd risk anything to save my grandmother. Bring on the peril!

I tried to get more information out of Opal, only she refused.

*Your channel is clouded with conflictions of love and anger. It's clear this is not the time for a lesson in life, love, and the meaning of everything. So I bid you adieu and shall return to this discussion when you are less restricted by emotional gravity.*

Then she was gone.

I still had no idea what she just said, and thinking about it was too confusing. Exhaustion imploded like a building crashing around me. I'd had such a full few days, leaving my parents' home and moving back in here, seeing wonderful friends yet also discovering Nona was only a handful of notes away from losing herself—which meant I would lose her, too.

After taking two aspirin, I slipped into my nightgown and then opened the cabinet where I kept my night-light collection. Every night I chose a different night-light to ward off dark spirits. I spent a few moments choosing the right one—a golden angel. Golden angels were great protectors. I hoped its golden guidance would reach out to protect Nona, too.

As I closed my eyes and stress eased away, some of Opal's words replayed in my head. Mostly they didn't make sense. But one sentence repeated itself. And I fell asleep thinking it would have been cool to learn about "life, love, and the meaning of everything."

\* \* \*

Penny-Love showed up early the next morning outfitted in slick black high-heeled boots, black jeans with glitter lips smacked on each pocket, and a black vest over a red shirt. Ruby rhinestone earrings sparkled from her ears and her lips glistened like dewy roses. Her naturally curly red hair hung to her midback in a twisted rope.

"It's cool going to school with you again," she said slipping in step with me as we walked down my long driveway.

"I've only been gone for a few weeks."

"Which felt like years and I didn't think you'd ever come back. Thank goodness your mom came to her senses."

"She just got sick of having me around," I joked.

"Isn't it usually the other way around?"

"Usually. But she's mellowed and almost treats me like a human being."

"What brought on this miraculous change?"

I thought of Jade, Crystal, and Dad. "Could be menopause. I heard that women her age have weird mood swings."

"Well, I'm glad she released you from captivity."

I chuckled. "It's not like I was in prison. I wasn't

locked in my room or anything. I had friends there, too."

"But they couldn't compare with your friends here. Namely moi," Penny-Love said with a flourish of her hand. "It's much nicer walking to school with you instead of Catelyn. She's sweet and all, but she can't stop talking about herself. That just gets so boring."

"Really?" I glanced away to hide my grin. "I never noticed."

"That's because you're too nice, which isn't that healthy. I'll have to toughen you up or people will totally tread all over you." Then she went on to tell me about every conversation she'd had during the few weeks I was gone.

I only half-listened as she described a blog quiz she'd taken that proved that she was a true romantic. I would have flunked that quiz. Romance was a tricky topic for me and I agonized over the serious decision I had to make today. I'd woken up thinking about Josh, and what a great person he was and what I'd feel when I saw him at school. Would I be happy to see him or just confused? I loved all the sweet things Josh said to me and the surprises like the heart-shaped balloon. But did I love Josh?

Should I break up with him or work things out?

Then I thought of Dominic and got this shivery excitement that made it hard to even think…only yearn to see him again. Did that mean I really should break up with Josh? I thought of my father and my resolve not to be like him. I couldn't be sure if he was cheating on my mother, but I could make sure I didn't make the same mistake.

So while Penny-Love talked, I wondered if Josh was going to greet me at my locker like usual (well, usual *before* I moved away). His last email had just said "C U 2-morrow." He didn't say where or when or how things really were between us. Was there even an us? He'd apologized for being so busy lately—just one of our growing problems. Eventually we'd have to talk. Seriously scary.

I should have been glad to find out that Josh wasn't waiting for me at my locker. But call me foolish or selfish or something worse because I was disappointed. I wanted him to show up with a kiss and say romantic things to me. I loved the attention, and I especially loved how other people thought we were great together. It was easier to fit in when I was dating one of the most popular guys at school. When I was next to him, no one noticed that I wasn't a typical teen. I could just relax with a semipopular status.

So where was Josh?

Had he heard I'd kissed Dominic? Was he avoiding me? Or was he waiting for the right time to break up with me before I could break up with him?

Sighing, I turned to my locker, spun the combination on my lock, and opened the door to find a giant poster with the words "TURN AROUND" spelled out in black ink. And when I turned around, there was Josh—strong and tall and totally hot Josh, holding out his hand to offer me a tiny gold-wrapped box.

"Wow!" I murmured, touched deeply.

"Well, aren't you going to take it?" He had these amazing dimples when he smiled and I felt myself getting all rubber-legged and mushy inside.

"Sure." My fingers closed around crinkly foil as I stared down at the tiny box.

"Go ahead. Open it."

"Okay," I said smiling. Sometimes I could look at gifts and know what was inside, much the same way I knew who was calling when the phone would ring. But just because I was psychic didn't mean I didn't like to be surprised. So I didn't ESP-peek.

When I pulled out a gold chain with a small

key, I wondered if it had some meaning. I hid my uneasiness with an "Ooh!" of delight. But inside I was freaking. A key? Like to his house? Was that like an invitation to spend some serious alone time in his bedroom? I wasn't ready to move that far that fast, especially since just a while ago I'd considered breaking up with him.

"Does this mean I won a new car?" I joked.

"You wish. Your prize is both smaller and bigger."

"Ah, a puzzle. What's smaller and bigger at the same time?" I shrugged. "I give up. What?"

Josh smiled mysteriously, then snapped his fingers with a magician's flourish. He gestured to himself, then pulled me close and whispered in my ear, "My heart."

Romantic. Corny. So perfectly Josh.

When he fastened the chain around my neck, my skin tingled from his touch and sweet feelings warmed me. A thrill ran through me, and I enjoyed Josh's warm touch. His fingers lightly pushed some loose hair from my face and I had no problem leaning against him. We fit nicely together, and I didn't pull back.

Was I feeling passion for Josh? I wondered. Maybe I really did love him.

I wanted to believe this. We melted into a very hot kiss right there in the school hall, not caring if anyone saw. My hands circled his broad shoulders, and I relaxed into our kiss. When thoughts of Dominic skirted the edges of my mind, I pushed them away.

I will make this work, I vowed. Josh is wonderful and we can be great together. I promised my love to him, and I'm sticking to my word. Nothing will change my mind. Not anyone else…especially Dominic.

As if my tiny key unlocked Pandora's Box, a whirlwind of dangerous things flew into the air, leaving me holding tight to precious hope.

# 5

Trick or Treats, a seemingly ordinary candy shop, was swathed in darkness except for a dim, yellow porch light, and appeared closed for the night.

The store bordered the edge of Sheridan Valley and attracted kids from nearby schools who craved sweets and carbs. But it also catered to a less obvious, more subtle clientele, and only those in the know were invited into the private back rooms.

A few months ago, Thorn introduced me to

Velvet, and I'd been invited into the back room of the candy shop. I'd been amazed to find everything mystical for sale. I loved all the crystals and candles and books on magic. I'd gone back several times, but only recently discovered Trick or Treats held even more secrets.

What does a girl wear to a séance? I wondered as I looked in my closet at clothes that were all wrong.

Maybe I should borrow something dark and wicked from Thorn. I hadn't had a chance to talk with her at school since we hung out with different groups, but I'd seen her across the quad with her Goth friends (one girl was wearing—if you can believe this—pink leotards and fairy wings).

Thorn and I shared an odd friendship. We didn't talk much, seldom hung out together, yet we completely respected each other. We had only one thing in common—being psychic. Thorn also had a talent for finding great clothes at thrift stores. She'd mix-and-match odd accessories like chains, dog collars, barbed wire, and jewelry shaped into skulls or snakes. She'd have advice on appropriate séance fashion. But if I told Thorn about the séance, I'd break the oath of secrecy I'd given to Nona. Only participants were in the know.

Ultimately, I combined a turquoise flared skirt

and white peasant blouse. I added a pair of laced black boots and dangling dreamcatcher earrings. Feeling a little mysterious, I climbed into the passenger seat of Nona's car.

On the way, she told me stories of past séances, where she'd witnessed grieving people briefly reunited with lost loved ones. Mostly it was joyous and healing, smiles mingling with tears.

"But sometimes it was downright funny," Nona added. "My friend Betty Jo was desperate to connect to her husband—to find out where he'd hidden the remote control. She'd been going crazy searching for it since he died while watching the Super Bowl. Fortunately he popped in long enough to tell her to look under the microwave. Another widow wanted to see her husband again because she missed their arguments—and when he showed she started nagging him. Poor guy couldn't get away from her even on the other side."

Chuckling over this, I decided the séance would be fun. And it would be great if we could connect to our ancestor Agnes and find out the ingredients for Nona's remedy. Then all of our problems would be solved.

Nona and I climbed the steps to the shadowy porch entrance to Trick or Treats. Although Velvet was a fairly new friend of mine, she was a long-time friend of Nona's. She spoke in a refined British accent, her mannerisms elegant and proper like a cliché uptight English woman. But after work hours, she let down her hair and invited in the mysteries of the moon, sun, and stars.

As we waited on the semilit porch for Velvet to answer our knock (three short taps and two long raps), I got one of my "feelings." Turning around, I searched through parked cars and bushes for the eyes I sensed watching. Tightening my jacket around my shoulders, I shivered not from cold, but from an icy aura of hatred. Whoever was watching was not a friend.

Nona rapped again on the door as I continued to scan the parking lot. A row of winter bare oaks bordered on one side and a credit union stood on the opposite side. The parking lot was still except for the pulsing red light of a surveillance camera and glow of outside lights. The aura of anger seemed to be coming from the back of the parking lot. Had something moved by that white compact car?

I couldn't see anything except a low-hanging tree branch reaching over the car. The branch seemed to point like a bony finger and accuse me of having a wild imagination. So I shrugged it off and turned back to the door just as it was whipped open.

"Darlings Nona and Sabine! I'm delighted you made it!" Velvet greeted at the same moment I was enveloped in warm air mingled with the heavenly aroma of chocolate. "Don't dally on the porch. The others are all here."

"Already?" Nona said with some surprise. "Are we late?'

"Not at all. We won't start for another ten minutes, so you're precisely on schedule." She spoke "schedule" so the c was silent and it sounded like "shedual."

When the door shut behind us, goose bumps lingered on my arms. The hateful aura lingered like an unpleasant smell. What kind of vibe had I picked up? Serious negative energy. Was it coming from someone close by? Or maybe the supercharged energy at Trick or Treats caused me to pick up on energy miles away. Yeah, it wasn't anything personal. It was paranoid to think someone was spying on me.

Spying.

Isn't that exactly what I'd done to my half-sister? I thought guiltily as I wandered over to a rock candy display case and ran my finger idly across the smooth glass.

Of course, my spying hadn't been malicious. Well maybe a little…but it wasn't like I'd done anything bad. Still, I felt a little ashamed of myself. Jade was an innocent bystander of my father's life. His actions weren't her fault and it wasn't fair to blame her. Resenting her wouldn't change anything. I had to accept the fact she was part of father's life. But I didn't have to like her—and I never would.

Feeling some resolve with myself, I peered into a glassed case of fruit-filled chocolates and read off the yummy flavors: blueberry, raspberry, strawberry, apricot, prune pecan, banana raisin, melon crush, boysenberry, cherry, and lemon. If I had to choose one, what would it be?

"Hard to resist?" Velvet asked coming up behind me.

"Always." I smiled. "Everything is so yummy, I want to taste them all—except maybe the prune pecan."

"It's actually quite scrumptious. When we're through tonight, I'll give you some free samples," she added before ushering us through heavy cloth curtains into a room I'd seen only a few other times.

The small room offered everything mystic:

herbs, candles, crystals, and books on topics like tarot cards, meditation, and spells. We continued down a short hall and into a large room I'd never seen. It was bordered in shelves with boxes, so I guessed it was a storage room during the day. But tonight the center held a circle of chairs and scattered tables with flickering candles and fragrant bouquets of flowers. Candles trails wavered like fiery snakes flying around the ceiling. Sandalwood incense wafted from a silver dish and all but three chairs were occupied. Nona said that Velvet was inviting members of her Wicca coven plus a few other trusted friends.

When I saw one of my own friends, wickedly attired in a black and crimson wig with skull jewelry dangling down a black leather jacket, I exclaimed, "Thorn! What are you doing here?'

"Well, duh. Same as you." She rolled her kohl-painted eyes.

"But you didn't tell me you were coming."

"Like you told me?" she retorted.

"I was sworn to secrecy."

"So was I." She grinned. "I always wanted to experience a séance. Of course my parents would freak if they knew, so to save them upset I told them I was babysitting. Come sit here."

I scooted in a chair next to Thorn then looked around at the rest of the group. I counted nine. Thorn and I were the only under-fifties, then five women including Nona and Velvet, plus two men. I recognized one of the men, a grizzled old bear named Grady who regularly played cards with my grandmother. I didn't know the others; most of them dressed like they were attending a PTA meeting. Only Thorn and a woman with stunning puffed silver hair had the exaggerated jewelry and makeup befitting a séance. While I admired their boldness, I was glad I'd gone with a more subtle look. I preferred to blend in, not stand out.

Candle trails swirled in subtle breezes from beneath doors and through small gaps in closed windows. My skin tingled with anticipation as I watched Velvet sit in the head chair and open a purple satin bag. She withdrew several polished stones, smoothed them between her palms, and murmured something no one could hear. Her pale skin glowed amber in the candlelight.

"A few of you are new, so I'll go over the rules," Velvet began. "First of all, please turn off any cell phones. And if anyone has to use the loo…I mean, the bathroom, please attend to that now."

Everyone looked around, but no one made a move.

"Splendid. Now we can proceed."

My heart quickened. I leaned forward so I wouldn't miss a word.

"There are a variety of methods for contacting the Other World: meditation, prayer, channeling, dreams, astral projection, and séance. Tonight, we have chosen séance. We shall call forth and invite a spirit within our circle."

I nodded and saw that everyone else was nodding, too.

"Our chairs are arranged to represent the circle of life," Velvet continued, "and although hand-holding can help focus, it can get tiring and sweaty. So we'll skip that old cliché. I've arranged flowers and candles around the room since spirits are attracted to light and fresh flowers. We will begin with a prayer for protection and an invitation to positive spirits. Please close your eyes."

With eyes shut, I joined the sea of energy floating with Velvet's words of reverence and gratitude. Peace settled over me like a loving caress.

"Take a deep breath and visualize a white light around the room. Usually we would invite any spirits with messages for each participant, but tonight we are united in the urgent purpose of contacting my dear friend Nona's great-great-grandmother, Agnes. You may keep your eyes open or closed, whatever you prefer, as we call upon the spirit of Agnes Jane Walker."

I'd seen an old black-and-white photograph of Agnes taken shortly before her death, surrounded by her four young daughters, so it was easy to envision her. I saw her gentle smile and braided hair in the photo. She was psychic, either the first in our family or a continuation of something that started centuries ago. Like her, I had a dark streak in my light hair—the mark of a seer.

Breathing deeply, I was keenly aware of smells around the room as Velvet summoned Agnes: acrid candles, flowers, perfume, and sweet chocolates. Shoes shuffled on hard wood and chairs creaked as several people leaned closer with expectation. Energy heightened and my pulse raced.

I could sense something coming.

"A spirit is with us," Velvet spoke with gentle invitation. "This young female spirit seeks her mother."

Heads jerked up and everyone looked around curiously. I couldn't see anything solid, but felt a cool chill and tickling sense of touch—as if something without form glided over my skin. Thorn must have felt it too, because she reached for my hand and grasped tightly. She'd never admit to fear, but she'd once confided that ghosts made her uneasy. In theory, she accepted them. But up close and in person, she'd avoided meeting them. Attending this séance was a big step for her.

"The spirit has short, curly dark hair and holds out a toy," Velvet spoke in a flat, monotone voice. "It's a stuffed animal...missing an ear...yellow with spots."

There was a sob from across the circle, and the women with frosty silver hair gasped. "Carrie's giraffe! She named it Dotti and we buried it with...ohmygod!" Her hands fluttered to her face. "Carrie, baby?"

Candlelight illuminated the surprise on the faces around the room, but Velvet stayed focused ahead and spoke calmly. "Gretchen, is Carrie your daughter?"

"She was..." The silver-haired woman collapsed in her chair, not falling over, but sort of sinking into herself. "She was only two...but it's been over twenty years...Carrie? Are you really here?"

"She's smiling and nodding at you," Velvet said.

"I never expected...in all the years of hoping to hear from her...finally it's happened. What's her message? Is she all right?"

"She says someone named Margaret is with her."

"My mother." Gretchen brushed her damp cheek. "I hoped they'd find each other."

"They have and they're both happy. They send their love." Velvet paused and the room grew warm. The sense of a presence was gone.

Velvet said a few comforting words to Gretchen, then called out to Agnes again, and I bit my lower lip anxiously.

For a few moments, we sat quietly in our serene circle. I concentrated hard on Agnes, imploring her to come here. I knew others were doing the same thing—but the next spirit that came through definitely wasn't Agnes.

It wasn't even human.

"Cap! You sly dog!" Grady exclaimed—and he meant this literally.

Velvet described a shaggy giant of a dog. Captain, nicknamed Cap, was a loveable, big black dog that had belonged to Grady. When I closed my eyes, I could even see a faint foggy outline of shiny, yellow-black eyes and a wet, red tongue that slurped

Grady's face. Grady must have felt something too because he said his face tickled.

It was hard to settle down after that. To be honest, I was losing hope. I knew that not all spirits were able to come through. Some weren't interested in earthly planes while others had gone on to other existences. When I glanced over at Nona, I knew she was discouraged, too.

Fortunately, Velvet didn't give up so easily. Once again she whispered a prayer, invoked a white protective light, and asked us to concentrate on calling forth Agnes.

Immediately, the air swirled with a breeze so chilly it made my bones ache. Thorn shivered and squeezed my hand tighter. The wind carried an odd odor of cigars and cinnamon, blowing through the room with swift force that snuffed out three candles. Gasps echoed, but Velvet urged for quiet.

"Agnes, is that you?" Velvet called out.

Silence…then the wind whooshed as if something invisible exhaled.

I peered around for a hint of a spirit, yet saw only my eight companions and their excited expressions. So I closed my eyes for a better look—and saw him.

A wavy figure of a man wore a bright orange

tunic over bell-bottom jeans decorated with embroidered rainbows, hearts, and flowers. His dark-blond ponytail trailed down to his midback. He had a nice, almost handsome, face with a nose a bit too long but blue eyes that seemed to laugh in good humor.

I'd never seen this hippie and didn't care what he had to say, so I looked away and tuned out Velvet. Where was Agnes? Why wasn't she showing up? Didn't she care about her own great-great-granddaughter? Obviously the answer was no. She wasn't going to come through and instead we got a little girl, a dog, and a hippie.

The séance was a failure.

So I wasn't paying much attention when Velvet called out the hippie-spirit's message—not until she spoke my name.

"Huh?" I blinked, opening my eyes to look at Velvet.

"Douglas is asking for you."

"Me?" I scrunched my brow, shaking my head. "Douglas who?"

"He didn't give his last name."

"Well, I don't know anyone named Douglas. And I've never seen this hippie before."

Velvet was quiet, nodding as if she was listening

to a voice no one else could hear. Then she turned back to me. "Douglas asks you to take care of your sister...there is some sort of danger."

"My sister!" I choked out.

"He's showing me a rag doll with red hair. Oh dear—there's a knife through the doll's heart. That can't be good. Are you sure you don't recognize him?"

"Totally."

"Well he seems to know you. He keeps saying 'sister' over and over. He's afraid she'll be hurt and asks you to protect her."

This made no sense at all. I didn't know this spirit. I couldn't even hear him and only had that one psychic glimpse of him. Why did a stranger want to talk with me? And what was his connection with my sisters?

I could hardly think clearly, my heart thumped so wildly. I could sense the spirit fading, though, which made me desperate to know more.

"Ask him what danger!" I cried to Velvet. "And which sister?"

Velvet nodded, closing her eyes. When she opened them, she stared at me with the oddest expression of confusion and worry.

"Well, tell me! Which sister is in danger?" I demanded. "Amy or Ashley?"

"Neither," she said with a look of puzzlement. "Who is Jade?"

# 6

Who was Douglas and why had he come through to me?

How could a spirit I'd never met on either side know my connection to Jade? Did spirits astral-eavesdrop on private conversations?

Of course I didn't believe this, but I didn't know what to think. Was Douglas an ancestor or spirit guide of Jade's? Why ask me to help her? Sharing blood ties with Jade didn't equal a relationship. I hadn't even known about her until a few days ago. Yet this spirit wanted me to protect her?

Utter insanity!

I had no idea how to answer Velvet. I couldn't just blurt out that Jade was my half-sister without breaking my promise to Dad. Besides I didn't want to talk trash about him. Sure, he'd made some mistakes, but it was all out of love and he'd always been a great father. I had to cover for him—even if it meant lying to my grandmother and friends.

Damn Jade anyway! I wanted to forget all about her—but how could I when she was complicating my life from the other side?

Thorn had let go of my hand and was tilting her crimson-black head to give me a questioning look. She wasn't the only one. A circle of curious faces stared at me.

"I—I don't know anything about Douglas," I finally admitted truthfully.

This wasn't really a lie. I had no idea why a spirit I didn't know asked me to protect the half-sister I didn't want to know. What kind of help would Jade possibly need? If her crowded driveway was any indication, she had plenty of family and friends. And let's not forget my—her—our father. If she was in trouble, all she had to do was flip her little cell phone in Dad's direction and he'd come running with open checkbook.

"It's all right, Sabine," Velvet said with a sympathetic expression. "Some messages aren't for now, but are for future reference. Someday this will make sense to you."

I nodded, pretending to agree.

Velvet smiled around the room. "Now let's return to contacting Agnes."

I exhaled in relief as gazes shifted away from me and back to Velvet. In a united circle, we concentrated once again on summoning Agnes. Only I had trouble focusing, unable to stop thinking about what Douglas had said.

A rag doll with a knife through its heart? Was it a symbol rather than a literal warning about knives or rag dolls? The knife might represent an end of a relationship and the rag doll could mean vulnerability. Maybe Jade was breaking up with her boyfriend or someone was going to break her heart.

Another thought jumped in my mind. Did the warning have anything to do with the guy with handcuffs? He wasn't wearing a uniform like a police officer or security guard. And he'd given me an uneasy feeling; a sense of something wrong that I couldn't define.

Not my problem, I reminded myself. Whatever problems Jade had were not my business. I wasn't going to get involved.

With fierce resolve, I forced my concentration back to the séance, cleansing my mind by envisioning a waterfall flowing over my thoughts. Agnes was the only spirit I wanted to see.

The room echoed with a silence so thick it was hard to breathe. Candle smoke swirled above the table like a spectral audience, and no one moved. All I could hear was the faint ticking of a watch and my own tap-tapping heartbeat. I closed my eyes and sent out a plea to Agnes.

Come to us now and help my grandmother. We're your family—your granddaughters—and we need your wisdom. You left the charms to protect and lead to the remedy because you must have known your descendents would need it someday. And you were right; we desperately need the cure for Nona. Please come to us—

I sensed something…not a presence so much as a palpable shift in the energy. The temperature dropped, and I wasn't the only one who shivered. The same negative aura I'd felt earlier in the parking lot gripped me. Someone—or something—hateful was nearby, seething with icy rage and coming closer…

Crashes exploded from outside the room. The floor trembled, walls shook, and windows rattled. Breaking glass cracked like sharp thunder. Mayhem erupted around me, shouts mingling with screams.

"What was that?"

"Oh my God! Earthquake!"

"We've been bombed!"

"It came from my candy shop!" Velvet jumped up so swiftly her chair toppled backwards to the floor, knocking into a table and causing a candle to teeter dangerously. She paused only a second to steady the candle before breaking into a run. The circle split and ran, too.

Since I was closest to the door, I found myself in the lead, racing down the hall, through the mystical sales room, and into the candy shop—where I gaped in horror.

The room was swathed in shadows and an eerie glow from outside streetlights. My hands flew to my face as I fought through my shock. Utter devastation. A demonic force had smashed through the sweet shop, tossing chairs aside and smashing display cases. Shattered glass and candy debris littered the floor. Glass crunched under my feet and I lost my balance, stumbling over something long and wooden lying among glittery shards.

Steadying myself, I looked down to see what I'd tripped over.

A baseball bat—studded with glass shrapnel as if the windows and display cases had fought back against brutal blows. Candy guts in gooey rainbow hues stained the wood like sweetened blood.

I flashed back to the first time I'd walked into the candy stop. It had been magical, like stepping into a beautiful anime cartoon come to life. Or the fairy tale of Hansel and Gretel, only the witch was good and kind and spoke with a lilting English accent.

Only now…the terrible destruction was sickening.

I couldn't bear to look, and turned away.

That's when I glanced out a window and saw a quicksilver movement. A lanky scarecrow figure ran from the store and into the parking lot.

The vandal! I thought angrily. The brutal candy killer is getting away!

"No, he isn't!" I yanked open the door and raced down the steps. "Stop!"

Cold night air sucked at my breath as I ran without thinking, chasing after the vandal who seemed freakishly tall and kept his face hidden in a hooded jacket. He dodged around parked cars, jumped over curbs, and disappeared.

Frustrated, I started to leave when shadows shifted and there he was—running to the same white car I'd noticed earlier. The long, black hooded jacket with red lining flared out behind him like a devil's tail. He paused and the wind whipped at his hood, revealing cropped hair as silvery as moonlight. Despite his gray hair, he moved like someone close to my age. With surprising grace, he sprinted forward to fling open a car door. A light flared in the dark—an interior car light—and in that flash I glimpsed a sharp-featured face with thick dark brows, a straight nose, and a cocky smirk.

The car lights died to darkness and the engine roared to life, twin headlights glowing like evil eyes. I watched the ghost-eyed blur speed away.

"Someone stop him!" I shouted.

But no one had followed me, so I took off after the car, plunging through the parking lot and out to the darkened street. My chest ached and my legs couldn't move fast enough. It was no use. The car zipped around a corner, gone.

I swore under my breath. He'd gotten away, and I hadn't looked at the license plate and had only gotten that brief look at him. Feeling like a failure, I slowly walked back inside the candy shop.

The circle of people that had only a short while ago been united in a mystic goal now huddled in sadness. While no one had been hurt physically, the brutal act of vandalism felt like a personal attack. And we all reeled from the aura of violence. In full lights, the damage was even worse. Overturned chairs, smashed displays, shattered figurines, and sweet chocolate corpses buried under shards of glass.

"Bloody hell!" Velvet's voice seemed cracked, too, like brittle glass. "Who could have done this?"

"It's horrible!" Nona cried.

"Why my shop? What did I ever do to deserve this?"

"Nothing but make people happy with your wonderful chocolate," Grady said as he came up to put a comforting arm around Velvet's shaking shoulders. His voice was gravely and his hands gnarled with age, yet his gentle gaze was full of concern. "I've already called the police. Make sure no one touches that bat. If there are any fingerprints, we'll get the brute that did this."

I was gasping for breath after running. "I saw him!" I exclaimed.

Heads swiveled in my direction.

"You did!" Velvet exclaimed.

"Where?" Grady's heavy brows narrowed.

"Out there! He was running…got in a car!" I pointed out the door I'd left open. "A tall man…but he drove away."

"Did you recognize him?" Velvet asked eagerly, coming beside me.

"No."

"What'd he look like?"

"I didn't see him clearly. He had gray hair, only his face looked young. It was hard to tell since he was hidden in an long, hooded jacket. He ran so fast, like an athlete. I chased after him, but I couldn't catch up…and he drove away."

"What make of vehicle?" Grady asked.

"It had happened so fast…I don't know…white, four-doors, midsized, I guess. It was too dark and I didn't see the license plate. Sorry."

"You have nothing to regret," Velvet said kindly. "You were very brave."

"Foolhardy," my grandmother criticized. "Sabine, what would you have done if you caught up with him? He could have hurt you! What were you thinking?"

"I wasn't, I guess…thinking."

"Well, I think you were wonderful." Velvet squeezed my hand. "Thank you for trying, but I'm relieved you didn't catch up with him. Anyone who could do such horrid damage is dangerous."

"This is awful," I looked around at the destruction with a grim shake of my head. Broken cabinets, smashed candy, and shattered display cases. How could one person do so much damage—even with a bat—in such a short amount of time? And we'd been just a few rooms away! What if someone had interrupted him or he'd come after us?

I wondered if this was random violence or the result of a grudge against Velvet. Was it revenge from a disgruntled employee, scorned lover, or ex-husband? I knew little about Velvet's personal life. I had no idea if she'd been married, had children, or anything about her life before moving to Sheridan Valley. Her accent hinted at years spent in England, but she never mentioned any family and she lived alone.

A sharp gasp startled me out of my thoughts.

I looked up and saw Thorn pointing to the

large front store window. The lovely painted design announcing Trick or Treats had been brutally
scrawled over with large black Xs. And underneath
the Xs dripped a bloody, red message.

Just two words.
*Die Witches.*

# 7

Who could sleep soundly after a séance and vandalism? Not me.

Spools of questions unraveled tangled knots in my head.

*Die Witches.*

I felt like I'd been raped with words.

Vandalism was so vicious and senseless. All that destruction from hate—for what purpose? To spread more hate?

Like that ever solved anything, I thought in disgust.

I didn't talk much about my personal beliefs, understanding that the things I experienced gave me a less-than-popular prospective on life and death. I'd found out what it was like to be ostracized and labeled a "Freak" once and didn't want to go through that again. Besides I figured everyone was entitled to their own opinion—although it was hard not to get angry at close-minded people who considered séances evil. Our private gathering was as reverent as a prayer and hadn't hurt anyone. It had been held in such secrecy that no outsiders should have even known.

So how had the vandal found out?

Had a member of the séance betrayed us?

This thought was jarring and totally ruined any chance of my falling asleep. So I snapped on my lamp, found a notebook and pen, and then sat in my bed with the notebook propped on my folded knees. I glanced for reassurance at my night-light, an illuminated picture of a peaceful forest, and began to write names. There had been nine séance participants: Nona, Velvet, Thorn, Grady, three older women, a short man wearing glasses, and me.

Well, I could cross myself off the list, and

Thorn, too, because she'd told me she kept the séance a secret. Velvet might have invited some others who couldn't attend, but I doubted she'd confide to anyone untrustworthy. Poker-face Grady would rather die than reveal any secret, so I eliminated him. That left the four people I didn't know...plus Nona. I wanted to cross off my grandmother's name, but how could I be sure she hadn't told someone in a moment of forgetfulness?

Looking at my list of names, all I saw were frustrating question marks.

This was all Agnes's fault, I thought angrily. If she'd come through tonight with the remedy for Nona, we wouldn't have taken so long with the other spirits and finished soon enough to prevent the vandalism. Or we might have stopped him before he could do any damage.

Why hadn't Agnes come to help Nona? I'd been so hopeful, so sure that our ancestor would reach across time and worlds to save her great-great-granddaughter. But she'd let us down. There was little hope left, and Nona would ultimately sink into a slow death.

I tossed aside the notebook and buried my face in my pillow. I couldn't lose Nona...not in such a cruel way, the light dimming from her eyes as her memory slipped away. I'd done everything I could think of to help her, but it wasn't enough. I felt so helpless. My dreams for her recovery were darkening into nightmares.

If I couldn't help the grandmother I adored, I sure couldn't help a half-sister I didn't even like. Douglas must be one crazy spirit. I was positive we'd never met—at least not in this life. If he wanted to get a message to Jade, he'd come to the wrong person. Even if I did want to talk with my half-sister (No way! Not ever!), I couldn't ask her about rag dolls and knives. She'd think I was nuts.

And she'd be right, I thought as I kicked off a heavy blanket. My pillow felt lumpy, so I pounded it with my fist, which felt really good. A punch for spirits that don't show, for spirits that have impossible requests, for half-sisters that shouldn't exist, and for fathers that lie.

Anger exhausted to weary sadness. All I could think of was glass-shattered candy and the fleeing vandal. Who was he anyway? And why did he seem intent on destroying more than candy?

*Die Witches.*

Obviously not a Wicca believer.

At first glance, I'd thought his message was scrawled in blood. But the gooey red liquid turned out to be cherry filling. He'd squished out his warning with a handful of chocolate-covered cherries—an edible death threat for the vandal in a hurry.

When the police showed up, it was obvious they didn't consider this a big crime. One cop even joked that we better not eat the evidence. They might have taken us more seriously if Velvet hadn't washed away the Die Witches message. But before the police arrived, we'd discussed whether or not to tell them about the séance. As public record, the crime could be reported in newspapers or on TV and become really humiliating.

The vote to wash away this telling piece of evidence had been unanimous.

Then we came up with a story about playing an innocent game of cards in the backroom when the vandal struck. Even with my description of the scarecrow guy I witnessed running away, the police chalked it up to a kid's prank and weren't going to put much effort—if any—into bringing the vandal to justice.

But this was far more than a childish prank. Hate this vicious didn't go away. The vandal might do something worse next time. What if he attacked Velvet?

Someone has to stop him, I thought.

Only I couldn't think of anyone—except myself and maybe Thorn. She was always up for a challenge and nearly fearless. But I wasn't sure where to start or what we'd do if we did find the hooded guy. Without proof, the police couldn't arrest anyone.

I longed for advice—even confusing advice from Opal would have been welcome. But when I called out to her, there was no reply.

Why wasn't she answering? What was the use of having a spirit guide if she wasn't around to guide me? She was probably off having fun—maybe hanging out with unreachable Agnes. While they were enjoying themselves, my life was falling apart.

Thank you very much for nothing! I thought.

Sinking farther under my blankets, I felt utterly alone. Why was everything so messed up? I'd thought my life would be perfect once I moved back with my grandmother. Instead things were all messed up. Nona's illness was critical and now Velvet had a dangerous enemy. There had to be some way to use my psychic skill to help, but I couldn't exactly hop over to the other side.

Or could I?

I remembered Velvet's list of ways to contact the Other World: meditation, prayer, channeling, dreams, astral travel, and séance. Scratch off "séance" for obvious reasons. Meditating was great for relaxing, but even Opal didn't come through that way. Prayer was more for giving gratitude, and dreams were too confusing. And forget channeling—after my scary experience with a haunted witch ball, I wasn't going to risk channeling an unknown spirit.

Some psychics could find answers in tarot cards, tea leaves, or even chicken bones, but I was still getting used to my psychic skills—like learning to ride a bike and wobbling on training wheels. While I understood concepts like astral travel (traveling in spirit form while your body sleeps) I wasn't sure if I could do it. Still it couldn't be that hard to make a quick trip over to the other side. I'd had a few experiences leaving my physical body and meeting spirits in neutral planes. I hadn't gone all the way to the other side, but I'd gotten close. Each time it just kind of happened. Could I make it happen on purpose?

One way to find out...

I tried to remember what I'd heard about astral travel. First I needed to lie in a relaxed position and free my mind of earthly weight. Easier said than done! I closed my eyes and struggled to release negative thoughts.

Don't think of Jade or the vandal or Nona's illness, I told myself. Visualize a wonderful, safe place on the other side.

An image came to mind of a beautiful room bordered with colorful murals and comfy pillows scattered around a plush carpet as colorful as a field of wild flowers. A large picture window with an amazing view of a perfect green-blue ocean was open so I could hear the sweet lull of whispering waves. Complete peace and beauty, a place where there were no worries.

Concentrating hard, I abandoned gravity and sailed away like an ocean breeze. I was filled with such a joyful sense of freedom. I wasn't chained to a body, no longer weighed down by humanity. Lifting up, up, up, I floated to an edge of a steep cliff, as if pushing myself to make a choice to stay or go.

I chose "go," and I leaped forward. Instead of falling, I was flying! There were blurred places I didn't know and dizzy images of shapes and others like me flying in soul. To stay focused, I thought of Nona losing her keys, Velvet's smashed candy shop, and a red-haired rag doll pierced with a knife.

There was a lurching sensation, as if I was

tethered by a rope and jerked in a new direction; I swirled through air so fast I couldn't think or feel anything except rushing movement. A high-pitched static surrounded me like a giant beehive. Then my momentum changed—spiraling downward, spinning and whirling, aiming right toward a solid wall. Only it wasn't solid—or maybe I was the one without substance. Buoyed with curiosity, I slipped through the wall like vapor and hovered high in a ceiling above someone sleeping in a bed.

Everything slowed, as if time hit a "pause" button, allowing my mind a chance to catch up with my senses.

I was in a bedroom, weightless and lacking a solid body, floating above a girl whose head was half-covered under a pillow.

Wow, this was cool—but scary, too. What if I was trapped in spirit and could never return to myself? I should go before it's too late. Yet I kept watching the girl, fascinated by the faint rise and fall of her breathing. Such a familiar face…as if I looked at it every day in the mirror. Could she be me? Had I traveled so far only to arrive back at the same spot? How strange to be down there and also up here floating in the ceiling.

Except the room didn't look familiar—and

there was no comforting glow from a night-light. So I had to be somewhere else, and the sleeper was someone else, too. She made a soft breathy sound, flinging an arm out and turning on her other side. The abrupt movement caused a pillow and cloth doll to tumble off the bed, landing down in shadows on a soft carpet. I could see the girl's face now, and she did look like me, except the curl that fell across her cheek was red.

Not blond.

Startled, something seemed to snap my essence through the ceiling. Quicker than a thought, I swooshed through air—sucked upward by a giant vacuum. Static buzzed loudly in my ears and wisps of other souls flashed by in a kaleidoscope of colors.

With a slamming force, I smacked into something solid. Gravity smothered me like a mountain of heavy blankets. I was back in my bed, trapped in a suffocating body. Gasping for breath, I bolted upright and grabbed a handful of my hair. Long and blond. Not red. I was in my own lavender room with a braided rug over the wood floor, a glowing night-light, and shades of lavender, not green and blue reflections of another personality.

Even when things started to make sense, I could hardly believe it.

I'd astral traveled over one hundred miles. But instead of finding Opal or Agnes, I'd found my half-sister, Jade.

And I'd spied on her.

Again.

# 8

Nona slept even later than I did, so I didn't see her before I left for school. I didn't mind because avoiding any talk about last night made it easier to pretend it hadn't happened. School was recess from my weird life.

Josh met me at my locker and everything seemed okay between us. His dark eyes lit up when he saw me. Then he pulled me close for a "good morning" kiss. It felt comfortable being with him.

He was so uncomplicated—things were either good-bad or right-wrong to him. It was tempting to lean against his dependable shoulders and pour out all my worries. But that would just complicate things.

So when he asked how I was doing, I lied. Everything was fine—never better. When he wanted to know what I'd done last night, I shut out the memory of the "Die Witches" threat. I shrugged like my life was boring.

"I played cards with Nona and some of her friends," I said.

"Your grandmother seems cool," Josh said with an approving look. "It's great how you hang out with her like a girlfriend."

"Nona doesn't seem old to me," I said with a wry smile.

Josh smiled back. "I know what you mean. When I'm at senior centers, I get to talking to the residents and sometimes forget the age difference, they're so interesting. Like this one woman told me all about driving alone to Alaska in an old jalopy before there were modern freeways."

I listened without saying much as I spun my locker combination. Josh always had something going on. It was cool how he could multitask so many activities: homework, school council, apprentice-magician meetings, and volunteer work.

Today he was excited about a new project.

"You know how I like to help kids?" he asked.

I nodded, pulling two textbooks from my locker. When Josh was young, his older brother was diagnosed with terminal cancer, and Josh spent a lot of time in hospital waiting rooms. His only happy moments had been when the Amazing Arturo—a stage magician who volunteered regularly at hospitals—taught him magic tricks. When Josh's brother died, Arturo took him on as an apprentice, inviting him into a secret society of professional magicians. Josh coped with his grief by performing some of these tricks at hospitals. Instead of wallowing in his loss, he used his new skills to help others—one of the many things I admired about him.

"I just found out about a program where disadvantaged kids are paired with teen mentors on a weekend horseback riding campout," Josh explained. "It's called Hoof Beats in Moonlight."

"Very cool! Are you going to be a mentor?"

"Yeah. It'll be great to help with homeless and foster kids who have never ridden a horse or gone camping. Some live in terrible conditions and are lucky to get fed regularly. A weekend outdoors will give them a different outlook on life."

"When are you leaving?"

"A week and a half."

"Isn't that Thanksgiving?"

"Only on Thursday—and most of these kids will be celebrating in a shelter anyway. The campout is from Friday to Sunday. This will be an adventure the kids will never forget," he added with shining eyes.

When he was like this—idealistic and passionate—it was easy to get caught up in his energy. Emotions stirred in me, and I hoped this meant I loved him. I certainly loved being with him and I loved his excitement over helping others. He made me want to do good things, too; to be a better person. He was good for me—without the complications of He-Who-Must-Not-Be-Lusted-After.

"I didn't know you rode horses," I told Josh.

"There are a lot of things you don't know about me," he said with an exaggerated air of mystery.

"Oh?" I raised a brow. "Like what?"

"Magic stuff. You know I can't tell you what goes on in our meetings."

"I'm not interested anyway. It's probably the usual card and hat tricks."

"It's way more than that. I'm learning illusions that would make you gasp. The society is all secret, but I can say it's been freaking amazing. Grey has been teaching me some cool tricks. Some of the stuff is so unreal, I can't figure it out."

"Maybe because it's real," I couldn't resist saying.

"Impossible. Magic is all illusion, and anyone who says otherwise is lying."

"Even the big stuff? Like when that famous magician made an airplane vanish?"

"I don't know how that was done, but Grey can explain any trick—usually science, clever machinery, or sleight of hand. Bodies aren't sawed in half and people can't really levitate into the air. Everything has an explanation."

I remembered Opal hinting she could tell me the meaning of everything. Maybe she could, but I was pretty sure that a stage magician didn't have a clue. To hide my doubts, I turned back to my locker and rearranged stuff. Josh was still raving about Grey's brilliance, and I was tempted to argue with examples of many things that defied explanation—ghosts, predictions, intuition, astral travel, and even love.

But why shatter Josh's beliefs?

"If you want to practice riding, come over any-time," I finally said with a slam of my locker. "Nona's horses are kind of old but at least they're gentle."

"Thanks. I may take you on up the offer—but not till I find out for sure."

"About what?"

"If the campout is canceled."

"Canceled? How could that happen?" We fell into step, heading to the first period class we shared. "I thought the kids were eager to go?"

"They are—but there aren't enough teen vol-unteers. We have twelve kids to only eight mentors. Most people our age just don't care." He gestured around at everyone rushing through the hall; talk-ing, laughing, and not noticing us.

"Some do," I insisted. "I'll bet Penny-Love and other cheerleaders would sign up."

"Already tried. Penny-Love says she doesn't want to get horse hair all over her because her boy-friend is allergic to horses. Jill used the job excuse. No one signed up."

"Well, this *is* kind of late notice."

"I know," he agreed. "I only just found out myself. But the kids have been really looking for-ward to it for months. They'll be bummed if it's canceled."

"That would be tragic," I agreed. "But not hopeless. You have over a week to find more mentors."

"I have to be realistic. It's harder to find mentors because not just anyone qualifies. They have to be under twenty, skilled on horseback, patient with kids, and willing to rough it in rugged woods without any comforts."

"No TV or Internet?" I asked teasingly.

"Or bathrooms."

"You're joking."

"No joke." Josh shook his head matter-of-factly. "The campers will get an authentic wilderness experience. The trail is so remote there aren't even outhouses."

"Then where does everyone…you know…go?"

"Anywhere they want."

"You mean…with no privacy? Outside in front of everyone?"

Josh chuckled. "Usually behind a bush or tree."

I started to say, "That's gross," until I realized how that would sound. I didn't want to come off like a prissy city girl who couldn't live without malls and makeup. Sure, I enjoyed nice clothes and shopping, but that wasn't all me. I may have been from San Jose, where my parents lived in a large house with gardeners and a housekeeping service, but I'd fallen in love with a rural lifestyle from my weekends and summers at my grandmother's farm. I didn't scream at snakes, wasn't afraid to get dirty, and could ride a horse.

"It's easier for guys in the outdoors," I said in a joking tone. "You just unzip and do your thing. Can you imagine Penny-Love squatting behind a tree?"

"Not in this lifetime." He chuckled. "I'm glad you're not like that."

"Lots of girls like the outdoors. I'm sure you'll find more volunteers. The important thing is helping the kids. The campout will be a wonderful experience."

"So you'll do it?" he asked, suddenly stopping in the middle of a stream of moving students to face me.

"Me?" Damn! Why didn't I see that one coming?

Okay, so snakes and dirt didn't freak me out. But squatting behind a bush would be embarrassing—not to mention disgusting. Besides, I hadn't ridden a horse in a while. I was competent on a well-trained mount, but I didn't know if I had enough experience to assist little kids.

As for camping...well, maybe there was still

some city girl in me. I almost laughed to think of my family on a camping trip. The closest we'd ever come was when Mom sent me to soccer camp when I was twelve. I wasn't any more skilled at sharing a cabin with a bunch of girls I didn't know than I was at kicking a soccer ball. Mostly I'd gotten bruises and stayed alone in my cabin talking to Opal. And at soccer camp, we'd had running water, electricity, and toilets.

Josh was looking at me in a sincere way that made me feel like a selfish jerk. Did I want to help others only when it didn't inconvenience me? And hadn't I promised myself to work things out with Josh? What better way than a weekend in the outdoors? This was a great opportunity to improve our relationship. Riding horses in the moonlight, sharing food over an open fire, cuddling close in sleeping bags. Very romantic—without Dominic around to confuse things.

"All right," I told Josh.

"Really?" He looked a little surprised, as if he'd expected me to argue. "You'll do it?"

"Sure. It'll be fun."

"Great! I'll sign you up ASAP."

"Wait—there's one condition."

He furrowed his forehead. "What?"

"Toilet paper." I smiled. "Four-ply and cushioned."

"You got it." He chuckled. "As much TP as you want. It's great you want to come. I wasn't sure you would...I've kind of wondered about some things..."

"What things?" I asked cautiously.

"Nothing really. Not anymore, now that you're coming with me." He gently squeezed my hands. "I promise you—this will be a weekend you never forget."

As he spoke these words, I had a mental flash of a dark brown horse galloping through dense pines, then disappearing like smoke. I heard a girl screaming from somewhere in the distant future, and I shivered with acute premonition.

Instantly, I knew that Josh was right about the campout. It would be a weekend I'd never forget.

But not in a good way.

# 9

It was my last period of the school day and I struggled at a computer to meet an impossible deadline.

"Beany, have you finished yet?" Manny asked for like the ten-thousandth time.

And for the ten-thousandth-and-first time, I told him, "No."

I didn't bother to add my usual, "Don't call me Beany" because it was a waste of stale classroom air.

Manny DeVries, editor of the school paper *Sheridan Shout-Out*, always did exactly what he wanted and badgered everyone else until they did what he wanted too. He didn't fit the image of a dictator in his khaki shorts, sandals, and dreadlocks, but he was one-hundred-percent tyrant.

"We're already a day late and in a crucial time crunch. I desperately need the column before school ends." He rubbed the silver arrow in his pierced brow. He leaned over my computer desk, his beaded dreadlocks jangling. The noise added to my annoyance.

I slapped my hand on the desk, sending papers fluttering to the floor. "It won't be done *ever* if you don't stop nagging me." I glared up at him. "This isn't like a Google search—I need to concentrate and wait for messages to come from you-know-where."

"Actually, I don't know where—which is why I need your expertise. Or my readers might realize my Mystic Manny rep is crap," he said with a cautious glance around the room where other students typed busily at computer desks. Our teacher, who was so mellow he was more like furniture than an authority figure, hunched over stacks of papers at his corner desk. "The *Shout-Out* has to go to press tonight."

"Stop pushing me." I waved him away. "Leave!"

"Can you be done in ten minutes?"

I glared at him. "Watch out or I'll hex you."

"You don't have that kind of power."

"I can learn. Then I'll curse you with an extreme case of zits."

"And ruin this work of art?" He gestured to his face. "Say you don't mean it, Beany."

"I'll show you mean. Zits and bad breath. See if you still have a female fan club with that combo."

"Cruel girl."

"Go ahead—insult me all you want. Just do it from over there." I pointed to the other side of the room. In a perverse way, I enjoyed arguing with Manny—not that I'd admit that to him.

"Do I detect a sour mood?" he asked. "Is it your bitchy time of the month?"

Manny was lucky I didn't have a stapler or paperweight handy. Instead all I found to throw at him was a paper clip. It hit him on his chin and I felt a small satisfaction when he cried, "Hey, that stung! Could you stop acting like a kindergartner and show some maturity?"

"If you let me work in peace. You're not the only one who wants to finish. Josh and I have plans after school. And I'd much rather be with him than you."

"I am crushed beyond words. Most girls beg for my company."

"Go annoy them."

"Definitely that time of month. I can see you're in a nasty mood, so I'll leave you." He glanced at his watch. "You have fourteen minutes to turn in your column."

"Tyrant!" I muttered.

I turned back to the computer and looked at what I'd come up with so far.

*Mystic Manny Sees All.*

The title of my weekly column. Or actually it was Manny's column, but we had this secret arrangement where I gave him real predictions and he helped me whenever I needed information (he was a whiz hacker type). Despite our insults, he was a true friend. Manny and Thorn were the only two people at school who knew I was psychic; they honored my secret and I'd grown to trust them.

It was ironic that while Manny pretended to impart psychic revelations every week in the *Sheridan Shout-Out*, I was the real source of his predictions.

Lucky numbers, romantic advice, campus gossip, the popular "Ten Years in the Future" profile, and whatever else popped into my head.

My accuracy rate was amazing—which added to Manny's popularity, especially with girls. Not that he needed any help. He didn't follow any trends or wear name brands or do any of the usual things that equaled popularity. But his whole "I don't give a shit" attitude won him admirers. I really didn't understand it.

And I wasn't getting any predictions either. That was the problem and why I'd been sitting in my chair, swiveling around, tapping my feet, staring into space and feeling like a total failure. Why was I having so much trouble today?

The answer was obvious to me, but I couldn't tell Manny because he didn't know about the séance. Although he'd heard about the vandalism at the candy shop. He'd even called Velvet to get an interview for the paper. But she hadn't revealed more than basic facts, thankfully not mentioning that I was one of the witnesses. Since I was a minor, my name wasn't revealed in police reports.

Lucky colors. Lucky numbers. Anything lucky at all?

I meditated, mentally opened up to the universe, and hoped for answers.

*Oh, all right already*, I heard Opal's snippy voice.

Then information flooded my brain—and I started typing.

Lucky color—pink. (Ooh! That wasn't going to be popular with Manny's male readers!)

No lucky number. Instead, an unlucky number: eight.

A girl with black hair whose named begins with "A" was warned to stay home and not run away to her best friend's house.

I also wrote the "Ten Years in the Future" profile on a random student. A sophomore named Erika Flanders would go into nursing, fall for a guy who wouldn't respect her, have twins, and move to Hawaii. I also saw divorce and some spousal abuse, but I had to be cautious about what I revealed. You couldn't rescue people from their life path…although a subtle warning couldn't hurt.

One minute before the bell, I ran off the column, then triumphantly handed it to Manny. Shutting off the computer and grabbing my stuff, I hurried to meet Josh as he exited his last class. It was nice to watch his eyes light up when he saw me. He slipped his arm around my shoulder and we left campus together.

On the short drive to his house, I gave Nona a quick call to check on her. I'd told her I wasn't coming directly home, but as her illness worsened, I was never sure what she'd remember. Fortunately she was having a "good" day. And she wouldn't be alone long since Penny-Love was coming over to work a few hours.

"Come on into the backyard," Josh said when we arrived at his home.

"Why?" I stepped out of his car, glancing down to step over a puddle left from the automatic sprinklers. The newly mowed dark green lawn glistened with shimmering water drops.

He crooked his finger at me. "Come this way and find out."

I smiled at his "stage" tone of mystery. He had such compelling charisma that if he went pro with his magic, he'd be famous. "Did you learn a new magic trick from your mentor?"

"Nothing to do with Arturo. I worked with Evan on this."

"Evan?" I grimaced as I said the name like I'd swallowed poison. And Evan Marshall was poisonous to me. At school he was Josh's best friend and my worst enemy. A conceited jock, Evan arrogantly wanted to handpick Josh's girlfriend and hadn't approved when Josh started dating me, so he tried to break us up by digging up the scandal of my being kicked out of my last school. Fortunately Josh didn't believe it. His loyalty was so sweet; I didn't deserve him.

The wood gate to the backyard creaked as Josh held it open for me. Overgrown oleander bushes brushed against my jeans as I followed Josh down the narrow bricked path to the backyard. It wasn't a huge yard, but it had ample room for a flower garden, a brick barbeque with built-in sink, and mini-basketball court.

A gruff bark made me jump. I braced myself as a whirlwind of padding feet and barking rushed forward.

"Horse! Down!" Josh ordered before his dog could knock me over.

Horse was a giant of a dog who deserved his name. Fortunately he was well-trained and sat politely at Josh's command. Still his tongue flopped out and his tail thumped happily against the ground.

While I scratched Horse on his head, Josh grabbed a basketball and I guessed he wanted to show me a new basketball shot. Definitely Super-Jock

Evan's influence, I thought sourly. I understood that Josh would want to hang out with his best friend, especially since I'd been gone the last few weeks, but I didn't have to like it. Josh needed a better best friend, someone who wasn't a stuck-up ass. His new pal, Grey, sounded okay. But then a mass murderer with the plague would have been an improvement over Evan.

"Watch this!" Josh announced with the ball poised between his palms.

Snapped out of my thoughts, I looked up, expecting Josh to shoot a tricky basketball shot, like ricocheting the ball off his head or throwing it backwards with his eyes shut. So I didn't expect him to bounce the ball to his dog.

With a sharp bark, Horse sprang forward and head-butted the ball so that it flew up and sailed down dead center into the basket.

"Wow!" was all I could say.

"Exactly the reaction I was hoping for." Josh grinned and slipped Horse a doggie treat. "Want to see it again?"

I nodded and stepped back to get a good view. Josh threw the ball again, but this time Horse sprang at the ball too soon and only hit the backboard. The ball bounced off into the garden. While Josh retrieved it, I patted Horse and said, "Good try."

Josh rewarded Horse with another doggie treat. "He's gotten much better and sinks the ball three out of four times."

"Very cool." I applauded.

"The credit goes to Evan."

Not what I wanted to hear, but I kept right on smiling.

"He came up with the idea to train Horse. At first I didn't think a dog could shoot a basketball. But Horse and Evan proved me wrong. Now I'd like to put Horse into my act, you know, like when I go into hospitals. Animals really cheer up sick kids."

"Horse would look cute with a little hat on his big head," I suggested.

"He would! Good idea."

Josh and I sat at a small table and brainstormed more ideas, like teaching Horse to bounce a balloon and standing on his back feet to dance.

We were still talking when Josh's mother brought out a tray with iced tea, cheese, crackers, and cookies. I really liked Josh's mother and secretly wished my mother were more like her. Mrs. DeMarco was like those moms you see in reruns of old sitcoms, all hugs and nurturing. Her only fault was fussing too much over Josh. She'd lost one child so it made sense she'd cling more to her remaining son. I noticed Josh's embarrassment.

I was thinking of the different ways my mother embarrassed me when I heard an odd, shrill sound. A dark flutter of wings swooshed over our heads and disappeared into a nearby tree. We all looked up, but I was the only one who recognized the sharp-beaked tawny falcon.

What was Dagger doing here? He was sort of a pet of Dominic's, except he was completely wild and free to go wherever he wanted. Usually that was near Dominic.

Did that mean Dominic was close by? Was he waiting to talk to me?

Conflicting emotions made me crazy. I was eager to see Dominic again yet anxious because I didn't trust myself with him. Could I ignore lustful urges and treat Dominic like a friend? But what if he wanted to kiss me again? Would I be able to resist?

Doubtful.

Why was staying honest and loyal so hard? Was it because of something lacking in my relationship with Josh? Or had Dominic cast a spell on me? Just thinking about him made me itchy under my skin, hot and lightheaded.

All of this passed through my head in microseconds, while I pasted a smile on my face and pretended to listen to something Mrs. DeMarco was saying about a pet pigeon Josh owned when he was young. I should have been hanging onto every word about Josh, eager to know what he was like as a child and thinking about our future together and even imagining the children we might have someday. That's how a typical girlfriend would act—yet seeing Dagger sent my thoughts flying back to Dominic.

Torture. That's what I felt not being able to rush out of the yard and look for him. He'd been gone for days and I'd tried not to think about him, wonder what he was doing and if he was thinking about me...

And I was dying to ask him the Big Question: Had he found the final charm?

You're overreacting, I chastised myself. The bird probably isn't even Dagger.

But as if to prove himself, the falcon flapped his wings with a squawk and launched himself into the air. He circled directly over my head, which set

Horse off. The large dog barked and jumped at the bird.

"What's that bird doing?" Mrs. DeMarco cried, shading her eyes from the sinking sun as she looked up.

"I don't know, maybe looking for food. But it's odd to see a wild bird in this neighborhood," Josh said with surprise as he gazed up at the circling bird. "Looks like a hawk."

"A falcon," I corrected.

Horse's barking increased as Dagger sailed lower and lower, stirring the chilly air around me. The bird shrieked in some avian language I didn't understand, then he swooped down near my face.

"Watch out, Sabine!" Josh shouted, reaching to shield me.

"It's all right. He won't hurt me."

"You can't be sure with wild animals."

"I'm safe...honestly."

"He's coming at you again! Get down!"

Josh's shout set off Horse, who barked and sprung high, knocking against the table, sending plates and glasses tumbling to the ground. Mrs. DeMarco screamed as iced tea splashed in her face.

I moved away and the bird followed me. He swished his wings and squawked, as if trying to tell me something. Although I couldn't understand his squawks, I had a mental picture of a hand reaching in the air. While Josh struggled to get past his excited dog, I lifted my arm up and opened my palm toward the sky.

Dagger's sharp talons uncurled and a tiny object sailed down into my hand. I curled my fingers, capturing the object. The bird flew away with a final shrill cry.

I glanced down at my palm—and saw a tiny glint of silver.

The missing charm had been found.

# Part Two

*Charmed*

# 10

Josh and his mother were so focused on the falcon dive-bombing in their backyard that they didn't notice me slip the small charm into my jeans pocket.

After Dagger flew away, things settled down, although it took a lot of talking to convince Josh that the bird wasn't vicious and hadn't attacked me and please do not call animal control.

"Too many wild creatures have lost their natural

habitat to urban overdevelopment," I appealed to his idealist side. "The poor bird was probably confused and more afraid of us than we were of him."

"But he attacked you!" Josh argued.

"No, he didn't."

"He dove at you with his claws."

"But he never touched me. See, no scratches."

I showed him my unmarked arms. Still, Josh and his mother were so worried, and I felt guilty for misleading them. But I couldn't tell the truth about Dagger without explaining Dominic's unusual ability to communicate with animals.

The whole time they were fussing over me, I was thinking about the tiny charm hidden in my pocket. My quick look hadn't been enough to tell the shape, only that it was rounded, with a flat side surrounding a hole. Leave it to Dominic to add mystery to this amazing moment by having Dagger surprise me with the charm. I could hardly contain my excitement and nearly threw my arms around Josh and shouted, "We have the charm! At last, we have all the charms! Nona is going to be okay!"

How agonizing to pretend like nothing had happened. For so long this elusive charm had seemed like an insurmountable wall blocking Nona from getting well. If only we had the fourth charm, I'd thought so often, dreaming of this miracle moment. And now the tiny charm of hope was tucked into my pocket.

All because of Dominic.

So was he waiting for me back at the farm or hidden beyond the fence? Was he watching me right now?

Dangerous emotions tingled through me. I reached up to smooth my hair, wishing I'd taken time to touch up my makeup. It felt like weeks since I'd seen Dominic. I imagined him reaching out for me with that arrogant grin which teased and challenged and made me want to slap him...or kiss him.

I took a moment to glance away as if admiring the garden, although there were few blooms in November. Taking a deep breath, I turned back to Josh, relieved that he couldn't guess my betraying thoughts.

Bad Sabine, I chastised myself. Don't you dare break Josh's heart. That would be wicked and a terrible way to treat someone who has only shown you love.

Reality splashed me with a harsh dose of shame. I reminded myself of all the wonderful reasons I fell for Josh in the first place: his honesty, humor, and kindness to small children and large dogs. I stared up at his handsome face, gentle dark eyes, and sexy dimples. He should be easy to love. Why I was making this so hard?

Josh is your boyfriend, I scolded myself. Don't forget it and ruin everything just because of some insane attraction to the wrong guy.

Fine. I wouldn't even look at the charm until later. For now, I was all about working things out with my wonderful boyfriend.

We went back into the house with Horse at our heels. Josh's mother stayed in the kitchen while we went into the family room and played computer games. Josh had quick reflexes, reaching high levels and gaining extra lives, but I was better at solving puzzles and uncovering hidden weapons. I whooped in triumph the fifth time I killed Josh with dragon dung bombs, but he had more life and retaliated by attacking me with an army of killer spiders. Game over.

Mrs. DeMarco invited me to stay for dinner, but I shook my head, smoothing my fingers over the charm in my pocket.

Josh drove me home, parking on Lilac Lane beside the large barn-shaped mailbox at the entrance to Nona's long gravel driveway. We didn't get out right away. A devoted girlfriend wouldn't just hop out of the car and dash off. She's supposed to say something sweet about having a great evening and hating to leave him. Then, if no one was watching, they'd make out for a while.

I can do devoted, I told myself, unfastening my seat belt and leaning across the seat toward Josh—which was awkward in bucket seats with a cassette holder between us. But I managed anyway.

He slipped his arms around me. His hands moved along my back and to my shoulders, pulling me even closer so I was almost sitting on his lap.

This is nice, I thought as we snuggled inside, while outside the sun was setting and long shadows surrounded us. I rested my head against Josh's muscled chest, inhaling a pleasant scent of lime shampoo.

"Sabine," he murmured huskily. "I want to tell you—"

"Yes?" I lifted my gaze.

He bit his lip, as if he was suddenly uneasy with me, which seemed odd.

"Just say whatever's on your mind," I spoke quietly. "You can tell me anything."

He sucked in a deep breath. "Sabine...I love you."

Anything but that, I almost replied.

Damn. Why did he have to go and complicate everything? Now I was stuck with having to make the expected reply of "I love you, too." But I just couldn't. I wasn't sure how I felt, and even if I did love him, I wasn't ready to talk about it yet.

So I just nodded—which seemed to be enough for Josh because he pulled me onto his lap and then we were kissing. I tried to relax and enjoy myself, but it was hard to with a steering wheel poking me in the back. And I kept wondering if I should keep my eyes open or shut them. And what about the whole tongue issue? Penny-Love once told me that guys were really turned on by deep kisses. I wanted to be deserving of Josh and not really bad at this. I thought about asking him to recline the seat, but that kind of implied I wanted to do more than kiss. So I scooted sideways and got jabbed by that steering wheel again. Damn. Someone should design cars with ample make out room.

When our kiss ended (a perfectly nice kiss, really, I had no complaints), we made plans to go out to a movie Friday night. Josh said I could even choose a "sappy chick flick," which was really sweet of him.

Waving goodbye, I headed down the gravel driveway, gazing up in the twilight sky on the lookout for a flutter of dark wings. The sound of Josh's car engine faded away, and I gave in to my curiosity, withdrawing the silver charm from my pocket.

Turning the charm in my fingers, I studied its shape. It wasn't bigger than my thumbnail; an elongated half-circle with an opening in the middle. There were some indentations that were too small to figure out.

A half moon? A wishing well? No...a horseshoe.

So what was significant about a horseshoe? Were we looking for horses or a ranch or a blacksmith? Not that any of the above would still be around after one hundred and fifty years. Horseshoes were supposed to be lucky, so maybe we were looking for a place with "Lucky" in the name. Like the Lucky Restaurant, Hotel, or Saloon. Of course, any saloon from that era would have been long gone too.

The horseshoe was just one of four charms. What did it mean? Locating this last charm was supposed to solve everything, only so far it just added more to the puzzle. The horseshoe, cat, fish, and house combined equaled nothing I could guess.

I hoped Dominic would know.

He waited for me on Nona's porch, sitting nonchalantly beside my cat Lilybelle on the bench swing. He kicked the ground with his western boots, causing the swing to rock gently. Back and forth, back and forth, like my swaying heart. Just minutes after kissing Josh, my emotions lurched in the wrong direction.

Against my will, I locked my eyes with Dominic's, aware of every small detail about him. His curled dark hair that fell across his forehead, his eyes as deep as oceans, the jagged hole in the knee of his jeans, the specks of mud crusted on his pointed boots, and that knowing half-grin that seemed to taunt me.

"Your grandmother had a headache and is resting now," he told me as he scooted over to make room on the swing. "Let's talk out here."

"About what?" I sat as far from him on the swing as possible.

"Your cat."

"My cat?"

"Serious situation. Lilybelle is very disappointed in you."

"Why?" I avoided looking directly at him and reached for my cat, not so sure the blue-and-green-eyed cat was really our topic. "She's purring, so she can't be very upset."

"Don't let her good nature fool you. She says that you've been ignoring her."

"Ignoring her?"

"I'm sure it was unintentional," he said in dead seriousness. "She puts on a brave front, but inside she's very hurt. She said you didn't give her any special treats this morning and she waited for you to come after school, but you didn't."

"I had a lot of things to do."

"With Magic Boy?"

"I doubt my cat called him that."

"Cat language is complex. I'm translating for her."

"Can't you just say Josh's name?"

"I could, but what's the point? It's not my fault Lilybelle thinks he's fake."

"Josh is the most genuine person I know. I don't have to answer to my cat...or you," I added accusingly.

"Never ignore a cat. Felines are notorious for

subtle revenge and have sneaky ways of getting attention."

"Do you mean stinky ways?" I knew full well the sort of revenge Lilybelle was capable of. There was still a lingering pungent odor on the living room carpet.

Dominic nodded. "Give her extra treats tomorrow and all will be forgiven. I'll tell her you're sorry."

"When are you going to tell me?" I held up the silver charm. "About this?"

"It's a horseshoe."

"Already figured that out—but why did you send it with Dagger?"

"So you wouldn't have to wait."

"Are you sure it didn't have anything to do with interrupting my visit with Josh?"

"Would I do that?" he said with a wicked grin.

Of course he would, but I didn't say that. Instead I asked him how he found the charm.

"Lucky," he said with a shrug. "I went to the address that woman in San Juan Baptista gave us for her sister."

"And the sister just handed over an antique charm?" I asked doubtfully because we'd been warned the woman was far from the generous type.

She'd stolen from her own sister—not the generous type to just hand over a family heirloom to a stranger.

"I smiled and said 'please.'"

"That seems too easy. She didn't ask for money?"

"She didn't ask for anything."

I didn't believe that, but whatever. We had the charm and that's all that mattered. Next step: decipher the clues.

"What does this mean?" I gestured to the silver charm in my hand.

"Don't know."

"But you have to—you work with horses, learning that horse-shoer stuff."

"The term is farrier."

"So how does the horseshoe fit in with the other charms?"

He frowned and shrugged.

"Don't you know anything?" I demanded, stopping the swing from moving by firmly planting my foot on the porch as I faced him.

"I know lots. Some things you don't want to hear," he added with a deep look.

I looked away and focused on the charm, idly running my fingers over the rough silver. The silver was an older pure quality, so instead of being smooth it was uneven in places. My thumb paused over an especially bumpy part in the center.

"I need a magnifying glass," I said as an idea struck me.

"What do you see?"

"Nothing yet—but I feel something…like a faded inscription."

"Really? Great!" He jumped up and rushed into the house, then returned barely a minute later with a magnifying glass. Then he aimed the glass over the tiny charm in my hand and whistled. "You're right. There are letters, but they're slanted in a fancy cursive style. I can only make out the first three letters…an M…no, it's an N. Then an E-V."

"Never?" I guessed.

"Nevada," he corrected.

"That must be it. Silver strikes were big in Nevada, and the trail of charms led there before. But we still don't know where in Nevada and what the shape of the charms mean."

I sank against the bench. Every clue resulted in more questions and no obvious answers. I'd thought the charms would solve everything. Agnes had left the four charms for her four daughters like a map to the remedy book's hidden location. But even with all the charms, nothing was clear.

A cat, fish, house, and horseshoe? Four charms equaled...what? This was like an algebra equation of $4 + X = Z$. And there was no way of figuring out the Z without knowing what X meant.

At least we had a starting place—Nevada.

Dominic and I sat without speaking, the swing creaking rhythmically back and forth. Lilybelle stopped purring, as if she picked up on our disappointment, and jumped out of my lap and scampered off the porch into the darkness.

What should have been a celebratory moment had deteriorated to frustrating. We needed to connect the charms—uncover the key to their secret. Even if we did achieve this, we still might not find the remedy that may have been lost decades ago.

"Now what?" I finally asked.

"We keep trying," he answered.

I gave a solemn nod. Nona hadn't given up on me when I was a young girl afraid of visitors in the night and voices in my head. She'd explained how ghosts were lost souls who were afraid and she showed me how to guide them to the light. She helped me see spirits clearer and hear the garbled messages they brought. Nona had always been there for me. I would do the same for her.

If Dominic and I couldn't solve this by ourselves, we'd ask for help. We'd do whatever it took to stop the shadowy enemy who was stealing Nona's memories.

Time.

Our worst enemy.

And we didn't have much left.

# 11

Manny had an internal gravitational pull to computers. If it was too early for the computer lab to be open, there was a good chance he'd be in the library—which is where I found him the next morning. I'd come to school early specifically to talk to him, as he was the closest to an expert I knew when it came to digging up information. Besides, he owed me for all my help with his "Mystic Manny" column.

I found him at a rear table in the school library, cozying between two dark-haired girls while he sorted through a pile of thick books.

"Since when are threesomes allowed in the library?" I teased.

"Everything's allowed for me. I got an in with the assistant librarian, which is like a license for rule-breaking." He winked at his bookend friends. "Besides, I'm doing research."

"Research?" I arched my brows, amused. "On twins?"

"Oh, we aren't twins or even sisters," one of the girls said, blushing. "Just best friends, and everyone says we look alike. Some people even think we sound alike, which is just so cool. Maybe it's because we do everything together."

"I'm all for that," Manny said wickedly.

I just rolled my eyes, refusing to rise to his bait.

Then I asked Manny if I could talk with him alone, resulting in nasty looks from his friends. I almost laughed at their identical pouts and would have gladly assured them I had no romantic interest in Manny—but it was more fun to watch them act jealous. If they had the poor taste to lust after Manny, then they had better get used to disappointment.

Manny was full of swaggering confidence and a self-acclaimed expert of everything. "Finding answers is as easy as falling in love...which I do at least once a week." He glanced slyly at his girl-friends. "Sometimes twice."

"Love?" I said. "Sure you don't mean lust?"

"Same thing."

"Only if you're a chauvinistic ass."

"Or irresistible to the ladies."

"You're impossible."

"Yet here you are, ready to ask for my help. I'm right, aren't I? Isn't that why you came to school early? Does this involve the missing charm?"

"Not missing anymore." I quickly explained as I showed him the tiny horseshoe. "Any idea how this fits in with the others?"

He squinted down at the new charm.

"Intriguing," he murmured. "It's like hold-ing a piece of history. After one hundred and fifty years, all four charms are back together."

"But what does it mean?" I asked, frustrated.

"My theory is that at least one of them repre-sents the town where Agnes hid her possessions. Last time I ran a search for you, I checked Ne-vada town names for any connection to the other charms. But nothing close to cat, house, or fish. The closest I came was Duckwater."

"Duckwater? I don't see a connection."

"You know…ducks eat fish. And one of the charms is a fish—but I guess that's stretching things."

"Could there be a town called Horseshoe?"

"I can check." He sidled up to the library desk and grinned at the student library assistant, who blushed and twirled an end of her streaked red-black hair. A minute later he led me to a computer and powered up.

"No Horseshoe," he announced a few moments later. "But there are town names with Silver: Silver Park, Silver City, and Silver Springs. Hey— what about this? There's a city named Smith."

"So?" I asked skeptically.

"Smith could be a reference to "blacksmith" —the dude that makes horseshoes."

"Smith." I repeated the word, hope stirring. "That could be the one—if the town is over 150 years old. Can you find out?"

"Have I ever let you down?" I started to answer, but Manny wisely held up his hand and stopped me from replying. Then, with a grin, he shooed me away and promised to let me know what he found out later.

I put all this out of my mind while I slipped back into the grooves of familiar school routines. But I couldn't pay attention in my classes. Not because I disliked my teachers or learning. But because during those weeks I'd lived with my family in San Jose, I'd done independent study—which jumped me ahead in all my assignments. In English Lit I'd already read the book and written the report. In science, I'd aced the quiz. In history, I knew who won the war and in what year. Only gym wasn't old news—but then who could study ahead for a volleyball game?

Sitting through boring classes left too much thinking time. I worried about Nona's illness, wondered if Velvet would get enough insurance money to reopen Trick or Treats, stressed over the whole Josh versus Dominic dilemma, and tried to figure out how and why my weird astral trip had sent me to Jade.

By lunch, I was eager to chill with my friends and catch up on the latest news. But after getting whacked on the head with a volleyball, I detoured to fix my hair in the only non-smoky/mostly clean girls' bathroom on the other end of campus.

It only took a few minutes to brush and twist my hair into a braid. I was just wrapping it with a hair tie when I heard my name called and the door burst open.

"Manny!" I exclaimed.

"Hey, Sabine." He leaned one arm against the door, grinning.

"Get out! Girls only, no guys allowed." I glanced around anxiously to see if the stalls were occupied and saw only one closed stall. White sneakers with pink laces shifted under the door.

"I've been looking all over for you."

I pointed to the occupied stall. "I repeat— you're not allowed in here."

"Sure about that?"

"Positive."

Manny tossed me a challenging look, then swaggered over with cocky confidence to the closed stall. He rapped on the door. "Hey in there, can I ask a question?"

"Sure," came a muffled reply.

"Are you okay with my being here? I wouldn't have done it if this weren't important."

"Is that you, Manny?" a girlish voice asked.

"The one and only."

"Cool! I'm a huge fan of your Mystic Manny

column. How do you come up with such amazing predictions?"

"It's a gift," he bragged, ducking as I reached out to swat him.

"And your editorial really made me think. I never knew my choice of ring tone could influence my entire life."

"Brilliant, wasn't it?" He grinned. "Well, go on with your…er…business."

"No rush," she called out.

"See. My being here is perfectly okay, Sabine. But we're leaving anyway." Manny grabbed my wrist. "Come on. We have to talk."

"Right now?" I asked as I tucked my brush into my backpack.

"Only if you want to hear what I found out." His black eyes sparkled. "About Nevada."

"Are you serious? You found the location?"

"Did you ever doubt me?"

"Always. But I love surprises. How did you do it?"

"Magic keyboard fingers," he joked, waving his hands. "Turns out there used to be a town called Horseshoe, only its name was changed. Want to hear more?"

I definitely did, but not in a public restroom.

So I slipped on my backpack and followed Manny. As we swung the door out, a girl I recognized from my calc class was coming in. She gave Manny such a surprised look, double-checking the "Girls" on the door, then back to Manny with confusion.

Manny and I burst out laughing.

Then I made him tell me everything.

*     *     *

That evening, Dominic, Nona, and I faced each other across the dining room table. There was hot raspberry sage tea, crackers and cheese, plus some shortbread cookies spread out before us. A fire spread out warmth from the nearby living room, and anyone looking in would have thought we were models for a quaint Norman Rockwell painting.

But there was nothing cozy about our purpose.

"Nona," I said in a solemn tone. "Dominic and I have something to tell you about the charms."

A blank look crossed her face, and she reached inside her pocket.

"You don't need your notes," I said, stopping her before she could pull out the papers. "I'll remind you."

"I don't need reminding about my own life," she snapped. "You think I could forget the charms that my great-great-grandmother left as clues to the remedy? There's nothing wrong with my memory. I'm the one who told you about the charms and showed you the one shaped like a house."

"A cat," I corrected. "That was the first charm. The house was the second charm and I found it."

"I knew that. Don't treat me like a child."

"I'm not."

"It's natural to forget small details. But I haven't lost all my marbles yet. I still remember the important things." She smiled at us, sipping her tea and nodding as if everything was fine—but the light in her eyes was dim. She was only partly there.

"You're doing great, Nona," I said calmly, although I felt like crying. Someone had to take the adult role, and without volunteering the job had quietly passed to me. I reached across the table and squeezed her hand. Her skin was sun-spotted and leathery from a life spent outdoors. Her fingers seemed smaller than I remembered.

"So what did you want to tell me?" she asked.

"Dominic found the last charm."

"That's wonderful!"

Dominic showed her the tiny silver horseshoe.

"Manny just told me today he found out there used to be a town called Horseshoe in Nevada, only now it's called Shrub Flats. The remedy has to be there."

"We'll find it," Dominic added with a protective glance at Nona. I knew he couldn't love her more if she'd been his own grandmother.

"We're leaving in the morning, so I'll miss school," I told my grandmother. "I'll need you to write an excuse."

Nona pursed her lips and shook her head. "No. That's not acceptable."

"Why not? Your health is more important than school. Besides, I'm ahead in all my assignments—I won't miss anything."

"Except our holiday celebration," Nona sat her cup down so hard it rattled.

"What holiday?" I demanded,

"Sabine, you must be kidding. And they say I have problems with my memory, but you don't see me forgetting a major holiday." She chuckled. "With company coming, I'll need your help getting ready. There are so many preparations: peeling potatoes, baking pies, preparing the turkey—"

"Turkey?" I felt sick and shared an uneasy look with Dominic. "But Nona...Thanksgiving isn't until next week."

"Next week? I was sure when I looked at the calendar…" Her voice faded and she seemed to shrink in her chair as if aging years in a few seconds.

"It's a mistake anyone could make," Dominic said with forced cheerfulness. "I've never had a real family Thanksgiving. By next week we'll have found the remedy and we'll have lots to celebrate."

Nona managed a faint smile. "I'm counting on it."

"We won't let you down." I clasped her small, withered fingers. "I promise."

Then Dominic and I made plans to leave in the morning.

On a road trip that meant life or death to Nona.

# *12*

It was early morning, chilly with an overcast sky that loomed ominous in the east. Rain wasn't predicted, but weather had a mind of its own, so I brought a hooded jacket, gloves, and an umbrella. Where we were going, over the Sierra Mountain pass, rain could quickly chill into heavy snow.

Dominic's truck still had that sharp "new car" odor.

I reached across my lap to fasten my seat belt

and my elbow brushed Dominic's leg. A jolt like a stun gun blasted through me. I jerked my arm back, heat rushing to my face. Abruptly, I turned to the window and faked an extreme interest in scenery.

What was wrong with me anyway? Getting all weird over being near Dominic? We'd spent lots of time together before, so why was now any different? It wasn't like he'd made a move on me or there was anything sexual about an elbow touch. This was all about me overreacting. He probably hadn't even noticed or cared...not that I cared if he cared or wanted him to notice because that would be totally wrong.

Damn, I was seriously losing it.

If I didn't get a grip on my emotions, this trip would be a disaster.

I put on a casual face like everything was normal. I was too aware of Dominic, longing for more than a brief elbow touch. I wanted...well, things that just couldn't happen.

Admit it, Sabine, I told myself. You're hot for Dominic and denying the attraction won't make it go away—only confuse truth with lies.

I wanted to get closer to him, yet wanted to get far away from him. I wanted to touch him, but couldn't risk where that would lead. I wanted to talk to him about everything, except I feared words could tumble into an avalanche I couldn't handle. I was keenly aware of his strong, calloused hands, one poised on the wheel and the other casually resting inches from me. His jeans were frayed at one knee and he was missing a button on the leather jacket he wore over a blue cotton shirt. I noticed a tiny feather in his wavy brown hair, probably from Dagger, and resisted the urge to pull it out.

I'd be resisting a lot of urges today.

"Do you have a map?" I asked after long, silent minutes. My forced casual tone gave no hint of my inner drama.

"Map?" He looked startled, as if he'd been lost in deep thoughts.

"So I can navigate while you drive."

"In the glove box, but don't bother."

"Why not?"

"Shrub Flats is so small it's not mapped."

"Then how do we get there?"

"I got it covered."

I waited for him to explain. But he slipped into his annoying habit of clamming up and focusing on the road, not on his passenger. What was he thinking about or who he was thinking about? Not me of course…

"Do you think it will snow? The mountains are so beautiful, but the sky has turned to such a dark gray. It'll be hard to find Horseshoe in a snowstorm." Okay, I was babbling without giving him a chance to answer, which happened when I got nervous.

"Snow would be cool," was all he said.

"Not if it storms while we're on the road."

"My four-wheel drive can get through anything."

"Then yeah, snow would be cool. My family stays at a cabin in Tahoe every winter and we have a great time sledding and skiing. Do you know anyone in Shrub Flats? How will we find where the remedy book is hidden?" Babble, babble, babble. God, I was pathetic.

"The charms should help."

"Once we figure out the fish, cat, and house. Maybe there's a statue of a fisherman holding a cat or a house shaped like the charm. Do you have any theories?"

"A few."

"Like what?"

"The house could be where Agnes lived."

"That charm isn't shaped like a normal house.

It has weird angles; rectangular with a steep pointy roof and round windows. Maybe it's a church."

"Or a hotel," he guessed.

"Would a small town have a hotel?"

"Maybe a boarding house—unless it burned down in the Pig Fire." He flicked his turning signal and passed a large semitruck.

"Pig Fire?"

"I read about it in a history book." Dominic had a quiet passion for reading and often went to the library; it was one of the things I admired about him.

"Nevada was rich in silver mines," he explained. "Towns would sprout up overnight but then vanish when the silver strike ran out. Horseshoe had a lucky streak until 1913, when a huge sow broke out of her pen and knocked a lantern into hay. The fire took out half the town, leaving only stones and shrubs. Horseshoe became Shrub Flats."

"What if the fire destroyed the remedy book? Nona won't ever get any better...only worse...until she slips into a coma and never..." My voice cracked. "Never wakes up."

Dominic pursed his lips determinedly. "We will find the remedy."

As he said this, my head went all dizzy and I had a flash of my great-great-great-grandmother

Agnes kneeling outside in the dark of night beside a sturdy metal box, digging into rough ground with a small shovel. That's all I saw, but it was enough to offer hope.

"You're right." I felt in my pocket for the small satin bag which contained the charms, letting my fingers glide over one. "The remedy is out there— we just have to decipher the charm clues. The fish could mean a fishing pond."

"Or someone named Fish."

"What about the house and cat?"

"House cat or cat house?" Dominic winked. "As in Nevada's oldest profession."

I knew he didn't mean gambling. "No way! Not Agnes."

"Desperate people will do anything when they're desperate."

"My great-great-great-grandmother would never sink that low. She was a devoted, respectable mother."

"And accused of poisoning her neighbor."

"She never poisoned anyone—her herbal medicines cured people. She was treated crappy by neighbors and forced to leave her little girls. By the time her girls received the charms, it was too late and they were split up into different homes." I'd had visions of Agnes and her daughters, and ached with an overwhelming sadness for them. Losing people you loved was so hard. And I thought of Nona.

Dominic seemed to guess what I was feeling. "Don't worry," he said gently. "We'll figure out the charms."

"Over a hundred and fifty years later?"

"You never know."

That was the problem, I thought with frustration. There were too many things I didn't know. Everything hinged on possibilities and hopes, elusive non-tangibles. We were following a tiny clue of silver to another state on the slim chance of finding an old book that may not still exist.

Impossible.

Yet impossible things were normal when you saw ghosts, chatted with spirits, and had prophetic visions. Ironically, this was not the kind of "normal" life I'd hoped for when I'd started a new school this year. I'd strived to create a new and improved Sabine—and on the surface, I'd succeeded. But sometimes I felt confused about my own identity. Despite my cool boyfriend and popular girlfriends, I was still a freak…and maybe that was okay. I'd rather be unique than a clone of everyone else. Sure, my inner freak got me into trouble sometimes, but my abilities helped people—which made me feel good. And I realized that I liked myself.

I wondered if Dominic liked...*more* than liked me.

Of course, I'd never ask. Why did my thoughts keep coming back to Dominic? I should be thinking about Josh. A loyal girlfriend wouldn't go on a road trip with a guy she lusted after. Although it wasn't like we planned to stay the night together. We'd only be gone for five or six hours that did not involve anything romantic. And I'd been upfront with Josh, explaining that I would be gone today because of Nona's illness. Okay, maybe I left out a few details...like who I was traveling with.

Did that make me terrible?

Don't answer that, I told myself.

As we climbed higher into the hills, the temperature dropped. Dominic cranked up the heater. Outside, pine trees shivered from chilly winds, but inside, close to Dominic, I was warm. At the 8,000-foot elevation mark, snow piled along the steep, rocky hillsides and the traffic slowed, flashing red brake lights as we neared ski resorts. Lots of cars had ski racks and I imagined how much more fun this trip would be if we were going skiing. My family used to go skiing.

But that was before Jade threatened our family. I sighed, thinking of laughter and snow fights and warming our hands around a fireplace. Dad didn't act like he wanted a divorce, yet he was hardly ever home and now I knew where he spent all that time away from us: with his other family, Jade and Crystal.

Was Dad willing to work to save his marriage? Or would he rather be with Crystal, who was as relaxed as my own mother was uptight? When he was home, he and Mom argued a lot. Not a good sign. How much longer would my parents stay together? A secret daughter wasn't something Dad could hide forever, and when Mom found out…it was too horrible to imagine. There would be shouting and ultimatums. War would erupt and everyone would lose— except Jade.

My parents' problems weren't Jade's fault, but she was undeniable proof that Dad wasn't perfect. If Mom found out about her, my parents' marriage was over. I had to make sure she stayed away from my family.

Dominic frowned at me. "Did I do something to piss you off?"

I shook my head. Traffic was moving again, although slowly as we curved around a spectacularly sharp drop. Far below, a beautiful emerald-blue lake shimmered with reflections of the frosty white-tipped mountains.

"Worrying about Nona?" he guessed.

"Yeah."

Dominic's expression softened. "Me, too."

"I appreciate all you've been doing for her."

"It's my job."

"You've gone far beyond your job description."

"I care about Nona, and I care about—" He shot me a sideways look.

"What?" I held my breath.

"Sure you want to know?"

"I asked, didn't I?"

Red lights flashed ahead and the truck slowed to a crawl. Dominic hesitated, studying my face as if searching for something.

"You," he finally said. "I care about you."

Fast breath, dizzy head, soaring heart. I couldn't think—only feel an insane rush of joy. There was so much I wanted to say, but I couldn't betray Josh like this. No matter how much I wanted to. That meant hurting Dominic instead…and myself.

He frowned and pulled away. "Sorry. I was out of line."

I shook my head.

"You're with Josh. I respect that."

"Well…that's…um…" Sinking into his clear blue eyes, I couldn't speak.

"I shouldn't have said anything."

"It's…It's okay."

"I've been a total ass. Once Nona is well, I'll move on."

"NO! You can't!"

"I never planned to stay this long."

"But you're such a huge help to Nona." I dug my nails into the armrest. "You love working for her and she thinks of you like family."

"I have no family."

The traffic moved back to posted speeds and Dominic slipped in a country CD, shutting himself off. He disappeared while sitting inches away, humming softly to a sad song. We didn't talk again; as if words, powerful or casual, would expand and steal the oxygen in the truck. There was too much to say and so much that could never be said.

*I care about you*, he'd told me.

Over and over I replayed these words, proving to myself they were real. I hadn't been imagining the vibes between us. He liked me! I wanted to shout and laugh and sing and tell him I felt the same way. But how could I?

Ohmygod! What was I doing? I was committed to Josh—"committed" like being strangled in a straight jacket. I couldn't believe that within twenty-four hours two guys had confessed to liking me. Be careful what you wish for, I thought miserably, because it might come true and mess up everything.

If only Dominic had told me how he felt *before* I'd vowed to work things out with Josh. If only I hadn't promised to go on the horseback camping trip with Josh.

If only…damn.

My romantic timing totally sucked.

# 13

A short distance later, a sign announced we were entering Nevada.

I opened the glove box and pulled out Dominic's map. It wasn't an actual map but a computer printout. I studied the paper, trailing my finger along red highway lines until the lines disappeared into high desert and only a tiny black X hinted at our destination.

We passed Boomtown and Reno, where casinos

and hotels beckoned with bright lights and gambling tables. Snow capped nearby mountains and prickly weeds rolled across vast, rugged hills. Wild horses still roamed Nevada's rugged hills, although I suspected urban sprawl would eventually corral them. Freedom was defined by landscape and society. Wild horses were restricted by roads and fences; I was restricted by duty and expectations. I imagined myself galloping off, shaking away the have-tos of life, and jumping over tall fences…

Dominic spoke my name.

"Huh?" I looked up, startled to realize we'd missed our turn-off.

Oops. I apologized for my lapse in navigating. We doubled back to find Gopher Hole Road, which wasn't much of a road; two lanes that climbed like a creeping snake up sage-brush-covered hills. Almost there, I thought, and I crossed my fingers for luck.

A faded arrow on a fence pointed two miles to Shrub Flats, and we left the paved road for a bumpy dirt road bordered by barbed fencing for cow pastures. Cows lifted their heads as if curious why a truck was interrupting their morning snack, then swished their tails and resumed munching.

I didn't expect much from Shrub Flats—and my expectations were met.

No longer than a block, the cheesy tourist trap claimed to be a historical mining town. Faux Old West shops were bordered by stilted wood walkways on each side of the main street. Yes, that street really was called Main Street. It was like driving onto on a movie set, and I half-expected gunslingers to ride up on their horses and shout "This is a holdup!" But the only horses were wood carvings outside the entrance to Suzy's Saloon.

Other shops included Candy's Ice Cream Parlor, Gold Panning Adventures, Silver Jewelers, Heart's Hideaway B&B, and Shrub Flat Historical Society. The latter piqued my interest. Would local historians know the history of our charms?

Main Street was quiet; probably more tourists were swarming to snowy slopes rather than quaint shops. Soft falling snow sprinkled on cars, curbs, and wintry trees. Dominic parked his truck in front of the Historical Society.

"The sign says it's open," I pointed out. "Although it looks dark, but then a lot of these buildings look deserted. I wonder if anyone's inside."

"One way to find out." Dominic stepped out of the truck.

I hesitated, feeling a chill of unease. Darkened windows like shaded eyes reflected cloudy skies, hiding secrets that I sensed swirled underneath the touristy façade. I glanced around but saw no one suspicious. Then I stepped up on the planked sidewalk.

As we entered the Historical Society, a sudden wind shook the door and slammed it behind us. The bang rattled the windows and caused some brochures to fly off a high shelf. I bent to pick up the brochures when a sudden voice ripped through the room.

"Intruders!" shrieked a raspy voice.

Startled, I jumped and narrowly missed bumping into a shelf.

"Shoot to kill! Intruders!"

"What the hell!" Dominic swore, jerking his head to look around. "There's no one here."

"So who shouted?" I didn't see anyone either, only tall chrome brochures racks, orange cushioned chairs, and an empty desk with neat piles of papers stacked in trays. There was also an odd odor in the air, musty like soggy newspapers mingled with strong coffee.

"Kill intruders!" the voice screamed again. "Go away!"

"I don't think we're welcome," I whispered to

Dominic. I still couldn't see anyone but I heard a rumble noise from the back. "We should leave."

Dominic shook his head, walking to the rear corner of the room, beyond a high shelf of books. I heard his burst of laughter.

"What's so funny?" I asked, hurrying after him.

"Meet our unfriendly host."

He pointed to a large metal cage with a bright-feathered bird inside. "A parrot!"

"Intruders! Go away!" The bird squawked with a flap of his feathers.

"Oh, shut up, Gwendolyn."

I turned to find a middle-aged woman with frizzy, straw yellow hair entering through a back door. She wore too-tight jeans for her wide butt and shiny spurs on her white cowboy boots jangled as she wiggled over to us. She held a cup of steaming coffee in one hand as she waved with the other.

"Don't mind Gwen," she greeted in a friendly drawl. "Y'all are welcome in Shrub Flats."

"Thanks," I said with some relief.

"Sorry, but I was in the back and didn't hear you come in." She set her cup down on the desk, then frowned at Dominic, who was bending over the giant-sized bird cage. "Be careful. Gwendolyn bites."

"I'll take my chances," Dominic replied.

"Last person who said that lost a finger," the woman said ominously. "Gwen's a very old African Grey and bad tempered. She detests strangers. Don't say I didn't warn you."

Dominic leaned closer to the cage, whispering rhythmic clicking and whistling sounds as he slipped a finger through the bars. Gwen tilted her blond head, her beady eyes fixed on Dominic. Instead of biting, she made a clicking sound, then fluttered over and perched on his finger.

"I've never seen her do that before!" the woman exclaimed.

I smiled, not at all surprised. Dominic had been astonishing me with his almost-magical spell over animals since I met him. To be honest, I found it very sexy.

"African Greys are fascinating birds," he said, tickling the bird with his other hand. "Some live over a hundred years."

"Ain't that the truth? Gwen's so old, no one knows her age. She's had more owners than Nevada has slot machines. Seems like it anyway," the woman added with a chuckle. "I can't get over how she's taking to you. I reckon that means you're good people and I'm glad to meet you. I'm Bea Hiverson, but my friends call me Bea Hive."

"Bee hive?" I repeated, amused.

"Silly, I know, but suits me." She reached up to pat her hair. "Spelled B-E-A, short for Beatrice."

Dominic held out his hand. "Pleased to meet you. I'm Dominic and this is Sabine."

I gave a small wave.

"Where y'all from?" Bea asked. She reached for a bag of seeds and offered some to Dominic. He slipped them through the cage and Gwendolyn gobbled them up with gentle pecks.

"Sheridan Valley, California."

"Never heard of it." She turned from me, clearly more interested in Dominic. "You raise birds?"

"No." He stroked Gwendolyn's silvery head feathers. "But I respect animals and they can tell I like them. Isn't that right, Gwen, old girl?"

"Intruder!" she squawked. "Nice intruder."

We laughed, then Bea gestured to a display of pamphlets, calendars, and videos on Shrub Flats. "We have plenty of history to share. You interested in a video of an authentic re-creation of a silver mine?"

"Not this trip," I said. "We're looking for information on someone who may have lived here a long time ago."

"How long?"

"A hundred and fifty years ago."

Bea stared at me. "Mighty long time. Back then Shrub Flats wasn't even called Shrub Flats. It was called—"

"Horseshoe," Dominic said.

"Yes. That's right." Bea gave a low whistle. "You must have been studying up on our area. Any particular reason?"

"We're looking for information on an ancestor of mine who may have lived here. Are there old records from the late 1800s?"

"Not around here." She gestured to the glass and chrome shelves and displays. "Nothing's left of the old town. The Pig Fire destroyed everything. But you can buy a video on the fire—a fabulous re-creation of real historical events. It's on sale, too, buy one and get an authentic nugget of imitation silver." She crossed over to a counter with small plastic containers and picked up a speck of silver smaller than my pinky fingernail.

Bea didn't look happy when we declined this "great deal."

But she persisted, leading me over to cases of jewelry and pitching hard for a sale. I finally broke away from her and went over to Dominic.

"If you're done playing with that bird, I'm ready to go."

He looked up. "You find out anything?"

"As if you care."

"What's wrong?"

"Coming here was a total waste." The door banged shut behind us. An icy gust slapped at my legs and stung my face. "Bea doesn't have a clue about history or antiques. She only carries 'authentic reproductions.'"

Dominic snorted. "Translation: Junk."

"This museum is a rip-off, limited to what she wants to sell. She kept hitting on me for a sale."

"Looks like she succeeded." He pointed at the plastic bag in my hand.

"Well…I felt like I should buy something."

"Sucker," he teased.

"It was on sale. I could hang the charms on it—at least they'd be good for something. I wish I knew what they meant." I dangled the silver necklace from my fingers. "Horseshoe has to mean this town, yet Bea said nothing was left of the original town. Everything went up in flames with the Pig Fire. There's nothing over a century old."

"Except Gwen," Dominic chuckled.

"Oh, yeah. Mustn't forget old Gwen."

"Seriously. Gwen was very talkative."
"But she's a bird."
"A brainy bird with a long memory."
Then he told me what Gwen had to say.

# 14

Bassett, Parrotten, Jackpot, Rebekah, Feather Brain, and Beak Boy.

These were a few of the names Gwendolyn had in her very long lifetime.

"Beak Boy?" I questioned. "Gwen is a girl."

Dominic shrugged. "Hard to tell with birds."

I shot him an amused look. "Unless they tell you."

The sky was darkening and the blustery wind

was now flecked with white puffs of snow. We returned to the truck, and I reached into the back for my jacket, warming up my shivery body.

Dominic's voice rose with excitement when he talked about something he felt strongly about, which would be anything to do with animals. His cheeks and nose were ruddy from the cold, although he didn't seem bothered enough by the dropping temps to put on his leather jacket. He gestured as he talked, excited about connecting so closely with a wise animal. His aura flared red and golden hues, drawing me into his energy, overly conscious of my own green-lavender essence reaching across the space between us.

"Gwen talked about her past," Dominic told me.

"Oh? Is she really over a hundred?"

"Older. Her earliest memory is of crossing the ocean on a large boat with many other birds. Her first owner was a wealthy little girl who dressed her up in doll clothes and took her for rides in a baby buggy. But the little girl got sick and died young. This was around 1890."

"Long after Agnes died," I said sadly. "Gwen never met Agnes, so how can she help us?"

"She also lived with a train conductor, farmer,

and midwife. She's seen a lot." Dominic started up the truck, glanced over and seemed to notice how I huddled under my jacket, then turned up the heater. But he didn't drive anywhere, not yet.

"Gwen went through many owners; most of them considered parrots lucky. One of her names was even Lucky—until that unlucky owner died in the Pig Fire. Gwen never liked him much anyway. He forgot to feed her and left her water dirty. His feed store burnt down along with *almost* every other building in Horseshoe."

"Almost?" I noticed how he'd emphasized this word, my interest piqued. I leaned forward, careful not to brush against him.

"This isn't the only museum," he said with a dismissive flick of his hand. "The Horseshoe Museum survived."

"How?"

"Brick doesn't burn."

I glanced around at the touristy faux Western shops. "So where is it?"

"Over that hill at the original town site."

"Which Bea said didn't exist."

My annoyance with Bea faded as I realized how close we were to finding my great-great-great-grandmother's remedy book. I crossed my fingers, hoping this museum was the real deal and not another "re-creation." If it was genuine, then someone there might know about Agnes. Did this mean our luck was improving? Old Gwendolyn may live up to her former name of "Lucky." If this panned out, I owed her a special bird treat.

Dominic clicked on the windshield wipers. They swooshed back and forth as we pulled away from the curb, flicking away snow flakes. The light snowfall was mesmerizing, each lacy flake awesomely beautiful, inspiring confidence that life happened for a reason. Nature's puzzling perfection was proof in powers larger than human worries. Somehow this made everything better, and I felt confident all the puzzle pieces were falling into place. Soon we'd find Nona's remedy, mostly because of Dominic. Aside from gleaning information from animals, he had a keen sense of direction for important clues. My grandmother had chosen wisely when she hired him as handyman/apprentice.

I wished my choices were as wise…

A rut in the road jolted the truck and smacked me against the door. The paved road changed to rough gravel and we wound around rugged terrain with only a few scattered ranches. Light snow softened the landscape of the high desert, adding an angelic frosting to tumble weeds and prickly bushes.

We slowed on a dirt road surrounded with vast fields with dead-looking flat patches that were the burnt remains of old buildings. There were other remnants of a forgotten town: crumbling rock walls, broken chimneys, and deep trenches grown wild with chaparral, twisted barbed wire fences, and gnarled trees littering a dead orchard. Only a few buildings remained. One had an odd rectangular shape with a high roof that sloped down to a row of small square windows that circled the building. On the front by the porch was a large brass horseshoe above large letters: HORSESHOE MUSEUM.

"Unreal!" Dominic exclaimed. "It's shaped exactly like the charm!"

"Wow." I pulled the house charm from my pocket and held it up, comparing it to the brick building. Except for a frosting of snow, it was an exact match with the same odd peaks, rounded windows, and double doors. Displayed at the front of the building was a large brass horseshoe.

"It's both the horseshoe and the house! Only it's a museum, not a house. Agnes was here!"

I jumped excitedly, snow sloshing on my jeans.

But who cared? We'd reached the end of our quest! Nothing could dampen this amazing moment. Over one hundred years ago, my great-great-great-grandmother had stood on this same bricked walkway and walked through that door. Where other descendents had failed to follow her clues, we'd succeeded.

But when we climbed the steep brick staircase to the door, we were stopped abruptly. A cardboard sign hung on the doorknob by a string so the words tilted off to one side.

Gone Fishing. Niles.

I could not believe it.

"Not fair! Someone has to be here!" I pounded on the door. "Who goes fishing in the snow?"

"Some guy named Niles." Dominic jerked on the door knob. "Locked. Damn."

"So what do we do?"

"Wait until he comes back."

"And turn into icicles."

"It's not that cold. But the snow is coming down harder. What do you want to do? Wait or leave?"

"If we leave that's like failing, and if we stay we could freeze to death."

"It's your call," Dominic told me.

How long would Niles be gone? Niles could be

fishing for a few hours or a few weeks. Why couldn't his note have included a "will return by" time? I hated to give up, but what else could we do?

*Excuse me, Sabine dear, but as usual you're over-looking the obvious.*

"Opal?" I asked, realizing I'd spoken out loud.

Dominic shot me a questioning look. "Your spirit guide is here?"

I nodded, then tuned in to Opal, closing my eyes so I could see her image. Gray shadows sharpened, defining a feminine shape, the dark-amber skin luminous and her shining ebony eyes rich with wisdom. She lifted her braided head, the purple ribbons twisted into a regal crown, with queenly elegance.

*I suspected you'd soon turn my direction for council.*

"Can you help?" I asked doubtfully. Opal acted like she knew it all but seldom gave me real advice.

*It is my chosen role and obligation, written down before your journey, to align with you. I profess to an enjoyment of challenges and am never disappointed in that regard. I find constant amazement in your penchant for trouble.*

I wasn't sure what she meant, but I guessed

"penchant for trouble" was her way of saying I attracted trouble. I couldn't disagree, although I bristled at her scolding. I never planned to get in trouble—it just happened. I swallowed my pride and asked her for help.

*You must be more precise in your query. Help is a vague term which can mean simply an encouraging word or more drastic involvement. I have always offered thankless assistance. Who do you think reminded you to bring the jacket and gloves?*

"You never said anything."

*I put the thought in your head. If you were paying attention, you would have sensed my presence. I knew the weather would prove challenging and you'd require substantial warmth. Despite the lack of gratitude I deserve, my considerable actions are woefully unnoticed.*

"I'm grateful…honestly. Thank you, Opal! You're the best, and I do appreciate everything you do."

*As you rightly should.*

"Do you know how long Niles will be out fishing?"

*That enters into the prohibited area of human choice, which is specific information out of the range of my knowledge.*

"So you don't know?"

*In a manner of speaking.*

"Just tell me what to do. We have all four charms and they led us to this museum. Only we can't get inside. Do we wait for permission or break in?"

*Breaking rules comes with consequences that you would not enjoy. Patience is a dependable ally. Rushing to quick solutions can lead to disappointing answers.*

"What answers?"

"Are you asking me or her?" Dominic whispered.

"Her."

"What's she saying?"

"That we'll be disappointed if we rush to quick solutions— whatever that means. Opal always says confusing stuff—it's like receiving garbled text messages."

*I am still here and do not appreciate your derogatory comments.*

I sighed. "Just tell us how to find the remedy book."

*To see clearly, you need only to utilize your eyes.*

"We *have* been using our eyes! But we need to get inside the museum, and we can't until Niles returns. The door is locked and the windows are too high."

*Really child, can you be any more dense? Your God-given free will binds me as your guide and not your servant. Search within your own resources. Anyone with moderate intelligence could look beyond solid structures to the place where grave answers reside. When you go behind the obvious, you'll find yourself ahead of the game.*

I just wanted the "game" to be over. But we had a long way to go, so I repeated these words to Dominic. I found some satisfaction when he scrunched his forehead, looking confused. Moderate intelligence indeed! Opal was impossible.

She must have heard these thoughts because I felt a heated wave of indignation and then a cold emptiness.

"She's ditched us," I told Dominic.

"Can she do that? I thought guides were supposed to help."

"She helps with massive amounts of sarcasm." I scowled as a huge snowflake plopped on my forehead. Had Opal caused that?

"So why do you put up with her?"

I paused to consider this. "I guess because

I love her—even though she makes me want to scream."

"So scream."

"You're joking, right?"

"Screaming is one of the emotion-cleansing techniques Nona taught me. Primal screams relieve stress."

"I'm not stressed."

"No one's around to hear if you need to scream."

Except you, I thought. And if I'm stressed, it's not only because of Opal.

"I'd rather figure out what to do," I said with a frown at the closed door. "Opal gave us some clues. Any idea what she meant by saying 'See beyond solid structures'?"

Dominic pointed. "This building is a solid structure."

"Beyond might mean behind."

"So let's look around back."

We had to walk through high weeds and around prickly cactus, and all along I felt skeptical, not expecting anything more than weeds. So I was surprised when we reached an old iron gate that stretched out to an old graveyard.

"'Grave answers,'" Dominic repeated.

I brushed snow from my nose, hugging my coat tighter as I looked around at dark skeleton trees hanging over crumbling gray headstones and broken angel statues. My skin tingled, not from the cold, but from the thought that jumped in my head.

Was Agnes buried here?

But the gate was locked, and the only way to get inside was with a key or to climb over. I could tell when I glanced at Dominic that he was already searching the gate for an easy spot to climb. The iron spikes were pointed and dangerous for climbing. But that didn't slow Dominic.

"Take my hand," Dominic told me. He pushed through weeds near the fence and started to climb. "This area over the gate isn't spiked. Follow me."

Anywhere, I thought.

Weeds scratched at my jacket. I looked for a foothold at the base of the gate, stuck in my foot, then reached to pull myself up. I hesitated, not from fear of a difficult climb but of touching Dominic's hand.

"Come on," he urged.

My fingers met his and our hands fit like they'd been molded together; his were large and callused, mine were smaller but strong, too. Purple-gold energy sizzled from our joined hands.

Then I was being lifted up and half-carried over the points of the gate, landing feet first, safely in the graveyard. Among the dead, alongside Dominic, I'd never felt so wonderfully alive.

"Do you think Agnes is here?" I asked him.

"Not anymore."

"But she was." I spoke in a whisper like I'd walked into a library. A library and graveyard were similar—places of peace and memories, filled with stories. While libraries nurture true and imagined stories, a graveyard was the caretaker for stories at their end. Some people fear graveyards, spooking easily at ghost stories, but there was nothing frightening here, only footsteps of memory.

"Do you see any ghosts?" Dominic asked, smiling.

"No ghosts or spirits." I pointed to a gravestone which read Myrtle Mae Fredericks, Beloved Daughter and Sister, 1895–1899. "She died too young."

"Even if she'd lived a long life, she'd be dead now."

"It's still sad."

"Look for Agnes's grave. She could be buried here."

"Along with her remedy," I added, hope rising.

The cemetery wasn't huge, but it took nearly an hour to read every tombstone, especially the crumbling headstones with names too faint to decipher. A few times a name would trigger my sixth sense. I'd get a mental image of a face: a laughing girl with blond ringlets, a baby crawling on a braided rug, or a wrinkled man hunched over a cane. So many lives lived and gone. But none of them related to me.

"The only Agnes I can find has the wrong last name—Hoggleworth. Have you noticed how strange the names used to be? Euphelia Tredeway, Docile Wagonwheel, Hibram Bridgeman."

Dominic chuckled. "And this one here, Katherine Trout."

"Trout?" I walked over to the grave. There were no angel statues or fancy inscriptions, and the faded, square tombstone had deteriorated so I couldn't make out the date, although the first two numbers looked like a one and an eight.

"Are you getting a vision?" he asked.

"No. An idea."

"What?"

"Fish is Trout. And what's a nickname for Katherine?"

He shrugged. "Kate? Kathy?"

"Or Kat." I pulled out the cat charm and dangled it in front of his face.

"Cat!" His blue eyes lit up. "Cat plus fish equals Katherine Trout."

"Exactly," I said with rising excitement.

"That means all four charms—"

"—lead to this grave," I finished.

"The horseshoe, house, cat, and fish. You found it."

"We both did."

"Yeah, partner." His grin went to my heart.

Suddenly hot all over, I glanced away and pointed to Katherine Trout's rock- and weedsplotched grave. "The remedy book has to be buried here."

"So we start digging," Dominic said.

Easier said than done, we both discovered. We searched for a shovel, but the closest we found was a metal rake. Dominic improvised with a metal bowl he found in his truck and the rake. Using leverage, we worked together to pry off the headstone. Then Dominic did the dirty work and I paced impatiently, brushing off light falling snow from my face.

"See anything yet?" I must have asked a dozen times, and his answer was always no. He'd dug about two feet now without even finding a casket (which was actually a relief). I mean, talking to the dead was okay when they looked almost alive, but I didn't want to see their yellowed bones.

The sky had darkened and chilly wind whipped like icy ropes across my skin. I kept my spirits up by thinking how happy Nona would be when we found the remedy. We were so close now...

I heard a sound behind me. Before I could turn, something pointed jabbed my back. "Don't move," a gravely voice ordered.

With a choked cry, I froze. The sharp object jabbed deeper, painfully, between my shoulder blades, and I knew what it was.

A gun.

# 15

My attacker ordered Dominic to stop digging.

"Okay. Don't do anything dumb." Dominic froze in his kneeled position; his back was to me so he couldn't see much. He tensed, seemed to think it over, then slowly lifted his arms in surrender. His makeshift shovel rolled away from his snow-crusted boots.

"We did what you said." I tried to sound calm.

"We don't want any trouble," Dominic added.

"Yeah," I agreed. "Put the gun down."

"Gun? Where'd you get that fool notion?"

The pressure on my back vanished.

I risked a look over my shoulder and saw a stout elderly man with a fuzzy black beard, and he wore a thick black jacket that made him resemble a bear. But the wrinkles around his eyes and smile took away the edge of danger. I looked for a gun...and saw a fishing pole.

"I didn't catch any fish today, but caught a pair of vandals. Aren't you too old for childish pranks?" the man demanded.

"We're not vandals." Dominic wiped dirt from his palms on his jeans.

"And this isn't a prank," I added.

"What do you call digging up a grave?"

"A rescue mission," I told him. "We're trying to save my grandmother."

"Your grandmother is in on this, too?" The old guy looked around, scratching his beard. "Where's she hiding? Behind a gravestone?"

"She's not here. But she's the reason we came." My heart was going so fast it made my head dizzy. "My great-great-great-grandmother hid an important remedy a lot time ago. It's a long story."

"Long stories are the best kind." The man's

voice spit out like gravel, and I guessed he was around eighty. "But only fools and penguins stand out in this weather. Come on inside for a hot cup of tea."

A hot drink sounded great—and much better than being stabbed with a fishing pole or arrested for trespassing. This grizzly man had a right to be suspicious, yet his golden and blue aura showed no malice.

The old man led us out of the graveyard, up rickety stairs, and through a back door, where we went down a narrow hall, past several closed doors with engraved labels reading "Library," "Artifacts," and "Records." We entered a living room with a comfy brown leather couch, coffee table, TV, and wood-burning stove. While we sipped tea, the man started a fire in the stove, which gave the room a cozy glow.

"The name's Niles Farthingtower," the old man said as he settled into the recliner and reached for his steaming teacup.

After Dominic and I introduced ourselves, we explained about my grandmother's failing health and how our only hope was to find my ancestor's remedy book. "All we had for clues were four charms." I pulled them from my pocket and showed Niles.

"Beautiful antiques," Niles said. "May I examine them?"

There was an appreciation in his tone that impressed me. I handed the charms over and he held them as if they were precious diamonds. "Exquisite! Look at the artistry and color. I have some silver pieces, but not of this quality. What do you want for them?"

"They aren't for sale," I said quickly. "They're clues from my great-great-great-grandmother."

"The horseshoe led us here," Dominic added. "The building is your museum, and cat and fish means Katherine Trout. We're sure the remedy book is buried here."

"A book could never survive that long."

"I think it's in a metal box of some kind," I explained, remembering my vision of Agnes. "So can we finish digging?"

Niles rubbed his beard. A soft patter of snow slapped against the windows and warm flames crackled from the fireplace. "I can't allow digging in the cemetery."

"But we have to!" I was ready to get down on

my knees and beg; anything to save Nona. "Please let us dig."

"No," he said with a shake of his head. "There's nothing under that grave—not after the flood."

A fire *and* a flood? Horseshoe had to be the unluckiest town in history. If anyone tried to put it on a map, a hurricane would whip through and blow it off again.

"The flood came when I just started working here," Niles explained with a faraway expression. "Heavy rains overfilled creeks and caused a flash-flood. Water came up to the porch, took out some trees, and unearthed dozens of caskets. It was quite a sight—caskets floating around, some ripped apart with bones hanging out. A skull stuck on a log and we never did find the rest of the body. We salvaged what we could, but had to guess where to bury some of the bodies."

"Katherine Trout?" I almost whispered.

"We found her casket about a mile away. No one could remember the exact location of the original grave, so we picked one at random. Nothing's buried there—well, except for Katherine. When the water receded, we searched through piles of debris for personal items since some folks were buried with jewelry and other mementos. We matched what we could with the proper remains, but most went into storage in case relatives ever turned up. You're welcome to take a look."

We'd found the right grave but in the wrong place. How messed up was that?

Niles invited us up into the artifact room. Holding the door open, he gestured toward wall shelves and display cases. "Those three boxes are what you want. Take your time. I'll be in the kitchen preparing bass burgers. You're welcome to stay for dinner."

Bass burgers? No, thank you.

I politely declined, explaining we still had a long drive home.

"You'd better hurry. The weather report says it'll storm by night. They'll close the roads, and no one will get over the pass."

"I know back roads," Dominic said.

Dominic didn't sound worried, but I felt a chill of apprehension. A few hours ago everything seemed so hopeful, we had the clues and a destination, but now bad news kept getting worse. Even the weather seemed against us.

Niles left the room, and Dominic and I tackled the boxes.

My first box was crammed with odd objects: a

spoon shaped like a boat, a black shoe with a broken heel, a hairbrush, a yellowy set of false teeth, and a toy rattle. The rattle must have come from the grave of a baby. This grim reality sobered me and I realized the rusted bits of jewelry, water-stained photographs, and other mementos were all that was left of real people.

"No metal containers or books," I said with discouragement as I closed the box.

"Not here either."

"Going through these things feels…I don't know…wrong."

"Are any ghosts complaining?"

"No, but there's a heaviness in the air."

"This room is just stuffy."

Like a tomb, I thought uncomfortably. Not haunted by ghosts or spirits, but by imprints of long-ago people. Strong emotions left imprints on object or places. The empty room felt crowded, claustrophobic. I had to get away. So I left Dominic with the last box and excused myself to go to the restroom.

I wandered out of the artifact room, wrinkling my nose at the strong fish odor coming from the kitchen. Not a savory fried fish aroma, but more like stinky socks and dead fish. If the smell was an example of Niles's culinary skills, I'd choose take-out any day.

On the way back from the restroom, I was surprised to see the library door open. I was sure it had been closed before. Curiously, I took a look and saw book heaven—the afterlife of books whose owners have died. At least that's what it seemed like because there were so many antique books. Most were crammed onto wall shelves while others, I guessed the most valuable, were locked inside glass display cases.

I wished Agnes's book could have been protected under glass.

My eyes blurred and I blinked back tears. We couldn't find something that didn't exist anymore. Why hadn't Agnes simply mailed the remedy to her daughters instead of leaving cryptic clues? Her descendents would have passed on the remedy to each generation and lives would have been saved. At the first sign of Nona's memory loss, she would have whipped up the remedy and felt great.

Instead my grandmother was deteriorating fast. Agnes's lifesaving remedies had died with her. If only the séance had worked. But it had been so disastrous no one would even consider trying again.

I wandered around the room. The lighting was dim, only a single bulb dangling from the ceiling. I glanced down at a glassed case, not really interested in the old coins, jewelry, buttons, and books on display. The books were brittle and faded, so they appeared to have no color. I had to squint through the glass to read the titles: books on Western lore, hunting, fishing, Nevada history, silver mines, and cooking.

One entire case held cookbooks. On a cookbook called *Varmint Vittles* there was a sketch of a squirrel and an opossum. I wondered if this was where Niles got his fish burger recipe.

When I was around ten, I'd asked Mom to teach me how to cook. Her answer was to sign me up for a cooking class where I'd learned 101 ways to cook an egg—which could come in handy if I was ever stranded on a chicken farm. Fortunately Nona had stepped up and taught me some recipes. She'd offered to teach more, but with school and friends and everything, I put her off for another time…as if we had all the time in the world.

"Recipes never age, only the cooks," Nona had quoted once.

Did she even remember that quote? Or was that piece of her memory gone? And what about her specialty recipes she'd never written down? Her spicy avocado dip and double delicious "Double Dip Chocolate Chip" cookies. Were these recipes already gone from her memory? Or did we still have time to save them…and Nona?

I won't give up, I vowed, even if it means digging up an entire cemetery in a snowstorm.

There was a gentle touch on my shoulder.

"Dominic?" I turned, but no one was there.

The room was empty, except for an unusual aroma—a soft, flowery scent like lavender. Goose bumps rose on my arms. I wasn't alone. The pressure of a hand on my shoulder remained. Not Opal, I could tell although I saw no one.

Closing my eyes, I breathed deeply to concentrate and see beyond. A shape appeared, a misty cloud of a woman with a dark streak running through pale hair. Hair like mine! I realized with shock. She wasn't much older than me either, and I recognized her face from the old photograph treasured among my great-great-great-grandmother's possessions.

"Agnes?" I called, hopefully.

It was hard to keep her image in my head the way I could with Opal. Shadows and light danced, shifted, and faded away. Still I could sense her presence; energy rippled like waves in the air, tingling through me.

"Agnes, it is you." I wasn't asking, I knew. "You came to help me?"

I sensed her nod.

The pressure from my shoulder vanished and moved to my hand. Her unseen fingers clasped mine, holding tight across centuries. The pressure increased and pulled me forward. I followed, moving across the room until I stopped at a glassed case with a plaque: Ledgers, Journals, and Diaries. Glancing down, I saw very old leather- and cloth-bound books.

I bent closer, studying the dozen or so odd-sized books. There was a thin black leather ledger dated 1898, cloth journals with uneven stitching on the spines, and a row of very old diaries.

Unseen fingers grabbed my hand and I watched in uneasy fascination as my second finger pointed to a plain, dark-brown diary, bound in soft, lined leather. There was tiny gold printing on the cover, and I bent low and squinted to read:

*Belonging to Agnes Jane Walker.*

Ohmygod! I'd found it!

The remedy book.

# 16

I shouted for Dominic.

"Sabine!" He rushed through the open door-way, pushing strands of his sandy brown hair from his forehead. "What's wrong?"

"Nothing's wrong! Everything's right!"

He wrinkled his brow as he stared at me. "What's going on?"

"It's here!" I threw up my hands and twirled in celebration. This perfect moment deserved to be wrapped in glitzy bows and ribbons and a marching band trumpeting a parade. "I found it!"

"Found what? You okay?"

"I'm great! And Nona is going to be great, too!" I pointed to the plain brown book under glass. "Look at the thick brown book!"

"A diary?" He tapped the glass case as he bent down for a closer look. When I heard his sharp intact of breath, I knew he'd read Agnes's name.

"I thought it was just another old diary until I saw Agnes's name."

"Wow," Dominic murmured.

"Yeah, I feel the same way."

"After everything, it's sitting here under glass. Unbelievable."

"Agnes led me to it. It's like a miracle!"

"Now we just need to open the case. I'll get—" Dominic broke off, tilting his head as if he'd heard something.

Then I heard it, too. Footsteps.

Niles appeared in the doorway. His hands were on his hips as he regarded us with a stern look. "What's the ruckus going on in here?" he demanded. "I left you in the artifact room."

"Sabine made a surprising discovery," Dominic said.

"She did?" The old man turned toward me. "What discovery?"

"The book we told you about—it wasn't in any of those boxes. But it's here!" I pointed to the glassed case.

"That's the Walker diary."

"Agnes Walker was my great-great-great-grandmother."

"Well, I'll be horse-whipped." His gray brows knitted as he let out a low whistle. "Why didn't you say Agnes Walker was your relation? All that talk about Katherine Trout, I assumed she was your ancestor."

"I have no idea who Katherine was. Her name was the clue," I tried to explain, even though I was still making sense of everything myself. I wondered about Katherine and why Agnes had chosen her grave. Had they been friends? Or did Agnes pick that grave because it worked for the clues?

"I could have brought you here if you'd asked for the Walker diary," Niles said.

"It's not a diary," I told Niles. "It's a journal of herbal cures. If you look closely at the bottom of the cover there's a faded word beginning with 'Re.' I'm sure it's 'Remedies.'"

He reached in his pocket and withdrew a pair

of wire-framed glasses, squinted down at the case, then shrugged. "I can't make it out. But if you say it says 'Remedies,' then it must be. This diary has always been a mystery around here."

"What do you mean?"

"Now that's quite a story." Niles's old eyes twinkled. "That book's been here since before I was born, when my uncle was the caretaker here. Uncle Zebron told me that a stray dog dug up a metal box after the Pig Fire. He found the diary inside—but there was no record of any grave for Agnes Walker. He checked records going back and found no one by that name in Horseshoe."

"But she must have lived here," I said.

"Maybe. Maybe not. That's the mystery." He grinned, showing a gap where a back tooth was missing.

"Have you read the book?"

"Look around at all the books." He threw back his grizzled head with a deep laugh. "If I lived a dozen lives, I'd never have time to read every document. We have over three hundred diaries, cookbooks, journals, etc. This book is the oldest we have on display. There are hundreds more stored in the records room."

Gazing at the overstuffed shelves and full cases,

I was amazed we'd ever found the right book. I had Agnes to thank.

I gestured to the lock on the glass case. "Can you open this, Niles?"

"Sure. Now just a sec while I figure out which key…"

I could hardly stand still as I watched the old man withdraw a key chain from his pocket. He flipped through several keys before settling on a small brass key no bigger than my pinky. He fit it into the lock and there was a soft click.

"Be careful," Niles cautioned as he gently handed me the book. "The spine is cracked and the pages have some water damage."

I held my breath as my fingers touched the treasure I'd been seeking for months. I could hardly believe I was actually touching a book that my great-great-great-grandmother wrote in so many years ago. On the opening page was her name in loopy cursive that was similar to my mother's writing: Agnes Jane Walker. I nearly gasped when I saw four drawings below her name: a cat, house, fish, and horseshoe.

My fingers trembled with anticipation. I couldn't wait to read every precious word, but that would take time. The book must have over three hundred pages, all brittle and penned in faded ink.

Flipping a page, I read:

*Scrape corn with sharp knife three times. First scrape corn to break off kernels. Second scrape remainder off corn halfway. Third scrape off rest of kernels off cob. Then use potatoe masher and mash all kernels until milk comes out...*

I skimmed over the long scribbles of instructions to a page where the word "warts" grabbed my attention.

*Cut a potatoe in half and rub both sides of potatoe on wart. Put the potatoe back together. Put in brown paper bag. Bury the bag in the ground someplace you will never return to. When the potatoe rots the wart will dry up and fall off.*

Too bad Agnes didn't have a computer with spell check, I thought. Or maybe potato was spelled differently a long time ago. There were other odd spellings; some so peculiar I couldn't figure them out. The old-fashioned language was like a puzzling code without any grammar breaks or chapter headings.

There were entire pages with odd words I couldn't understand. It would take days—and possibly the help of a linguist—to find the memory-loss remedy.

I glanced up to find Niles and Dominic staring at me.

"Find it?" Dominic asked hopefully.

"Not even close." I shook my head. "It's harder than I expected."

"Take your time," Niles told me with a kind smile. "I don't usually allow visitors to handle old documents, but I'll bend the rules for such a nice young lady."

"Thanks." I wiped my dusty hands on my jeans.

"Glad to help. When you're finished, give me a holler so I can return the book and lock its case."

"Return it?" I asked, startled.

"Of course. It's property of the museum."

"No, it isn't." I stared at the old man in disbelief. "This book belongs to my family."

"History can't belong to any one person, only protected for posterity. As curator, it's my job to protect all property of the Horseshoe Museum."

"But this is mine. Agnes left instructions so her descendents could find it. She was my great-great-great-grandmother."

"So you say." His voice sharpened. Instead of a kind old man, he reminded me of a formidable bear protecting its cubs.

"It's true!" I insisted. "Look at the drawings on this page. They're of the same charms I showed you. That's proof this is mine."

"Museum property is museum property."

"But who owns the museum?" Dominic countered.

"Technically, I do. But I consider it a sacred trust for the community."

"What community?" I argued. "Horseshoe is a ghost town. This is the only building still standing around here. It's all about Shrub Flats now. Besides, I'm related to Agnes Walker. That book rightly belongs to me."

"I believe you, but I'll need to see official documents such as birth and death certificates or a will."

"I don't have anything like that."

"Too bad. I can't just let people walk off with museum property."

"Can't I borrow it? I promise to bring it back as soon as I'm done with it."

He pursed his lips stubbornly. "The diary stays in this room."

"But you have hundreds of old diaries. You won't miss this one, and we desperately need it to save my grandmother."

"I've never allowed even one piece of history to leave this building, and I will not start now." He folded his arms across his chest. "But I sympathize with your problem, especially since you've obviously been searching for this for a long time. You have my permission to copy as much of the diary you want."

"Do you have a copy machine?" I asked.

"No. I couldn't allow you to photocopy it anyway. Pressing the book flat causes damage to the spine. It's already cracked and might fall apart." Niles shook his grizzled head. "I'll loan you paper and pens."

I turned to another page, squinting at odd words like "alum," "laudanum," and "efficacious." How could I read something when I didn't understand half of the words? I felt like crying but had to hold myself together for Nona.

"It'll take hours to find the right remedy," I pointed out.

"In that case," Niles said cheerfully, "I'll put out two more plates for dinner."

He supplied us with paper and pens, then returned to the kitchen.

"That stubborn old fool!" I was so angry my hands shook as I tossed the paper and pens to the floor. "I'll tell him what he can do with his stinky fish dinner. This is so unfair!"

"Totally," Dominic said quietly.

"We worked so hard to find this book and now we can't keep it, even though Agnes wanted me to have it."

"It's yours."

"You bet it is. Why can't Niles understand?"

"I'll go talk with him." Dominic's gaze drifted to the door. "He has to see reason."

"Don't bother. He won't change his mind." I scowled. "Let's just find the remedy."

We couldn't both look at the diary, so we took turns.

I went first, struggling to make out words and phrases that seemed from another language. It wasn't like any English I'd read before. I could pick out some words and phrases, but others had faded away to faint scribbles, impossible to decipher.

After a dozen or so pages, I found the word "memory"—only to read further and discover it was a cure for hairballs for cats.

Groaning, I set the diary down on top of a glass case.

"Nothing makes sense," I griped. "It's impossible."

"I'll give it a try," Dominic offered.

He took the book and I watched over his shoulder. I could tell he was having trouble understanding the words, too. He'd sigh and shake his head, flip to a new page, then shake his head again. Finally, he closed the book.

"Damn," he said. "You'd have to be a cryptologist to read this."

"A historian could probably do it."

"Like Niles?"

"I didn't see him offering to help. He only cares about rules." I tightened my fists, the violence inside surprising me. "Nona would know what to do."

"If she's having a good day," Dominic pointed out.

Nona's good days had been fewer lately. I hoped Penny-Love was watching out for her like she promised, making sure Nona didn't drive anywhere alone or leave stove burners on. Seeing my grandmother lose her memory was like watching her slowly bleed to death with my arms tied behind my back.

The world outside through the windows looked cold and white. The predicted snowstorm was fulfilling its dire promise. Not a winter wonderland, but as empty as a blank sheet of paper.

When Dominic and I had discussed the charms earlier, he'd joked that the cat and house could mean Agnes worked in a cathouse. I'd argued that she would never resort to something so disgusting. But Dominic had replied, "Desperate people will do anything when they're desperate."

He was right.

And I had run out of options.

After a moment of soul-searching, I bent down to pick up the paper and a pen from the floor. I ripped out a sheet of paper. The storm raged outside while inside all seemed quiet.

I put pen to paper, then folded the paper and placed it on a glass case.

"What's that for?" Dominic raised his dark brows.

Shaking my head, I answered, "You don't want to know."

I thought of Nona, who was so proud and strong, who would do anything for me. Losing her memory was a slow death. She'd taken me into her home and loved me unconditionally. I'd do anything for her, too.

"We've run out of choices." I summoned courage in a deep breath. When I blew it out, I felt a chilling calm. "There's only one thing we can do."

Dominic eyed me uneasily. "What?"

With the precious book secure inside my jacket, I reached for the door. "Get out of here."

Then I started running.

# 17

Dominic's boots thudded behind me, but I didn't slow, clutching the remedy book inside my jacket. I had no plan, only desperate impulse. Escape, my brain screamed. So I ran faster, racing down the hall, spinning around a corner and yanking open the back door, swept into a blustery snowstorm. Ducking underneath the hood of my jacket, snow stung my face and I struggled against brutal wind, slowing but never stopping.

"Sabine, what are you doing?" Dominic caught up with me by his truck, grabbing my shoulder to spin me to face him.

"What does it look like?"

"Stealing?"

I bent over slightly, gasping for breath and tasting snow. "It's not stealing when it's mine."

"I can't believe you're doing this!"

I laughed bitterly. "I can't believe it either."

Remorse and guilt might hit me later, but in this wild moment I felt proud. Wrong, right, whatever—it depended how you looked at it. I'd done something wrong for the right reason, totally out of my comfort zone, something no one would ever expect from a "good girl."

"Your sisters look up to you," Mom used to drill into me. "Forget all that ghost nonsense and set a good example."

Even Nona praised me for my honesty. "I can always trust you, Sabine," she had said many times.

Penny-Love had a different twist on it. "Sabine, you're so goody-goody, you make me want to barf!"

Watch this bad girl now, I thought.

Dominic's keys rattled as he opened the truck door. "Get inside before we freeze."

I pushed my damp hair from my eyes. "You aren't going to make me go back?"

"Hell, no! The book is yours. I hope you know what you're doing."

"Absolutely no freaking idea."

"I figured as much," he said with a laugh.

"You got any ideas?" I stretched my seat belt across my shoulder.

"Nope—except getting out of here." He twisted his key, the engine roaring to life. The windshield wipers flicked off snow in icy clumps. "Let's hit the road."

"Hurry, Clyde."

"Clyde?" He arched a dark brow. "What's that about?"

"We're breaking the law and going on the run like Bonnie and Clyde." I wiped moisture from the window with my palm and peered nervously at the museum. "Hey, at least I didn't compare us to Thelma and Louise."

He glowered at me. "Just let me drive."

I started to laugh—until I looked back and saw the museum's door burst open. Red-faced, Niles stormed outside, stomping through snow as he ran into the road. He waved his fist and shouted, but we couldn't hear.

"Hurry! Drive!" I shouted over the noisy engine.

"I'm on it, Bonnie."

"Go! Fast!"

The engine revved loudly, jolting me forward then back in my seat. Exhaust smoke spewed dark against snowy flakes and the truck lurched forward. Snow spun off tires and showered a waterfall as we roared away.

My last glimpse of Niles was of his black beard frosted white.

\*     \*     \*

The storm was bad—and growing worse.

Snow piled high on the sides of the road, shutting off everything like speeding through clouds. Red taillights glowed ahead and overhead electronic boards flashed "carry chains" warnings.

But I was too exhausted to care, and grateful for the warmth of the truck's heater. I sank back against the seat, too tired to even talk and not sure what to say anyway. I was now officially a criminal.

I couldn't get my last image of Niles out of my head. Red-faced, outraged, and…hurt. He'd been kind, invited us to his house, made us hot tea, and offered us dinner. He'd bent museum rules and allowed us to hold the old diary. And I'd betrayed this kindness by stealing from him.

In the note I'd left, I'd apologized and promised to return the book after we had the remedy. But that didn't make me less guilty. Niles had every right to have me arrested. Would they handcuff me? I was a minor and this was my first offense so I should get off light, maybe community service. But what about my future? Could a criminal get into a good college?

I glanced down at Agnes's remedy book. Small, old, and fragile. Somewhere within those old pages was a cure for Nona. Was getting this book worth going to jail?

Damn right.

Still I looked at Dominic, wondering if he thought I was a terrible person. Not that his past was squeaky clean. He hadn't exactly explained how he'd gotten possession of the horseshoe charm. And my psychic glimpses of his past showed abuse and violence. His uncle used to chain him like an animal outside and beat him. Dominic wouldn't say how he escaped, except that his uncle was gone. He'd hinted at murder…although I didn't believe it. But desperation changed people. Ten minutes ago, I'd been a "good girl." Now I was a thief on the run.

"You okay?" Dominic asked. He slowed at a crosswalk in Shrub Flats then hit the gas hard, leaving the town behind us.

"Yeah. Sorry for getting you into this."

"Hey, no apologies. We're partners, remember?"

I gave a faint smile. "Thanks for being my getaway driver."

"Anytime."

"I still can't believe we got out with the book."

"It was a narrow escape," he admitted.

"Yeah—we narrowly escaped eating bass burgers."

Dominic laughed. "Now that would have been a crime."

I joined in the laughter—not that anything felt funny. It just felt good to laugh…especially with Dominic.

We didn't say much after that and listened to a road report on the radio. Snow came down harder, freezing the wipers with knotty icicles that scraped like knives against the glass. I could barely see anything except blurry flashes from car lights.

I glanced down at the remedy book and flipped

to a random page, but there wasn't enough light to read. The truck's panel showed it was only 5 PM, yet it felt like midnight. Nona would be starting to worry, since I'd told her we'd be back before dark. That is, if she remembered I was gone.

Now I was the one worrying. I dug into my purse and found my cell phone. It lit up at my touch, casting green light on my hands, but when I punched in Nona's number nothing happened. No signal.

"Too many mountains. Try later," Dominic suggested.

Then he announced that we were entering California.

"We crossed the border without being arrested." I tried to sound like I was teasing but my voice quavered.

"No one is going to arrest us."

"Maybe not you—I stole the book."

"Don't worry. Ninety percent of things people worry about never happen."

"What about the other ten percent?"

"We keep moving so it doesn't catch up with us. We should be home in less than two hours."

"Home." I whispered the word, tasting its

sweetness and aching with longing to see Nona. I tried the cell phone again, but still no signal.

I reached into my pocket and gazed at the tiny silver horseshoe. Horseshoes were supposed to be lucky, so I rubbed it between my fingers and made wishes. I wished for the remedy to cure Nona, Niles's forgiveness, my parents happily together, and answers for my own confused heart. I even added in world peace and a cure for common allergies.

The windshield wipers jammed, ice clinging to them like crystal snakes. Even with the heater blasting, I was shivering. On the side of the road, cars were pulled over and people bundled in heavy jackets and gloves struggled in the snowy wind to put chains on their tires. Four-wheel drive vehicles with snow tires weren't required to put on chains, so we kept driving—until we came to an abrupt stop.

"What's the problem?" I tried to see through the frosty windshield. But I couldn't see anything other than red taillights from the line of cars stopped in front of us.

"Don't know."

"What if the police are stopping cars, looking for us?" I asked, the remedy book feeling heavy in my jacket.

"We aren't important enough to stop traffic."

"I guess that's a good thing. So why aren't we moving?"

"Could be an accident or snow slide. There's a flashing sign up ahead. It says…" He reached up to wipe moisture from the window. "Road closed."

"Oh, no! They can't do that!"

"Happens all the time."

"How can you sound so calm?"

"It's no big deal." Dominic shrugged. "Soon as the snow plows clear the road, they'll open up again."

"How long will that take?"

"Could be ten minutes or a few hours."

"And we're just supposed to wait?" I looked through the frosty windows at the line of red taillights.

"Waiting is the safe option." Dominic leaned closer, tossing me a challenging look. "Or we could take a chance."

"I'm all for taking chances."

"Exactly what I'd hoped you'd say. I know another road."

"What if it's closed?"

"It's not busy enough to shut down," he assured me. "You want to go for it?"

"It's better than being parked on the highway."

"Okay. Hold on!"

He whipped the steering wheel sharp, making a U-turn. We double-backed a few miles, then made a sharp turn on a road that wound up being a narrow white-shrouded road. I wasn't sure this was a good idea, but Dominic seemed confident. I tried to relax but failed. My stomach rumbled and I remembered we'd missed lunch. I was sure there weren't any fast food places on a back road. Thinking about food made the rumbling louder. I couldn't even remember when I'd last eaten. When Opal had me bring my jacket, why couldn't she have told me to bring snacks, too? Even a stale granola bar would have tasted great right now.

Dominic swore.

"What's wrong?" I gripped the seat tightly as I turned to face him.

He didn't answer, his knuckles white on the steering wheel.

"Dominic, what is it?"

"Sit tight," he ordered through gritted teeth.

He kept his gaze straight ahead, squinting at

the glow from his headlights. The truck seemed to be going so fast—too fast—into a void of white. And we were zooming forward with a horrible grinding of gears.

Dominic slammed on the brakes, but the truck kept sliding, slipping, careening—until it slammed into a mountain of snow.

# 18

I lurched forward, then was snapped back in my seat belt as the truck came to a shuddering stop. Light flashes exploded in my head, and I was nauseous. I fought not to throw up, gulping in deep breaths.

Dominic dizzily lifted his head toward me. He rubbed his forehead where there was a small cut, blood smearing on his palm. "Sabine...you okay?" he asked.

"Am I? Yeah, I think so." I did a quick body check. "Bruised a little, but nothing's broken. But you're bleeding."

He shrugged at his hand. "It's nothing. There's more damage to my pride and my truck. Damn— I haven't even made my first payment yet."

"The truck's not that bad."

"But I screwed up and put you at risk, too."

"Hey, we're in this together. You tried your best."

"My best sucked." He smacked the dashboard.

"Can't you just back up and turn around?"

"Not like this. One of the back wheels isn't even touching ground."

The truck was at an odd angle, so I had to shift sideways to look through the window. I couldn't see much but vaguely made out the dark shape of a tire about a foot off the ground, spinning snow. I had to shift in my seat to stay upright, looking in all directions and seeing only shadowy white-frosted trees and endless snow.

Dominic unfastened his seat belt and grabbed the door handle. He pulled it, jerked hard, pounded, and kicked.

"It won't budge," Dominic swore. "What about your door, Sabine? Can you open it?"

I grasped the handle, pulled hard, shoved my weight against the frame, but nothing happened. "It's stuck, too. Can we tunnel out though a window?"

"And then what would you do? Walk and freeze your ass off?"

"You have a better suggestion?"

"Not yet. But we need to have the window open a crack so we don't get asphyxiated by running the engine." Dominic hit the window control. There was a mechanical click, yet the window, like the door, didn't budge.

"Open, dammit!" Dominic smacked the button so hard there was an awful clunking sound. The glass whirred open an inch—then stopped.

Chilly air and snowflakes gusted inside, powdery puffs attacking my jacket. I brushed them off, my fingers stinging from cold. Through the small slit of air, the snowstorm swirled inside. Shivering, I found my gloves and slipped them over my hands.

Dominic hit the button again and again, only it wouldn't rise up or down.

"Now what?" I asked uneasily.

"Is there a signal on your phone?"

I checked, but no signal bars.

"I was afraid of that."

"How will we get out of here?"

Dominic gnawed his lower lip, avoiding meeting my gaze. "We wait."

"Wait for what?" I tried not to panic.

"The storm to let up or someone to call a tow truck. I'll run the engine off and on for warmth, but we have to conserve gas. If we're lucky, someone will come along soon."

"And if we aren't lucky?" I remembered what he said about this being a remote back road.

"Maybe you should check with your spirit guide."

He was joking, probably trying to lighten the tension, but contacting my guide wasn't a bad idea. So I closed my eyes and ran a mental "Google" search for Opal. Only I guess she wasn't answering her psychic line.

"She's not around," I told Dominic. "Or this must be one of those experiences she wants me to handle alone."

"You're not alone. I'm here."

As if I hadn't already noticed that? Thinking about how close he was, looking at his face, hands, lips—especially his lips—put ideas into my head that didn't fall under the category of "just friends."

"Don't be afraid," he said, mistaking my trembling for fear. "We'll get out of this."

That's not what I'm afraid of, I was tempted to say. But I restrained. I didn't want him to read my real emotions and turned to the window. Not that I could see much of anything. It was almost completely black outside; strange, considering we were surrounded by white snow.

Dominic checked windows and gages, his frown deepening to a scowl that gave me a sick feeling, probably fear only I didn't want to admit being afraid, even to myself. How much trouble were we in? I mean, what if this was the end…as in dying? I'd heard of people lost in the snow and not discovered for weeks. Some survived, losing fingers and toes to frostbite, then sharing their true stories in cable movies. But the ones who didn't survive became only brief mentions on the evening news.

Is that what was going to happen to us? We were going to freeze to death?

Dominic had said worrying didn't solve anything.

Of course, he'd also said we could get through on this back road.

Even with the heater cranked high, cold air swirled through the partially opened window. I snuggled tighter inside my jacket, thinking wistfully of sunshine and hot tea. It was torture when Dominic apologetically turned off the engine. The silence was awful, sucking out every breath of warmth. I understood that saving gas was important, but damn it was cold.

"Sorry for getting you into this mess, Sabine," Dominic said, looking more miserable than I felt. "I was an ass for taking this road."

"At least you tried to do something."

"Tried and screwed up."

"Blame isn't important. Let's just figure a way out."

"I hate being so damned helpless." He slapped the steering wheel. "Hell with the weather. I'll get the door open and walk back to the main road."

"No, you won't. You don't even have a heavy coat. And my gloves are too small for you. We'll just wait."

"It could take all night."

"Then we'll wait all night."

My eyes had adjusted to the dimness so I could see his frown. He twisted over to look in the back seat, and although it was totally inappropriate considering our dire situation, I admired his firm butt. Working on the ranch gave him a fine body, as good as pumping iron in the gym. I bet his biceps were muscled, too, and I had an urge to reach over and find out.

He spun around and caught me looking at him, which immediately revved up my body temperature. "Here," he said, pushing a heavy brown blanket in my hands. "This will warm you."

"I'm warm enough." No lie there, I thought as my cheeked flamed. "You wear it."

"I don't get cold."

I didn't believe that. His leather jacket might keep out wind but wouldn't hold in warmth. And his clothes were damp from the snow blowing through his window. He had to be freezing—not that he'd admit it.

"We'll share the blanket," I insisted.

"Would your boyfriend approve?" he challenged.

I ignored that, not wanting to talk about Josh. "Sharing body heat only makes sense. Just as friends," I added quickly.

"Sure about that?"

I knew better than to answer. It was hard enough to act casual as I scooted across the seat and leaned against his hard body. The only sounds were hissing wind and our breathing. I draped the blanket over us, telling myself this was all about staying warm and not about his being so hot. I fit snuggly against his chest. His arm curled around my shoulders. Just as friends, I reminded myself. But tingles shot through me. The energy sizzling between us was like a third person demanding attention.

"Close your eyes," he told me. I looked into his face, my breath catching. Sharp angles, tanned rugged skin, yet such soft lips. "It's going to be a long night."

"You have no idea," I whispered.

"Try to get some sleep."

"I doubt I'll be able to."

"Scared?"

That was only part of it. "It's just…too quiet. Can you turn on the radio?"

"Sure." But when he turned the dial, there was only static. So he bent over to the floor where his CD case had fallen and popped one in. "Best of 80s country," he said with a chuckle.

"Don't you have anything better? Like from this millennium?"

"You got a problem with country?"

"It's not my first choice. But it's okay." Having music, even corny old songs, was a connection with the outside world. "Is your truck totaled?" I asked, remembering the last accident, when he'd swerved to avoid a cow. I'd been hurt seriously, but recovered. Dominic's truck didn't survive, though, and he'd only bought this one a few weeks ago.

"The truck will be fine."

"What about us?"

"We'll be fine, too. Relax and sleep."

Sleep was the last thing on my mind.

"Let's just talk," I suggested.

"About what?"

"I don't know…whatever comes up." I blushed. "I mean, just about anything. We're always rushing around and never stop to just talk. I've wondered about some things."

He propped up on his elbow, keeping a safe space between us. There was caution in his tone as he asked. "Like what?"

There was so much, I hardly knew where to begin.

How old was he? Had he graduated from school? How did he discover he could understand animals? How had he survived on his own after he escaped from his uncle? Where had he lived before moving in with us? Had he ever been in love?

I gave him a serious look. "Will you answer anything?"

"Depends."

"We could freeze to death out here, and this may be our last night alive, so we might as well be honest. Only the truth."

He looked amused. "Truth goes both ways, you know."

"So I ask you a question and then you ask me one."

"That could be the biggest risk you've taken tonight," he warned. But he agreed.

This was my chance to finally find out important things about Dominic; secrets of his past and his deepest thoughts. But I hesitated, rattled by the way he was staring at me, and asked the first inane thing that popped into my head.

"What's your last name?"

Dominic leaned back with a laugh. "That's your question?"

"It's a valid one," I insisted. "You've never told me your full name. I asked Nona and she said I had to ask you. Is it a big secret? Are you related to someone famous or infamous? A rock star, serial killer, or politician?"

"None of the above."

"So what is it?"

He hesitated, then sheepishly told me.

I didn't believe him at first, especially after we'd discussed how people used to have names fitting their professions. Then he pulled out his wallet and proved it.

Dominic A. Smith.

I skimmed through the other info: blue eyes, dark hair, born in Bend, Oregon, on November eleventh in nineteen eighty—

He slapped the wallet shut and shoved it into his pocket.

"What's the A stand for?" I asked.

"My middle name."

"Anthony, Andrew, Arthur?"

"Good guesses."

"Which is it?" I persisted.

"You already asked your question. It's my turn."

"Fine." I folded my arms and gave him an annoyed look. "What do you want to know?"

"Who is Jade?"

I gasped, completely stunned.

How did Dominic know about her? I hadn't told anyone! Yet somehow Dominic had found out. Was he a mind reader? Had someone told him? Or maybe he heard from one of his animal posse. Did I have to hide my secrets from my own cat?

If the question had come from someone like Penny-Love or Josh, I would have denied everything to protect Dad's reputation. But Dominic was different. I knew he'd keep whatever I told him in confidence, and he never seemed to judge others. He expected people to have flaws and didn't like them much anyway.

The crazy thing was—I was actually relieved. I didn't have to hold all the secrets in alone. Now that someone knew, I could talk about Jade.

So I did.

"I found out last week," I admitted with a sigh. "Jade's my half-sister."

I closed my eyes, seeing Jade as clearly as if she was trapped in the truck with us. It was like being haunted, only Jade was alive. "Dad's been hiding his other family for years. He didn't want me to know, but when I saw Jade and heard her call him 'Daddy,' the brilliant lawyer was quick with damage control. He whisked me off to a restaurant, figuring I wouldn't make a scene in public. Then he made me promise not to tell my mother. Not that I ever would."

"What's your sister like?" Dominic asked.

"Half-sister," I corrected.

"Okay…half-sister."

"She wears too much makeup, has long red hair, and is so thin she looks anorexic."

"But what kind of person is she?"

Low-life, greedy, family wrecker. "We've never really met but I don't think I'd like her," I said. "She's using my father, which makes me sick. She'd better keep away from the rest of my family. Let's talk about something else. What about your family?"

"I told you—I don't have any."

"But you used to."

"No father. Mom dead. You already know I had the uncle from hell."

"Despite all that, you turned out great."

"Not so great." He gave a bitter laugh. "You don't really know…and I don't want you to. My uncle was evil. But he's gone now."

"I'm sorry you had it so tough."

"Life is tough. I went through some bad times and did stuff I'm not proud of. But coming here…showed me life has a good side, too. I decided not to let the past shape me anymore."

"I'm glad."

"Yeah." His voice grew husky as he gazed into

my eyes. "I never trusted anyone until I met Nona and—"

"And who?"

"You."

It happened so fast.

One moment we were just talking, then he was saying my name in this husky way that gave me shivers, and I was in his arms. I should have pulled back. But it didn't even occur to me. This was what I was waiting, yearning, longing for…

Wrapping my arms around his neck, I lifted my chin at the exact moment he dipped his down. Our lips met as if every movement between us was in sync.

And we were kissing…

# 19

The first time we kissed we'd been dancing and I'd been possessed by a ghost. So that didn't really count. The second time I was close to death and his kissing was more like mouth-to-mouth resuscitation…at least it started that way. Still that only happened because of danger, and I'd kept dating Josh.

Nothing accidental about this kiss.

I clung to Dominic, shifting on his lap, my legs twining with his as our bodies pressed closer. I held tight, feeling amazing. My emotions rocketed in dizzy colors like fireworks.

The kiss deepened, fierce yet sweet. No words could define what was happening. I didn't stop to think, plunging heart-first into deep feelings. Whenever I'd kissed Josh, I could always think and sometimes even made lists and plans in my head. Josh was easygoing, not making any demands. But Dominic was fire-and-ice different. Without saying a word, Dominic demanded everything. Warmth spread from my legs to my head, and all reasonable thoughts flew away.

More taboo-breaking for this former good girl. Cheating on my boyfriend. How could being so bad feel so good?

A logical part of my brain (perhaps Opal lecturing me) warned that this moment would eventually end. We'd have to return to reality: school, family, friends…Josh. There would be consequences. But I shut out that voice. For now, Dominic was my reality. I wanted to be with only him…

Suddenly he pulled away. "This isn't right," he said.

"Feels right," I murmured and held on tight, pulling him back. "Besides, it's cold, and we're conserving heat. It's all about survival. More kissing please," I requested like a child at the dinner table asking for seconds.

"Sabine, be serious. Where is this going?" His voice was ragged. "You belong to another guy."

"I belong to myself."

"What about Josh?"

"It's over."

"You mean it?" Dominic's hand caressed my jaw line, following up to my hair and brushing it away from my face.

I hesitated only a moment before recognizing my own truth and nodding. No more pretending with Josh, even though he was a great guy and our friends thought we made the perfect couple. That wasn't grounds for a relationship. I may have let others influence me, dating Josh to be popular and accepted. Now I was accepting myself.

Josh would always be special to me and I loved him the way you loved a good friend. But friendship had nothing to do with my feelings for Dominic. We fit together; my head nestled against his chest, my lips molded into his, and his arms folded around mine. This was more than lust. It was real.

No more lying to myself or Dominic or Josh.

I'd turned a corner and there was no going back. Dominic was the guy I wanted.

"So you'll break it off with Josh?" Dominic persisted.

"Yes, yes, yes." I trailed kisses down his tanned neck.

He groaned, then gently pushed me away. "We better stop."

He was right, and I knew it, but that didn't ease the empty feeling when he moved away from me. I glanced in the rearview mirror and was appalled. I was a mess! My hair tangled like shredded blond rope, my cheeks and lips reddened. I ran my fingers over my lips, remembering, savoring. I couldn't stop smiling.

We didn't say much after that, listening to a CD for short periods when he turned on the engine. When our stomachs growled, he crawled into the narrow backseat and dug into a backpack, where he found a box of Wheat Thins. They were stale and crumbly and tasted like heaven.

The storm battled on, wild bursts of wind rattling the truck. The snow fell harder, so it was almost impossible to see out the windows, but we could hear the lashing snow and whooshing gusts like giant snow creatures stomping around us. I should have been scared, only I wasn't. Under a blanket, curled under Dominic's strong arm, nestled against his warm body, I felt safe.

So when he urged me to rest, I yawned and closed my eyes.

And fell asleep.

\*     \*     \*

I don't know why I thought about Jade.

Maybe the whole conversation with Dominic had opened a door in my mind that I'd kept locked, flooding me with unsettling emotions. Anger, hate, jealousy. The emotions wouldn't go away—so I went to them.

One moment I was cuddling under a blanket beside Dominic, then there was a ripping sensation. My body and soul separated, rising up, up, up. I flew above my physical body, lighter than snow, drifting like clouds through the truck roof and into the sky.

Strange how I could look down, through solid objects, and see the two sleeping figures. Dominic smiling in his sleep, cradling the small, blond figure. In a dim corner of my mind, I knew she was me.

I had this urgent sense of needing to be someplace else. So I let go and sailed away. Traveling without a body was wicked cool. The buoyant freedom made me dizzy with joy. I heard a buzzing, like I was moving at a speed faster than sound. I glimpsed flashes of other travelers, but never saw actual faces—more colors of personalities like auras.

I didn't know where I was going until I saw a house far below, yellow wood bordered in red brick with a driveway full of cars. I'd been here before. I surrendered to the gravity pulling me to this house. As strong as a thought and weightless as a whisper, I hurdled through space and solid objects. I braced myself for a crash—only there was nothing except surprise.

I was a ghost of myself out for a night's haunting.

The concept of my ghostly self saying "boo!" and scaring someone was so ridiculous I laughed. Not really laughed; there was no sound, just a sense of amusement. It was like waking up with a super power, only I wasn't going to use my power for good. Deeper emotions pushed me: resentment and suspicion. I would not allow Jade or Crystal to destroy my family.

Jade was sleeping just like the other time I'd

spied on her. One arm tossed aside and the other curled around a floppy rag doll. Jade's lips were partly open, her breathing soft and even. It was like looking at myself, which made me angry. She'd stolen my father *and* my face. Thief.

But wasn't I a thief, too?

I'd stolen the remedy book.

Confused, I wavered in the air like smoke. I sorted through my feelings—and came up empty. I had no right to judge Jade. I had no right to be here, spying in the hopes of finding some dirt. Blaming Jade didn't change anything. I had to accept that my father wasn't perfect, anymore than I was.

I pulled away, but instead of up I drifted into a room lit only by the faint moon glowing through a high window. I was above the window, invisible as a breath of air, looking down at two people who seemed to be arguing. The woman wore a long white robe and had wild, unnatural-looking wine-red hair that shadowed her face, and the man was lanky, with thin, bowed legs and a receding hairline. I figured the woman was Jade's mother, Crystal. I'd only seen her once, when I'd been waiting in Dad's car. I wondered about the man. Was he Crystal's boyfriend? Did that mean Dad wasn't having an affair with Crystal? I know he'd denied it, but I wasn't sure what to believe.

I swept down for a closer look, impressed that anyone could keep a room so immaculately white. The walls, carpet, furniture, and even the comforter on the rumpled bed were white. The only splash of color was from a red velvet heart-shaped box of candy on a white-gold dresser.

The man and woman were talking; I could tell because their mouths were moving, but the sounds came out like someone pushed a fast-forward button. I was on a different vibration level, I guessed, which made hearing difficult—but not impossible. I swirled overhead, struggling to understand. I shut out everything and focused on hearing. Slow everything down, I told myself. And with intense concentration, I made out a few words.

The woman was saying, "…don't…understand."

"I gave…everything!" he shouted.

She backed away from him, shaking her head. "Never made… promises…"

"Slut!" he raged. His hand slashed out and he slapped her hard across the face. I heard a shrill scream as she reeled backwards, tumbling across the bed. She lay there, shaking, tears dampening her thick, curly hair.

"Leave her alone!" I shouted. Only without a body, I made no sound.

Frustration made me crazy. I had to do something, stop that terrible man, but I was helpless. No hands to grab, legs to run, or voice to scream.

But I could go for help.

So I swept back through the wall, into Jade's room. I zoomed close to her ears and screamed out her name. I shouted loud enough to wake the dead, but apparently not the living. I tried to shake her, only my hands slipped through her shoulders—which really freaked me out.

I drew back, unnerved but not ready to give up.

Spirits and ghosts often communicated to me through thoughts, and since I was like a ghost, it might work for me, too. So I thought-screamed an SOS message.

Jade, wake up! I sent her an image of the room next door and the bow-legged man hitting her mother. You have to wake up and get help. Open your eyes. WAKE UP!

Jade stirred as if she was having a bad dream.

I was her bad dream—she must hear me on some deep level. But it wasn't good enough.

Panic propelled my concentration, and I sent another mind message. I added a sense of urgency and repeated the mental picture of the woman again. Jade moaned and covered her pillow over her head.

I heard a scream and zoomed back to the adjacent bedroom.

Crystal lay on the bed with her face buried in a pillow, her body heaving with hysterical sobs. The man hurled a fury of dark-aura words at her, although I only made out a few.

"Whore!" he raged. "told…came to you….. were lies!"

His hands tightened into fists and I worried he'd hit her again. How could I stop him? His dark aura trembled the air. Rage was like a furious cloud, pushing me back, making it impossible to get close. I didn't have hands to dial 911 or stop the man in any physical way. I could watch and hear, yet do nothing to help.

I couldn't just float around while Crystal was beaten. I had to wake up Jade.

While Crystal sobbed facedown on the bed, the man stopped moving. Even his aura changed from dense and dark to a pale shadow. He unclenched his fists. His mouth curved into a distorted smile.

Then he reached for the red velvet box of candy...

I hoped he was going to apologize and offer her some candy. But he didn't open the candy box. Instead, he flicked a twist of gold ribbon off the top. A golden bow fell to the floor, and he stomped on it as he moved toward the bed.

Then he lunged forward and looped the ribbon like a noose around Crystal's neck. He yanked hard and quick. Strong, jerky movements. A topaz ring on his right hand reflected moonlight from the window, tangling in red hair and sparkling like embers.

Crystal clawed at the ribbon, struggling. With her face buried in the pillow I couldn't see her terror, but I felt it. Her body jerked like an erratic puppet, frantic at first, then slower, weaker...

The man gave the ribbon a ferocious twist, waited a moment, then let go.

Red hair flopped forward with the lifeless body.

I screamed and screamed and screamed.

Then woke up back in the truck.

# Part Three

*Hoofbeats*

## 20

"Sabine!" Dominic called softly, his arms holding me as I shuddered with sobs. "What is it? What's wrong?"

"He killed her! I couldn't do anything...to stop him!"

"Stop who? What are you talking about?"

"Crystal! And that man...Ohmygod!" I covered my hands over my face, sobbing.

"I don't know what this is about, but you're safe here with me."

"I know I'm safe—but Crystal isn't! He killed her!"

"Nobody died." Dominic gently pried my hands from my face and made me look at him. "You had a dream."

"I wasn't dreaming! I was in Jade's room, then I heard a noise and went to look and saw this man—and he killed her!"

"Jade? Your half-sister?"

"Yes…no! I mean, it was her mother! The man strangled her!"

"Listen to me, Sabine. What you're saying isn't possible. You never left here. You've been next to me the whole time."

"I did go to Jade's! Just not in my body."

"You're not making sense."

"I astral traveled."

Dominic didn't laugh or call me crazy, but I could tell he didn't believe me. Talking to animals made sense to him, but not traveling without your body.

"It's happened before," I insisted before he could argue. "I can leave my body and travel far away."

He pushed his fingers through his hair, blowing

out a deep breath. All was dark and silent around the truck, except for my thudding heartbeat. The storm had died down…and Crystal was dead, too. I started shaking, the reality sinking in. I'd watched her die and wasn't able to save her.

Dominic put his arms around me. "It's okay now, Sabine."

"So you believe me?" I sniveled, wiping my face with my coat sleeve.

"I don't know. Tell me everything."

I started with my first out-of-body experience, to prove that I wasn't imagining anything. I made it sound scientific, how the soul is a separate entity from the body. I added in some of my experiences with spirits who could travel between worlds, making traveling a few hundred miles sound easy.

Dominic didn't say anything, so I kept trying to convince him. My voice shook when I got to the part about the ribbon around Crystal's neck…

"He killed her with a ribbon?"

"From a heart-shaped candy box." I would never enjoy Valentine's Day again.

"Are you sure she was dead?"

Sick to my stomach, I nodded. "And I couldn't stop him…it was over so fast."

"You have any idea who he was?"

"Crystal's boyfriend, I guess. He seemed really mad, called her awful names. I thought maybe she was cheating on him and he found out. But I don't know his name."

"The police will find him. Don't worry."

"Does that mean you believe me?"

His brows knit together, studying me, and he cleared his throat.

I'll never know what he was going to say because right then there was a roaring noise. The ground rumbled like an avalanche and glowing lights cut through the snowy night.

A voice echoed into the darkness, "NEED HELP?"

The snow plow had found us.

We were rescued.

\* \* \*

I couldn't talk about astral travel or murder in front of the burly, black-haired woman who drove the snow plow. Her name was Dyanne and despite her tough appearance, her voice was shrill like a little girl's. After calling for a tow truck, she'd invited us into her heated truck and offered us steaming coffee from a thermos and some chocolate chip cookies. I couldn't remember the last time I'd eaten.

But I only managed a few sips of coffee and turned down the cookies.

I couldn't stop thinking about…murder.

What was happening at Jade's house? Had the killer gone after her next? Or had he gotten away with murder because I hadn't been able to stop him?

Poor Jade.

Finding your own mother dead had to be the worst thing ever. What would happen to Jade now? Were there other people living in that house that would care for her or would Dad have to step up to being her father? She was older than me, at least seventeen, so maybe she could live on her own— funded by Dad, of course.

But nothing could replace her mother, I thought guiltily. Too awful to think about…and I'd watched without saving her. The killer might go after Jade next unless I called the police. But if I called them, how could I explain knowing about a crime that took place over two hundred miles away?

Totally unbelievable. If I hadn't been there, I doubt I'd believe it myself. It was already starting to feel like a bad dream. Shock and exhaustion confused my thoughts. Was there any chance I had dreamt it?

Dreams came out of subconscious thoughts, and on some level I may have wanted revenge on Crystal and Jade. Hadn't I wished they would go away and leave my family alone? I resented them for stealing my father.

Could the whole murder scene have been a bad dream?

No. Everything inside me said it was real. I may have wanted Crystal out of my father's life, but I never wanted her dead. Besides, with her dead, Jade would be motherless and more reliant on her natural father.

My father! I thought with a snap of my fingers. I had to call him right away. He'd know what to do.

I still had no signal for my phone, but Dyanne's had worked to call a tow truck, so I asked to borrow hers. She graciously handed it over. Then I moved out of hearing range and quickly dialed my father.

"Sabine?" my mother asked sleepily.

Damn—not my father. "Mom, can I speak to Dad?"

"Do you have any idea how late it is?"

"I have to speak with Dad."

"Your father is asleep. Can't it wait till morning?"

"I have to speak with him now," I repeated firmly. I added that it had nothing to do with her or our family; that Nona and I were fine. Then I insisted again on speaking only to my father.

With a huff of indignation, Mom left the line.

Seconds later, Dad came on, groggy, wanting to know why I was calling at two in the morning.

Two? Was it that late? I'd totally lost conception of time, only moments marked in fear. Something about his concerned voice broke me down and I sobbed, "Daddy, something awful's happened."

"What is it?" Dad was instantly alert. "Where are you?"

"The snowstorm is over and the tow truck is on the way to pull us out of the snow, so we're okay now. But that's not what I'm calling about...it's Crystal—" I cut off, afraid to say more.

How could I tell him that a woman he once loved had been strangled and that I'd watched it happen without doing anything?

He whispered for me to wait a moment, and I heard him tell Mom that he needed to finish this talk privately. I knew she wouldn't like that, but that was the least of my concerns. Dad was using his lawyer voice, feeding Mom a story about how I needed some legal advice for a friend from school who'd been unjustly arrested.

I cringed at the word "arrested." Dad's fictional excuse came too close to reality. What would he think if he knew I'd become a thief?

A few minutes later, Dad said, "We can talk freely now. What about Crystal?"

"Oh Dad...I'm so sorry." Then I told him everything that happened while I astral traveled. I tried to make astral travel sound ordinary, but this went against his belief system. Dad always stayed clear of my arguments with Mom about being psychic, humoring me but never accepting my connection with the other side.

When I got to the part about Crystal's killer, I sensed he shut off.

"You had a nightmare," he told me.

"No. It really happened."

I tried to explain but he just wasn't listening. Still, I wouldn't let him off that easily and challenged him to prove I'd dreamed the whole thing by calling Crystal. If she was fine, then I'd accept it was all a dream.

I only wished it were.

Dad argued against calling anyone at this time of the morning. I said if he didn't, I'd call the police and they'd go to her house. He wasn't happy with me, but he agreed to check it out.

Feeling like I'd finally done something right, I returned the phone to Dyanne. She stuck around until the tow truck arrived, then drove off with a hearty wave. It didn't take long for the tow truck to pull Dominic's truck free. I was glad there wasn't any real damage to the truck, and it started right up.

Once we were on the road again, I told Dominic about calling my father.

"Good idea," he approved.

"I hope Jade's all right…not that I like her or anything…but it'll be hard enough losing her mother."

"Yeah, that's rough…if it's what happened." From his tone I realized that he didn't believe me about Crystal. He thought it was a dream…which hurt.

I avoided talking by pretending to sleep. Only I guess I pretended too well because suddenly the truck was slowing, and when I opened my eyes we were driving down Nona's gravel road.

The ranch house was darkened, except for a yellow glow from the porch.

All at once, I felt a jump of excitement. Home— at last! And we had the remedy book. I couldn't wait to see Nona's face when we told her. She would be so happy. And once we found someone to decipher the book, she could throw all those memory notes away forever.

"Are you going to tell her tonight?" Dominic asked as I stepped out of the truck.

"I hate to wake her up. It's almost morning anyway."

"So get some sleep first."

"I already slept enough." I didn't add that I was afraid of where I might travel if I fell asleep again.

Dominic came over and slipped his arms around my shoulders. "After everything settles down, we have some talking to do."

My heart soared. "I know."

"But Nona comes first." He bent down and brushed a soft kiss across my forehead. "See you at breakfast."

Smiling, I reached up to touch my forehead. My fingers smoothed over the spot where his kiss still warmed my skin. So many emotions played inside me that I wasn't sure what to feel. Happy, nervous, scared? I yawned. I'd sort it all out in the morning.

The house was dark. As I stepped inside, I

flipped on a light—and saw a blanketed figure sleeping on the couch.

"Velvet?" I did a double-take. "What are you doing here?"

"Shush, Sabine," Velvet said with a finger to her lips. She sat up halfway, blinking at the light. "Don't wake your grandmother. She's had a rough day."

"Oh, no. What happened?"

"No reason for alarm, she's fine now." Velvet yawned, adjusting her blanket around her shoulders. "Nona's assistant, that dear girl, couldn't get in touch with you and found my number under an emergency contact list. So she called me and I rushed right over. When I got here, Nona was just sitting at the kitchen table, staring down at her hands without talking. She didn't even recognize me."

"No!" I sank into a chair by the couch.

"I kept talking to her, trying to prompt her memory," Velvet said. "She gave me quite a fright and I nearly took her to a hospital. But I know I wouldn't appreciate being treated like an invalid. I made her a warm supper and she started sounding like herself again. I convinced her to go to bed. She fell right asleep and I stayed to watch over her."

"Thank you so much. I appreciate you coming here—especially with all the trouble you've had lately. Did they ever catch the guy who trashed your shop?"

"No, but insurance covered the repairs and I'm back in business. There haven't been any further threats either."

"I'm glad." I added softly, "You're a wonderful friend to Nona."

"She'd do the same for me. But I wish she had swallowed her pride and confided that she wasn't well, although I knew something odd was going on." Velvet reached out for my hand. "Tell me the truth—does she have Alzheimer's?"

"No, but she is sick."

"With what?"

"A hereditary illness that affects her memory and will worsen without the cure."

"If there's a cure, then why in heavens hasn't she taken it?"

"We only found the cure tonight. I just hope it isn't too late." I sighed, feeling the lump of the book through my jacket. "But the remedy book is old and hard to read. We have to find a linguist to decipher the writing. Then the ingredients might be hard to find. That could take days or weeks even. What if Nona doesn't have that long?"

"Your grandmother is one tough lady and has friends like me who will do anything to help her. No matter how rare the ingredients, I'll find them. As for a linguist, I may be able to help you there, too."

I stared at her. "You know a linguist?"

"Not a professional, but someone with a degree in history and languages."

"Who?"

"You're looking at her." Velvet chuckled. "Close your mouth, dear, and please hand over that book."

# 21

Velvet insisted I go to sleep, and I didn't have the energy to argue.

I slept heavily with no dreams—or any way-ward astral traveling.

When I awoke, the sun had replaced stormy clouds and shone brightly through a slit in my curtains. I hoped it was a good omen, that sunshine would banish all dark clouds. Nona would get well and she'd be thrilled to find out I was dating Dominic. Everything would be great—for me anyway.

But not for Jade.

How selfish and inconsiderate could I be? A woman had died and I was only thinking about myself. I mean, Jade had lost her mother. *Her mother*. That was beyond horrible. As much as I disagreed with my mother on almost everything, I loved her and couldn't bear to think about losing her.

What kind of hell was Jade going through? Her whole world had changed in one horrible night. Add the violence of murder, and that made it a zillion times worse. If we were real sisters, like I was with Amy and Ashley, I'd go to Jade and offer support. I hoped she had tons of friends and relatives with strong shoulders to lean against.

Did that include Dad?

Okay, this thought made me a little jealous. But I understood he had to be with her. She'd already lost her stepfather (I guessed he was the spirit named Douglas who was concerned enough about Jade to contact me through the séance).

If Dad was with Jade, that explained why he hadn't called me. He was busy shielding her from reporters and the police. That was the right thing for him to do—no matter how I felt about it. Jade would need a father and a lawyer. With a police investigation, all the sordid details about Dad and Crystal would probably come out.

But would the killer be caught? What if he'd gotten away without any witnesses (other than me) and no evidence connecting him to the crime? I'd seen enough crime dramas on TV to know that the person who a) found the body and b) reported the crime was always a prime suspect.

Had my call to Dad put him in the "b" category? What if the police suspected him?

I sat up in bed, hugging my pillow to my chest and staring at framed pictures hanging over my dresser. One of the pictures showed Dad and me together, decked out in ski suits, when I was just nine and trying out the bunny slope. I'd loved this picture because it was just the two of us. The twins were too little to ski, so they'd stayed behind in the lodge with Mom. There hadn't been too many private moments with Dad since then, but I always felt special as his eldest daughter.

But Jade was older than me.

I tried to guess the sequence of events after I called Dad last night.

Logically, when he tried to call Crystal, Jade would have answered. If she didn't know about her mother, she'd go into the room and make that horrible discovery. Or if she already knew, she'd be hysterical. Either way, Dad would rush right over to take care of her. And at some point, he'd call the police. He was a lawyer after all, sworn to uphold the law. But he also didn't want Mom to know about Crystal, and bringing in the police meant exposing his secrets.

Not an easy choice for Dad.

Would Jade be able to answer questions without involving my father? She'd been sleeping when her mother was murdered, so she wouldn't know much. Still, she must know the identity of the bow-legged guy since he was dating her mother. Jade would know his name and probably where he lived. She could lead the police to the murderer, and Dad wouldn't have to be involved.

Unless Jade didn't know about the guy.

Then the police would turn their suspicion to the reporter of the crime: Dad. If they asked Dad how he knew what happened when he lived way across town, what would Dad say? That his psychic daughter witnessed the murder while astral traveling?

No one would believe that. Dad didn't even believe me, so he'd have to come up with a lie or refuse to answer—which would make him look even guiltier.

Oh, no, Dad, I thought, we're in deep trouble.

I dug into my handbag for my cell and punched in Dad's number. I waited for him to pick up. But all I got was his voicemail.

Should I try his office or the house? A glance at the clock told me it was too early for him to be at work. But it was about the time Mom drove my sisters to their private school, so I might be able to catch Dad at home.

But after five rings, the machine picked up.

With a bitter taste of fear in my mouth, I stared at my phone. Why wasn't Dad answering? Was he still helping Jade? Or had he been arrested for murder?

I groaned. This was all my fault. I got Dad into this mess, so it was up to me to get him out. I'd go to San Jose and describe the real murderer to the police.

There were plenty of holes in this plan, but I couldn't just wait around doing nothing. So I jumped out of bed, hastily tossing on jeans and a green-striped sweatshirt. I tried to think of everything I'd need: my wallet, money, keys to Nona's car, and my cell phone. I knew Nona wouldn't mind me borrowing her car in an emergency, and she was one of the few people who wouldn't blink at the words "astral travel." Besides, until she was well, she shouldn't be driving anyway.

My cell rang.

"Dad!" I grabbed the phone.

The ID showed it wasn't my father, which was such a huge disappointment I had to force myself not to snap at my caller. "Hi, Pen...What's up?"

"About time!" Her voice oozed accusation. "I tried calling you yesterday when your grandmother was going psycho on me. It was scary, her losing it and no one else being here to help. Dominic was gone. You were gone. I would have totally freaked if I hadn't found Velvet's number."

"I'm sorry you had to go through that, but Nona is better now."

"Well...that's great to hear. But I still have issues with you. Like where have you been? Why haven't you returned my calls and emails?"

"I've been busy."

"Busy doing what?"

"Dominic and I had to go get some...uh...special medicine for Nona."

"So she is sick. I thought it was something mental like bipolar. But you could have told me—

we are best friends. And why didn't you return my messages?"

"I never got them. My phone didn't work in the snowstorm. Then the road was shut down and by the time I got home it was so late I went to bed."

"Let me get this straight—a snowstorm? Struggling to stay warm with that hottie Dominic? Does Josh know? Ooh, tell me all." Penny-Love may only be a C student in math, but when it came to adding up juicy details, she was a genius.

But I couldn't tell her I was breaking up with Josh. Not before telling Josh. So I put her off, insisting that it was no big deal. I used that well-used line about Dominic being "just a friend." Then I told her that I wouldn't be at school because I had to see my father (another half-truth). She was all questions, but I cut her off by saying I had another call.

Then I grabbed my stuff and headed downstairs. I figured Nona would still be asleep, so I'd just borrow her car keys and explain later. But as I walked by her office, the door was open and she was working at her desk.

"Wow," I murmured with an astonished shake of my head. "Nona, you're working? How are you feeling?"

"Embarrassed. I don't remember much about

last night, but from what Velvet told me before she left this morning, I owe Penny-Love an apology."

"You talked with Velvet?" I stepped closer into the room. "Did she tell you about the remedy book?"

"Yes. It's wonderful news! Thank you."

"And Dominic," I added.

"Of course. I owe you both so much." Nona smiled in a way that was so familiar that my heart warmed. "Velvet is confident she'll have the remedy within a few days."

"I know she can do it—and then you'll be totally well." I bent over to hug her.

"I already feel better." She reached for a crumpled pile of notes. "Soon I'll be able to get rid of these reminder notes."

"I'll help you burn them."

"A big celebratory fire," she agreed.

I was thrilled she was doing better, but still worried about Dad. I didn't want to burden Nona with the whole murder crisis; not when she was feeling better than she had in weeks. So I tried to sound casual as I asked to borrow her car.

"Sure." She set a paper on a thick pile, her brows arched curiously. "Are you running late for school?"

"School?" The word startled me. "Not today. I have to go to see Dad."

"You plan to drive all the way to San Jose?"

"It's important. Dad wants my advice…about a case."

"Then he'll have to call me himself and give permission, because I don't approve of your missing another day of school."

"Nona," I complained. Why did her memory have to come back so strong? "I really have to talk to him and he's not at home or answering his cell."

"Did you try his office?"

"He's never there before nine."

She reached over for a blue phone on her desk. "What's his number?"

"He won't answer. His secretary won't even be there yet."

"Can't hurt to try." She gave me a firm look, then asked for the number.

This was a waste of time, but I was trapped by my lies. So I rattled off Dad's office number.

"It's ringing," she said, handing me the phone.

"He won't be there," I insisted.

But he was.

I nearly dropped the phone. My grandmother had this annoying "I told you so" smirk. I had a feeling she knew he'd be there all along. Nona had been psychic long before I made my first prediction. I never got premonitions about myself. So I had no forewarning about what happened next.

"What is it, Sabine?" my father asked coolly.

"You didn't call back." My heart skipped. "I was worried you were in jail."

"I deserve to be for listening to you." Yup, he was definitely angry.

"I don't understand—what happened? How did Jade take it? Did you talk to the police? Did they find the killer?"

"There is no killer."

"What?" I felt behind me for a chair and sank down. "You mean he got away?"

"I mean there is no killer because there was no murder." His voice sharpened. "But thanks to your wild story, I had an embarrassing, uncomfortable evening and ended up sleeping at my office to avoid questions from your mother."

"But…But…I saw Crystal strangled!"

"You dreamed it."

"No, I was there! I know it happened."

"Sabine, stop it!" he shouted. "I'm sorry if you're having trouble dealing with my other family, but there's no reason to make up wild stories."

"I didn't make it up. I saw Crystal…dead."

"No, you did not."

"How can you be sure?"

"Because I spoke to Crystal and she was very much alive."

Then my father, who always treated me with respect and never lost his temper, hung up on me.

# 22

It was bad enough that Dad was mad and Nona insisted I go to school. But to add pimples on the face of an already scarred morning, when I stopped at my locker Josh was waiting for me. How could I talk to him like everything was normal?

I couldn't. So I just stood there limply while Josh kissed me and said sweet things like he missed me and was glad to be with me again.

All the while, I was trying to think of the words that might break his heart.

"So how did yesterday go?" He casually draped his arm over my shoulders, which made me flinch.

"Um...okay."

"Your grandmother feeling better?"

"Yeah. Much."

I turned to my locker, spinning the combo as I tried to remember what lie I'd told him, something about getting medicine for my grandmother. A safe half-truth...I hoped.

"Where exactly did you go?" he asked, coming to stand behind me. He was tall enough to easily see over my shoulders.

"It seemed like I was in the car all day," I hedged. "But I was able to get what Nona needed."

"When I visit hospitals, I hear a lot of medication problems. It's cool how you watch out for your grandmother. Did you run into any bad weather? We had a wicked storm come through yesterday."

Don't I know! I thought with irony. My mind flashed back to Dominic's snowbound truck, pressing against him, sharing body heat. My face flamed, and I was glad I was facing my locker and not Josh.

"Yeah, bad weather. All that rain left huge

puddles in our driveway." I grabbed my lit book and a notebook. "So what's been going on around here? Did I miss anything in English yesterday?"

"Nah. Only a boring lecture. Blah, blah…" He grinned, showing dimples that reminded me why I'd been attracted to him in the first place. He really was a hottie: smart, funny, and considerate. Lots of girls tried to hit on him, but he remained loyal to me. So why was I dumping him back in the sea for some other girl to catch? I must be crazy.

But then there was Dominic…

"I typed this up for you," Josh was saying.

"What's this?" I took the paper Josh held out to me. "Homework?"

"Sort of, but no essay questions. It's a list of what to bring on the Hoof Beats in Moonlight campout. We have a week to get ready."

The campout? Three days and two nights up close in personal camping space with Josh? Once I broke up with him, everything would be awkward between us. Spending a long weekend in the wilderness with my ex-boyfriend was out of the question. There was no way I could go now.

"Did you get more mentors?" I asked, hoping he'd say yes and I could gracefully cancel.

But he shook his head. "No. But one canceled."

"Oh, no!"

"You may have to be in charge of two kids instead of one if we don't get more mentors. You won't believe how many people turned me down with some lame excuse. It burns me when everyone always has something better to do than help others. I'm so glad you're not like that."

"Yeah...sure."

"It's not like it'll be all work—it'll be fun. Riding horses, eating around a campfire, and getting to know the kids. I can't wait."

Here was the part where I was supposed to say "me, too." But I couldn't. Instead I kept thinking I had to tell him the truth. He was going to hate me anyway.

"What if the weather's bad?" I asked.

Josh shook his head. "I checked the weather report, and it's all clear. We're not going into the mountains, only the foothills where the elevation is too low for snow. It'll get cold at night, though, so bring a warm jacket. And you'll need a sturdy hiking pack, too."

"I have a backpack already." I pointed to my backpack, which bulged from books, papers, pens, hair ties, snacks, makeup, and other scholastic essentials.

"You're joking, right?" He pushed back his dark hair. "We'll stow some gear on the horses, but the rest is up to us. You're supposed to be a role model for the kids, so I'm counting on you to be prepared."

"Do I look like a Boy Scout?" I asked sarcastically.

"No, you're way cuter."

How could I break up with a guy who said stuff like that? Josh was too sweet—damn him. Breaking up was going to be harder than I thought.

I slammed my locker. Just say it, I told myself.

"I've been thinking about…us being together for a whole weekend."

"Yeah, it'll be cool." He grinned. "But we have to keep it PG since we'll be setting an example for the kids. Still, I'll figure out a way to sneak off alone."

"No! I mean, that wouldn't be…um…fair to the kids."

"They have to sleep sometime," he said with a chuckle. "Speaking of the kids, I pulled some strings so you could be assigned to Lindsay."

"Lindsay?"

"She's nine and crazy about horses. She showed me this notebook full of horse pictures she'd cut from magazines. Such a cute kid—too bad about her mother."

"What do you mean?"

"Her mother's in jail again. Her dad isn't much better, although he's trying, I guess, back in rehab. Lindsay is staying with her aunt, along with five other kids. Two of her cousins signed up for the ride, too. Now if I could just get more mentors. If you think of anyone, let me know."

I nodded, feeling like my skin was tightening around me and I could hardly breathe, much less be honest with Josh. How could I cancel on him now?

But I couldn't go either.

While I was struggling with my conscience, he tugged on my hand and pulled me close like we'd done hundreds of times before. Except now everything was different. I stiffened and jerked back. Hurt flared in Josh's eyes. He was going to question me, ask what was wrong. This was the moment to admit the truth. It's over, we're done, adios forever. Only I wimped out.

"What's that on your arm?" I pointed to a design on his forearm I hadn't noticed before. "A tattoo?"

"It's nothing."

"But I thought you hated needles and would

never get a tattoo," I said, now genuinely puzzled. He pulled back his arm, but not before I read the three tiny cursive letters tattooed inside a sunburst below his elbow. "What's PFC mean?"

"Doesn't matter. Let's talk about the—"

I squinted to make out the letters. "Those aren't your initials."

"I never said they were. They're not important."

"Important enough to permanently etch into your skin."

"Well…" Josh frowned. "Okay, it does mean something, but it's confidential. I can't talk about it."

His secretive tone made me even more curious. I didn't even care if he had a tattoo or what it meant. I'd only asked about it as a diversion to stop him from kissing me. Kissing him felt wrong…dishonest. Until we broke up, I was cheating on Josh with Dominic, although it felt like being with Josh was cheating on Dominic. Did that even make sense? This whole falling in love thing was complicated.

"What's PFC?" I persisted.

"Drop it."

I really should have, but he was pissing me off. "I asked a simple question. What does it mean?"

"None of your business."

"Since when aren't you my business? Why are you shutting me out? Don't you trust me?"

Some kids hurried by us, but we were stone in a rushing sea and didn't move. His expression was pained, yet stubborn. "It's not about trust."

"Then why does it sound like you don't trust me? If that's how you feel, then maybe we shouldn't be together. Let's just end everything."

"Sabine, you're making too much out of this. It's only a tattoo. I didn't even want to get it and only did because…well, just because." He glanced away for a moment. When he met my gaze, his voice was soft and pleading. "Would you feel better if I got another tattoo with your name?"

"No!" I said sharply, horrified at the idea of my name branded on his skin. That would make breaking up impossible. And breaking up was a must. A startling thought hit me. "Are they the initials of another girl?"

"Hell, no! What kind of guy do you think I am?"

"If there is someone else, you can tell me."

"When I commit to someone, that's it. There's only you, Sabine." His voice softened and he leaned close to my face. "You're my girl, okay? I would never ever cheat on you."

Too bad, I thought. Then we'd be even and I wouldn't feel so damned guilty. "So what about the tattoo?"

"I'd tell you except I made a solemn vow—'Indocilis Privata Loqui.'"

"Which means?"

"It's Latin for 'keep your trap shut.'" He flashed a half-smile. "Let's just go to class—the bell is about to ring."

I folded my arms across my chest. "I don't care if I get a tardy."

"I do. Come on, Sabine, don't be that way."

I looked down at the PFC tattoo. A vision popped in my head of a dark room with glowing sconces and gold-framed portraits staring down from a high ceiling and a robed figure passing out cards to shadowy people around a long table. I realized what this was all about. Not another girl, which I really hadn't thought anyway, but passion—Josh's passion for stage magic.

"Does this have something to do with your magician society?"

Josh didn't answer, turning abruptly to walk down the hall.

"Tell me." I slammed my locker, hurrying after him. "What sort of magic stuff is so secret?"

"I'm not discussing this," he snapped without slowing or turning around.

"I'm not asking you to explain tricks—just the tattoo. Why did you have to get it? Does it symbolize something? Are you in some kind of cult?"

"No way—it's the opposite! We crusade against frauds and charlatans."

"Huh?" I had a feeling he was parroting someone else's words. "What do you mean 'crusade'? And who is 'we'?"

"I can't say any more, except this weekend is gonna be huge for me. Arturo is honoring the junior members at his private estate, so I won't be able to go out on Friday."

I'd forgotten we had a date on Friday, and I would have canceled it anyway, but having him say it first made me mad. How dare he take me for granted? For weeks he'd been sneaking off to magician meetings and canceling dates. If I wasn't going to break up with him...well...I'd break up with him.

Only we reached our first class, took our chairs, and didn't get another chance to talk alone. Instead of listening to my teachers, I jotted notes about the best breakup lines. "It's been great, but it's time we moved on." Or "You're a fantastic guy and it's really not you, it's me…" Or "Well, if you'd rather spend all your time with dumb magicians, then they can have you."

Okay, I might have been a little bitter—which was not how I wanted to end things.

During lunch I tried to get Josh off alone, only Penny-Love hooked her arm into mine and steered me to the cheerleading table. Josh showed up with a hot food tray and went along, sitting next to me. He gave me an uneasy look, as if he was afraid I was still mad over the date-canceling thing, but that was the least of my concerns. We wouldn't be dating much longer anyway. I would tell him after school.

Only that didn't work out either.

When the last bell rang and I bolted from my class, I couldn't find Josh anywhere. I checked his last class, his locker, my locker, and the parking lot. His car wasn't there either. I tried his cell and got his voicemail. I texted a short "Where R U?" message and waited for a reply.

I probably still would have been waiting, except Penny-Love found me and invited herself to my house. She wasn't scheduled to work for Nona today, but she was really concerned about Nona and wanted to see how she was doing.

"Much better," I assured her. Penny-Love knew Nona had trouble with her memory, but not that the illness was so serious it might be fatal. "It took a while to find the right…uh…medicine, but I think we have it now."

"That's great for Nona! But what's the 411 with you and Dominic? Don't think I've forgotten how you guys were snowbound together, which sounds so romantic and scandalously naughty, too. Did you get naked and wicked together? No—don't tell me, it's obvious from your shocked expression. Knowing you, nothing happened—which is a damn shame. I mean, if it had been me, I would have melted like a hot snowball in Dominic's muscular arms."

"What about Jacques?"

"Jacque's cool." She waved her hand, dodging out of the way of a mother pushing a baby stroller. "I get really turned on when he talks about art and shows me his paintings. But a girl can have some dessert with the main dish, you know. So dish, Sabine—what really happened last night?"

I cheated on my boyfriend. I committed a crime. And I witnessed a murder—that turned out not to be a real murder, just a realistic dream, so now my dad hates me.

"Nothing," I told her.

"You are so pathetic," she said with a playful tug on my long hair. "But I kind of respect it. I mean, you're like the most honorable person I know...well, except for Josh. You two really are the perfect couple."

"No one's perfect," I said with a sad smile.

I didn't say much else, listening and letting her talk until we reached Nona's house.

The ranch house was strangely silent. I could sense this as I approached. Lilybelle wasn't in her usual perch on the porch rail, and even the penned farm animals made no sounds. No music or scent of herbal tea drifting from within the house. With curtains drawn and windows closed, the house seemed like a tomb.

"No one's inside," I said knowing this for a certainty.

"How can you tell?" Penny-Love asked as she opened the door and peeked inside the dimly lit living room.

"It's too quiet."

"You're right—her office door is open but she's

not there. The kitchen is all dark, too. So where is Nona?"

I looked around, noticing for the first time a car parked beside Nona's car. "Velvet's car," I murmured. With a look over to the barn I saw that Dominic's truck was here also. There were lights on upstairs in the barn loft, and I sensed strong energy emanating from them.

I headed for the barn, pushing open the double doors and going up the staircase that led to Dominic's loft room. Mixed in with fresh manure and hay scents, I smelled something unusual; a strong aroma that made my nose tingle and my heart pulse. The whole barn seemed aflame in a lavender aura.

I pushed open Dominic's door and stared at the three figures gathered in a candle-blazing circle where crystals hung from the ceiling to ward off darkness and a small pan bubbled with an eerie green-black liquid.

Dominic, Nona, and Velvet looked up.

At the same time I heard a gasp behind me, realizing too late that Penny-Love had followed me—and I'd led her right into a den of sorcery.

# 23

"What's going on?" Penny-Love exclaimed, her eyes almost bugging out.

Dominic's expression was bland except for a slight arch of one brow. Velvet covered her mouth and shook her head. I had no idea what to say, so I remained silent. It was my grandmother who stepped up to the situation.

"I'm so glad to see you, Penny-Love," Nona said, smiling.

She came over to her "Love Assistant" with a casual manner, as if being caught stirring up a mystical brew was nothing out of the ordinary. I wanted to applaud Nona's quick reactions. You'd have never known she recently had memory lapses and would have died if we hadn't found the remedy.

The remedy! Velvet must have deciphered the book. That's why Nona, Velvet, and Dominic were gathered in shadows and candlelight. Secluded in the privacy of Dominic's room, they concocted the cure for Nona's illness.

"Penny-Love, I could use your help," Nona was saying.

"My...My help?" Penny-Love looked around uneasily. "Doing what?"

I watched with admiration for my grandmother as she convinced Penny-Love that they were mixing up scented soap to sell at Trick or Treats. I didn't think she'd had time to take the remedy yet, so it must have been the healing fumes—or perhaps hope—that sharpened her mind. She answered questions before Penny-Love had a chance to ask them. Why candles? Because the scent of burnt candles was part of the recipe. Why were they in Dominic's room? Because when the soap hardened it let off a noxious odor and Dominic's room had large windows to quickly air out bad smells. Then Nona sent Penny-Love to the house for a small electric fan to clean the smoky air.

"Soap, huh?" I asked my grandmother. "With poisonous smells?"

"There is a strong odor in here," she replied.

"Which we all know has nothing to do with soap," I said with a pointed look at my grandmother, Velvet, and Dominic.

"I can always use herbal soap for my shop," Velvet said.

"Sabine knows what's going on," Dominic said.

"But Pen didn't." I chuckled. "She sure left here fast. I'll bet she takes her time finding a fan so the 'poisonous smells' go away. Nona, you knew how to handle her."

"Just think how brainy I'll be when I take the remedy," my grandmother joked. "I can almost feel my memory improving. You two really came through for me."

"Dominic did most of the work," I said, scooting next to him on the rug.

"Teamwork," he added. Stirring the bubbling concoction, Dominic gave me a private look that

I knew meant we'd talk about us when we were alone later.

Still our eyes met a lot as we stirred, clocked the boiling time so it lasted no more than seventy-five seconds, shredded odd-smelling herbs, and mixed them in slowly. It was all complicated and tedious. Velvet showed us a typed paper with the translated remedy. Even spelled out in simple language, it looked like a chemistry-quiz nightmare.

We were all exhausted and sweating when at last Velvet pronounced the remedy finished. She and my grandmother took it into the house for cooling.

Dominic and I were alone.

Naturally he asked the one question I dreaded.

"No, I didn't," I answered with a sigh.

"Why not?"

"I never found the right moment. You have no idea how hard it is. Josh thinks everything is great with us."

"You can't have us both."

"Why not?" I asked half-joking.

"Sabine," he said firmly. "You have to tell him."

"I know...I know." I sank onto a cushioned chair, draping my hand over my forehead. "But I can't do it yet."

"Don't you want us to be together?"

"I do, only our timing sucks. There's this horseback campout in a week and I promised to go along as a mentor for the young riders. The kids are disadvantaged or homeless. This campout will mean so much to them, but there aren't enough teen mentors. If I drop out, some kids might not be able to go."

"Tell me more about this trip," he said as he sat across from me.

"It's called Hoof Beats in Moonlight, and a dozen kids are signed up. You know how Josh loves kids."

"Yeah, he's a real hero," Dominic said sarcastically.

"I know you don't like him, but you have to admit he's a good guy. He's working hard on this campout and is counting on me to go."

"So go."

"But if I break up with Josh, the trip will be torture." I noticed Dominic's blue eyes narrowing and added, "I will break up with him. I promise."

"When?"

"Um…" I hesitated. "After the campout."

"You want to spend two nights alone with Josh?"

"Who can be alone with a bunch of kids and other mentors?"

"What will you do if he wants to kiss you?"

I glanced away, guiltily. Josh had kissed me at school and talked about finding some way for us to be alone on the ride. "I don't know…"

"I do." Dominic stood, his mouth set in a grim line.

"What do you mean?" I demanded.

He walked over to his dresser, turning to ask me. "What's Josh's number?"

Automatically, I rattled off the number. Then I looked at Dominic's hand on the phone with horror. "Wait a minute! You wouldn't actually call him…would you?"

He lifted the receiver.

"No!" I choked out, rushing over ready to wrestle the phone from him. "Don't you dare! You can't call Josh!"

Dominic shook me off and turned his back on me.

"Please, don't do it!" I begged. "I said I'd break up with Josh and I will. It has to come from me— not you."

But he ignored me. My gut twisted when I heard the dialing tones on his phone. I held my breath, afraid of what would come next. My intuition wasn't buzzing in with any advice, only dread.

My new boyfriend shouldn't break up with my old boyfriend. That went against all the dating etiquette rules. But there was no predicting what Dominic would do.

Unable to watch, I shut my eyes, as if not looking could stop it from happening. I'd handled this badly. All my fault. I should have let Josh down at school today. Because I was a major wimp, Josh was going to be hurt far worse. But if I argued too much with Dominic, he might think I was still hung up on Josh. Guys were weird that way. So I waited helplessly, hearing a rumble of a one-sided conversation, but unable to make out the words.

Minutes later, Dominic hung up and faced me solemnly.

"Well?" I asked in a miserable whisper. "Did you do it?"

He nodded. "Yeah. I told him."

"Oh, no." I groaned. "How did Josh take it?"

"Good."

"He didn't get upset?"

"No. He thanked me."

"I don't believe it."

"It's true." Dominic smiled wickedly. "He thanked me—twice."

"You can not be serious!" Pursing my lips, I shook my head. "Are we talking about the same person? Josh DeMarco? The guy I've been dating for the last three months?"

"That's him, all right. A little pompous, but overall a decent guy."

"What was his reaction when you told him I was breaking up with him?"

"We didn't talk about you."

"You…You didn't?" I felt dizzy. "Then why did you call him?"

"To volunteer as a mentor for the Hoof Beats in Moonlight ride." Dominic playfully punched my arm. "I'm going on the campout with you."

\* \* \*

The next few days relaxed into my usual routine of homework, talking to my friends, and helping Nona prepare for the upcoming holiday. Now that she was taking the remedy, she was busy with her business, on the phone or meeting clients, with a renewed excitement about life. And she never forgot her keys or client names. She was feeling so great she wanted to celebrate by inviting friends and family for Thanksgiving.

Unfortunately a lot of people already had plans. My parents and sisters were invited to a party by one of Dad's law partners. Penny-Love couldn't come (she came from a large family and was in charge of cooking the turkey this year). I invited Thorn, too, but her mother (a minister) had the whole family volunteering at a homeless shelter.

I was saved from inviting Josh when he emailed me that his family was going out to dinner with Evan's family. Once upon a romance, Josh choosing Evan over me would have hurt, but now I didn't care.

I was truly over him.

Unfortunately, he didn't know it yet.

Until he did, I had to act like everything was normal. So it was a relief not to see him, although I did wonder why he seemed different lately. Now that I thought about it, his aura had been different, too; still bright in the center but edged in gray. And that whole tattoo thing was out of character. Josh was a big talker and liked to tell stories about his achievements. I always loved to listen and admired his dedication and ideals. Sure, sometimes he came off a little arrogant—like when he talked trash about slackers who didn't give back to their community—but everything he did came from his heart.

So his furtive behavior struck me as odd. Not that it was my concern. Soon we'd be completely yesterday's couple. Girls would be all over Josh once the news got out that he was available. He'd be happier with a nice, normal non-psychic girl.

Because of a combo of teacher in-service days plus Thanksgiving holiday, I had the entire week off from school. I kept mega-busy making pies, cleaning the house from closets to cupboards, and getting some riding in on Nona's oldest horse, Stormy (a name that so didn't suit this gentle horse).

Being busy kept me from thinking too much and left me so exhausted each night, I slept without dreaming or astral traveling.

The night before Thanksgiving, Nona, Dominic, and I had a solemn ceremony outside under a full moon. Dominic fanned a small fire in a dirt pit while I recited a harvest prayer about "refilling the well of time and seeding renewal of life." A little mysterious, deep, and meaningful. When Nona pulled a bunch of wrinkled papers out of her skirt pocket then flung them into the fire, I almost cried. We watched reverently as the papers flamed yellow and red, edges curling black until there was nothing left of Nona's memory notes. We'd come so far to reach this moment; months of searching for charms that crossed several states, always haunted by the fear that Nona might sink into a coma and never recover. I whispered thanks for all my friends who helped on the way.

The fire faded to smoke, but we didn't move to go inside. The night was so beautiful, the shimmering moon casted shadows that followed our footsteps. Although it was past midnight, no one was ready for sleep.

It was Nona's idea to carve pumpkins for Thanksgiving, and although I argued that it was too babyish, I had to admit it was fun, sitting on the porch in the quiet night with only rustling wind through trees and soft chirping of insects. I couldn't even remember the last time I'd carved pumpkins. My mother always hired a professional decorator for major holidays so Thanksgiving at the Rose house was a glittery event with wax-fruit centerpieces, life-sized automated scarecrows, and holographic pumpkins with creepy faces. No messy pulp oozing over Mom's manicured fingers.

But being messy didn't bother me—and I couldn't resist flinging a glob of pulp at Dominic. When it landed on his cheek, he faked like he was mad, then flicked a sticky orange seed at me. I retaliated, of course, which led to a full-scale pumpkin-seed war. Nona came out to see why we were laughing and pretended to be stern, ordering us to stop acting like children. So we pummeled her with pulp.

I awoke on a foggy, cold Thursday morning feeling happier than I had in a long time. When I'd first come to Sheridan Valley, hurting over betrayals and being kicked out of my home, all I'd wanted was to be "normal." But that hadn't really happened…and it was okay. At school I had good friends like Manny, Thorn, and Penny-Love, and at home I had a wonderful (healthy!) grandmother…and Dominic.

On this day of thanks and giving, I was very thankful.

Nona and I made four different kinds of pies: apple, pumpkin, pecan, and banana cream. The table was set and there was a toasty fire in the fireplace. The aroma of herbal dressing and a nineteen-pound turkey wafted into every room of the house.

Our Thanksgiving party consisted of Nona, Velvet, Grady, Dominic, and me—a cozy group with enough food prepared to stuff a small city. We planned to have an early dinner, play cards for a while, then return for dessert. Thanksgiving was like an Olympic event that lasted an entire day and gave our stomachs a workout.

I also had a special surprise planned for Dominic. While everyone else headed to the dining room, I pulled Dominic aside and handed him a wrapped package.

"For you," I told him. "Open it."

He ripped open the paper to reveal a boxed set of books by James Herriot, a famous veterinarian. "Thanks, Sabine. I love this author," he said. "But what's the occasion?"

"As if you didn't know." I grinned. "Happy birthday!"

He blinked. "Say that again?"

"I saw the date on your license. Sorry, it's a few weeks late."

"Actually..." Dominic looked embarrassed. "It's a few months early."

"But your driver's license showed November 11," I pointed out.

"All fake. With my past, I couldn't risk putting down the truth."

Before I could ask what was the truth, Nona called us into the dining room.

"Thank you all for sharing this wonderful day with me," my grandmother declared as we took our seats. "May this be a Thanksgiving we'll always remember."

Nona had just asked Grady to do the honor of carving the turkey when there was a knock at the door.

"I'll get it," I offered. I guessed it would be one of Nona's friends or clients coming over to wish her a happy Thanksgiving.

Wrong.

When I opened the door, I thought I was seeing a ghost. In fact, I would have preferred a ghost over the girl standing on the doorstep.

"Hi, sis!" Jade said with a confident flip of her red hair. She smiled like we were old friends instead of strangers. "Aren't you going to invite me in?"

# 24

I didn't invite Jade into the house—not that that stopped her. My half-sister breezed in past me like a force of nature in disguise.

Unfortunately, her disguise looked an awful lot like me.

Jade tossed her brown leather jacket on a coat rack, revealing a sexy, red midriff blouse that showed off her flat stomach. A belly ring flashed with a fiery red jewel above snug bleached-denim jeans with a large red star on a wide leather belt buckle and three-inch red heels. I didn't have to read the brand-name labels to know who was paying her high-priced bills.

While I was trying to figure out a polite way to say "Get the hell out of here," she was already on her way into the dining room. I hurried to catch up.

"Nona! You're exactly as I imagined." Jade's voice was deeper than mine, with enthusiastic power that demanded attention.

My grandmother's face wrinkled in confusion. "Do I know you?"

"You do now." Jade bent down to give Nona a quick hug.

"Oh my! You look like…but how can that be?"

"Genetics."

"I don't understand," Nona said with a shake of her head.

"Didn't Sabine tell you?"

"Tell me what?"

Jade tilted her head toward me. "Sabine, do you want to tell or should I?"

Like I had a choice? I couldn't trust what Jade might say. I tried to figure out how to explain her without breaking my promise to Dad. Apparently Jade had never promised Dad she'd keep his secret.

Or if she did, she sure wasn't honoring it. What was she doing here anyway? Shouldn't she be with her own family on Thanksgiving?

All eyes shifted toward me. Grady set down the carving knife. Velvet leaned forward with a curious lift of her brows. Dominic tilted his head, his expression slightly amused. And Nona, her face flushed, slowly rose to her feet.

"This is Jade," I spit out the bitter words. "She's my...my—"

"Cousin," Jade finished.

"Um...yeah...cousin," I echoed the lie.

"But how is that possible?" Nona's silvery brows knit together. "I was certain I knew all our relatives."

There was a lack of confidence in Nona's tone that bothered me. She was still sensitive about her memory lapses, so I quickly amended, "Distant cousins. Jade's from Dad's side of the family, and we only met recently."

"Surprise! It's a girl!" Jade whirled around with a laugh.

I wanted to vomit.

"Sabine, you have no idea how I've looked forward to this moment." Jade flung her arms around me, trapping me in a hug. "I've dreamed of coming here since we met."

I've dreamed of you, too, I considered saying.

Her perfume was strong, a heady floral scent that wafted in my throat and made me feel like I was suffocating. I pushed her off, struggling to keep my cool even though I was steaming inside. How could she act like this was all normal? Didn't she realize what her existence meant to my family? Divorce and heartbreak were a serious risk. Lying about being a cousin wouldn't fool anyone for very long.

"How did you know I was here?" I asked.

"Your father mentioned you'd moved back. This farm sounded so sweet; I just had to see it myself."

"Sabine, why didn't you ever tell us about Jade?" Nona chided.

"I only found out recently."

"But you said nothing about her. How could you keep such an astonishing secret?" Nona asked with an incredulous expression.

"It wasn't easy," I said.

"You two girls look sweet together." Nona smiled at us. "For distant cousins, you're amazingly alike. Except for the red hair, Jade could be Sabine's twin."

"Close." Jade winked at me.

"They don't look that much alike." Dominic

shook his head. "Sabine is taller and has your eyes, Nona."

I sent Dominic a look of pure gratitude.

Jade smoothed back her hair and looked appreciatively around the room. "Hmmm, all this food sure smells good. I hope you don't mind my showing up like this. In Sabine's last email, she said to drop by anytime, and I didn't have plans today."

I had not sent her an email. We had not had any real conversations. And the last time I saw her was in a killer dream, which gave me a scared feeling, like I expected her to break down into sobs because her mother had been murdered. Only her mother was fine. Yet my intuition warned that Jade's whole cheerful attitude was as fake as the emails we never exchanged.

"No plans on Thanksgiving?" Nona asked in astonishment.

"Mom left on a business trip and said we'd skip Thanksgiving this year."

Nona looked appalled. "Well, we can't let that happen. Of course, you'll join us. Sabine, find another chair and I'll put out another table setting."

"You're all so sweet! I hardly know what to say, except thanks! Thanksgiving here would be so totally fabulous!" Jade flashed a sugary smile.

She never seemed to stop moving either, whether it was twirling a curl of red hair around her finger or shuffling her feet like she was hearing music. I wondered if she was buzzed on energy drinks or just naturally hyper.

If I'd been in her place, I would have politely refused and said I didn't want to intrude on a holiday. But I was quickly learning that my half-sister was nothing like me. Her aura pulsed with splashes of scarlet and violet blue; strong, dynamic, and volatile. Being near her was like tiptoeing around the edge of a bubbling volcano.

"Do tell us about yourself," Velvet asked while Nona rattled plates in the cupboard and I dragged over another chair.

"What's to tell? My life is dull compared to Sabine's."

I wondered what that was supposed to mean.

Jade slipped into the chair I'd added to the opposite side of the table where I sat. "I was born in San Jose and still live there with my mother in the same house as always. It's in an older area, not the ultra-fancy subdivision Sabine's family lives in."

Velvet smiled. "So how long have you known about Sabine?"

"About a year." Jade shot me a challenging look.

"So what do your parents do?" Nona asked.

Please don't say your dad's a lawyer, I thought.

"Nothing." Jade's shoulders sank and she blew out a sad sigh. "Dad died when I was twelve."

"Oh, I'm so sorry," Nona said.

Even Grady, who had stayed out of this until now, seemed moved. "Tough break," he said with a sympathetic nod.

"You poor child," Velvet chimed in softly. "My own mum died when I was small, so I understand."

"I'm glad you found Sabine." Nona patted Jade's shoulder. "And now us."

Jade bent her head, her red hair sweeping down like a curtain to hide her face. In that moment I sensed something real—grief or sadness, I wasn't sure. Then it was over, and she was smiling again in that fake, sugary way.

"This food looks fabulous," Jade said, gesturing at the table. "My mother is away a lot and even when she's home she doesn't bother cooking. It's always fast food or frozen dinners. Last year we had tacos for Thanksgiving. I can't remember when I've ever been to a real traditional Thanksgiving. Thanks so much for inviting me."

I didn't point out that she invited herself. And it really burned me to have to go along with her lies. Dominic knew who she really was and he kept shooting me concerned looks. I think he wanted me to stop the lies. But I couldn't just blurt out the truth in front of everyone. Instead they all fell for Jade's act.

This was not the Thanksgiving I imagined.

I was forced to nod at Jade's comments as if we *were* long-lost cousins. According to her, we'd been emailing each other for a year, ever since someone mistook her for me when she'd gone blond at a costume party. She tracked me down through web searches and we'd started sharing emails. She exaggerated a dramatic story about meeting me when I was staying in San Jose—which was close to the truth. Only when our father had accidentally brought us together, we hadn't talked to each other. I'd stayed in the car, shocked and not wanting to believe my father had a second family. It had been horrible: the complete opposite of the happy reunion she described.

Jade went on to talk about her interests. She described things that could have been from my own life, only better. She didn't just hang out with cheerleaders like I did; she was the head cheerleader.

She wasn't an anonymous contributor to her school paper; she was editor-in-chief. She'd even taken fencing lessons and won some competitions.

It was like she'd copied the script of my life, but edited minor accomplishments into major successes. Did I believe any of it? No way. But with each of her lies, I was in deeper. I couldn't confess the truth without ruining everyone's holiday.

After dinner, I told Nona to relax and offered to wash dishes. Nona took Jade into the living room to show her family pictures. Velvet and Grady followed, but Dominic stayed behind to help me.

"So that's the half-sister?" he asked in a low whisper.

I ran water in the sink, waiting for it to heat up. "Yep. How'd you know?"

"Not too many girls who look like you named Jade." He grabbed a dish towel and added with a grin, "Even if you hadn't told me, you were bristling like a cat getting her fur rubbed with a rake."

"I'm still in a state of shock," I admitted. "Seeing her was bad enough, but then she told all those lies and I couldn't stop her."

"Why not?"

"What was I supposed to say?"

"How about 'Excuse me, but she's a lying bitch.'"

I laughed, loving him even more. "I wish I had! My feelings are all mixed up. At first I hated her, but that's not fair because Dad was the one who hid his second family. So I decided to forget her—until that nightmare where I thought her mother was dead."

"That was just a dream. You don't owe Jade anything."

"I promised Dad not to tell anyone about her."

"You told me."

"I probably shouldn't have—but I'm glad I did. Only now that she's here, it'll be hard to keep her a secret. If Nona figures it out, she'll go straight to my mother."

"It's not your job to protect your parents."

I frowned, not sure who I was trying to protect. Dad? Mom? Myself? If only Jade had stayed away. What was she doing here?

From the other room I heard laughter and guessed Nona must have been showing Jade the famous picture of me eating from the cat's food dish. I was only two; what did I know?

I was sick of Jade and didn't want to think or talk about her.

Dominic seemed to know this without my saying anything. He switched the topic to the campout—which didn't exactly improve my mood. Camping with my old boyfriend and new boyfriend would be a disaster. I tried to convince Dominic not to go, but he stubbornly refused. Was he insane?

When I rinsed off the last dish and Dominic was drying it, Nona appeared in the doorway. Her arm was draped cozily around Jade's shoulders.

"We have news," my grandmother announced.

"Is Jade going home already?" I tried not to sound hopeful.

"On the contrary." Nona beamed. "I've convinced her to stay a few days."

"Stay? Here?" I was glad I wasn't holding any glassware that might have slipped from my hands and smashed to the floor.

"It'll give you two girls a chance to get to know each other better. Doesn't that sound fun?"

"Yeah...tons of fun," I said with zero enthusiasm. "But I'm sure she had other plans with her friends."

"No plans." Jade shook her head. "My mother

is out of town and I don't have school until Monday. I'm all yours."

Nona could have her—I was headed for a camping trip. But I didn't remind Nona of this or tell Jade. My dear half-sister would figure it out when she woke up in the morning and I was gone.

Nona asked me to show Jade to the guest room, then left to get fresh sheets for Jade's bed. Dominic covered his mouth, as if hiding his amusement. But the traitor didn't offer to go with us. Instead he hurried off to join Grady and Velvet, who were starting up a poker game in the living room. Lucky me was left with Jade.

"Come this way," I said as I started up the stairs. "Your room is right across from mine."

"I'm sure yours is nicer," she said, scowling.

"Actually the guest room is bigger—not that it matters." I tensed but kept my voice polite. "I hope you'll be comfortable here."

"What you really mean is that you hope I'll go to hell," she retorted. "Don't pretend to like me."

I stopped midstair, my hand tightening on the polished wood railing. "I don't know you well enough to like or dislike you."

"You hate me, admit it. I saw your expression when I showed up. You wanted to slam the door in my face."

"I was surprised. How did you find me here?"

"What makes you think I'm here because of you?"

"Why else?"

"I got my reasons, and they aren't out of sisterly love," she said sarcastically. "All that stuff I said about us being friends was crap."

"Then why even say it?" I demanded, getting angry.

"Can't disappoint dear grandma, can we?"

"She's my grandmother, not yours, and she would prefer honesty to lies. I should have told her we were half-sisters."

"And spill Daddy's shameful secret?" she sneered.

"Whatever." I refused to rise to her bait and led her into the guest room. I gestured to a chestnut dresser. "There are empty drawers you can use. If you need extra clothes, you can borrow some of mine."

"Keep your nasty castoffs." She stuck a pointed finger at my face. "You're not any better than me."

"I never said I was."

"But you implied it. Don't think I'm naïve; I know how it is with princesses like you. Handed everything since you were born, never having to work or go without nice things. We share a father—and that's all we're ever gonna share."

Her hostility rocked me. It never occurred to me that she might resent me as much as I resented her—maybe even more. In a way I was relieved because we were being honest.

"Fine," I told her. "Then let's agree not to be friends."

"Agreed."

I started to leave the room, but paused and shot her a questioning look. "I don't get it. If you hate me so much, why even come here?"

Her lips pursed defiantly. "I can go wherever I want."

"Does Dad know you're here?"

"No. And don't you go tattling to him."

"I wouldn't do that."

"You better not or you'll regret it."

"Is that a threat?"

"What do you think? Just get out of my room."

She shoved me out in the hall and slammed the door.

I looked across the hall to my bedroom, which I'd found comfort in since I was a little girl, then back to Jade's closed door. The slam still rang in my ears.

Jade may only be my half-sister, but she was a full bitch.

# 25

During the night, I awoke from a weird dream where I was drowning in a pool of tomato soup and trying to escape by climbing up a slimy strand of red yarn that turned into a snake and wrapped around my neck. Gasping for air, I felt disoriented and startled to be dry in my own bed. I glanced over at my glowing unicorn night-light and breathed easier, calmed.

Still, there was a pit of anxiety in my stomach.

An odd feeling of not remembering something important. And I tried to figure out what had woken me. An unusual noise, music. Yeah, like someone playing a musical instrument.

Then I heard it again. A short burst of rap music. But it stopped abruptly and made me wonder if I'd imagined it—until it blared again. Not a musical instrument, but a cell phone. Since it wasn't my ring tone or Nona's, that only left one person.

I jumped out of bed, tossing on a robe, then tiptoed across the hall. I could see a light from under the door and heard a murmur inside. Jade must have been on her cell phone.

Pressing my ear against the door, I eavesdropped. Spying on my half-sister was beginning to be a bad habit. But I had no shame and was proud of it.

Jade's voice was low at first and I could only make out a few scattered words, "How could you?...finds out...have to ...dead." The last word gave me chills as I remembered my nightmare. But I assured myself it meant nothing. Jade's mother was alive; my father had been positive.

I waited there, crouched down and getting a cramp in my neck from straining to listen. I didn't hear anything for a few minutes then Jade cried out "No! When?"

There was a long pause before she asked in a trembling voice, "But I can't…don't understand…there's no…what am I going to do?"

Then only silence. I guessed that Jade's caller was answering. I closed my eyes and tried to visualize who this person was, but all I got was a feeling of an older woman; someone close to Jade.

When Jade said "bye," her voice quaked with fear.

And I felt afraid, too, although I had no idea why.

The end of the conversation was my cue to hustle out of there. I made it back to my own room within seconds, slipping under my warm blankets and waiting for my heart to slow. It was hard to relax into sleep with my mind buzzing with questions about Jade.

Who had called her so late at night? This was more evidence that she was hiding something. Had she come here out of curiosity or did she have a darker reason? Logically I knew she hadn't just showed up on a bitchy whim. But my psychic radar wasn't picking up any answers.

Worry slithered up my spine and I wondered why Jade had sounded so scared.

Did it have anything to do with me?

*   *   *

It was still dark outside when my alarm buzzed.

Groggily, I fumbled for my bedside lamp and snapped it on. For a moment, my head swam with confusion. Then I saw my backpack on the floor by my desk and realized the reason for the early morning wake-up buzz. The Hoof Beats in Moonlight camping trip started today.

The good thing was I would be out of Jade's toxic reach.

The bad news was it was almost five in the morning and I hadn't finished packing. I had to hurry because Dominic insisted we leave by six. He wanted to reach the stables early enough to choose a good horse. His exact words had been, "I don't want to get stuck on an old nag." The small, gentle horses were reserved for the kids, but expert riders would be allowed more spirited mounts.

Yawning, I stumbled out of bed, showered, and dressed. Then I consulted Josh's trip list and started pulling clothes from my drawers. I needed three sets of warm clothes, waterproof gloves, a flashlight, and other supplies. When I had checked off everything on the list, I had a feeling I was forgetting something. I double-checked my backpack (not the one I used for school, but a rugged outdoor pack Nona had found for me). Then I grabbed the heavy pack and left my room.

Jade's door was closed.

I paused in the hall for a moment, mentally replaying the partial conversation I'd overhead. Had Jade really said "dead"? Or maybe she'd said "Dad." That made more sense. She'd probably been talking to her mother—nothing mysterious about that. Maybe Crystal was mad because Jade was visiting me, which could ruin their sweet (and profitable) situation with Dad if my mother found out. Dad had been generously doling out money for years to his secret family. Why risk making him mad?

My father's demeanor was usually relaxed— unless someone pushed him too far. Then watch out. His flash flood fury swept fast, taking down anyone in its path. I'd incurred this anger when I'd sent Dad off to Crystal's home and insisted she'd been murdered. I'd been wrong; he'd been embarrassed. Dad still wasn't speaking to me, which hurt, although I knew he'd get over it eventually.

If Crystal was angry at Jade for coming here and

Jade was afraid of making Dad mad, that almost explained everything—except why Jade was here.

Not my problem. Adios, secrets and lies and drama. I was getting out of here and wouldn't have to deal with Jade anymore. By the time I returned, Jade would be gone. Good riddance.

Dominic was waiting by his truck when I stepped outside. It was a chilly, damp morning with darkness trapped under overcast skies. There was no hint of rain, though, which was encouraging.

"I'll take that," Dominic offered, reaching for my backpack and sleeping bag.

"Thanks."

I climbed into the truck while he stowed my belongings in the back, then we set off for Manzanita Stables. We'd been driving for almost an hour when I realized what I'd forgotten.

I smacked my forehead with my palm. "I'm an idiot!"

Dominic turned down the radio. "What did you say?"

"My purse! I was so busy checking off everything I had to bring, I forgot my purse because it wasn't on the list. I don't have my ID, money, or my cell phone."

"Should I turn back?" he offered.

I bit my lip, angry with myself. Here Nona was improving her memory and I seemed to be losing mine. How could I be so careless? My purse had been sitting right on my desk, in plain sight and impossible to miss. Yet I'd left it behind. And we'd already driven too far to return home. That wouldn't be fair to Dominic. If he got stuck riding an "old nag," it would be my fault.

"No need to go back." I shrugged. "I can live without my purse for a few days."

"You sure?"

"Our food is provided, so I won't need any money. I don't need my license because you're driving. And I can borrow someone's cell phone if I need one."

"There won't be a good signal in the hills anyway," Dominic added. "I'm leaving mine in the truck." So he kept driving.

Manzanita Stables was a sprawling ranch with over fifty acres of stalls, pastures, and out-buildings. Frost sparkled from bushes and trees, shining like crystals in the early sunrise. As I stepped out of the truck, I inhaled fresh air mixed with manure and hay smells. Not a smell most people enjoyed, but it reminded me of Nona's barn.

Dominic parked in a gravel lot near the staging

area where we'd gather to start the ride. Josh had given me a small map showing me the trail route, which would start at the ranch and wind up hills into the wilderness, eventually circling back to the ranch.

We stepped out of the truck. I looked around for other cars but saw none.

"I told you we didn't have to get here so early," I teased Dominic. "I'll bet even the horses are sleeping."

"They don't need much sleep."

"I do," I said with a yawn.

"Sleep all you want tonight under the stars. Want to share my tent?" he asked with a devilish grin.

"You're so bad." I hit his arm playfully. "I'll be bunking with the girls."

"As long as it's far from your ex."

I chuckled. "Jealous?"

"Should I be?" he challenged.

"No, but I'd like to know I'm appreciated."

"I'll show you appreciation."

He pulled me close and would have kissed me right there in the parking lot if a middle-aged woman wearing a plaid quilted jacket and tawny boots hadn't shown up.

"Are you here for the Moonlight campout?" She ran her hand through her short black hair and stepped through a white gate surrounding the front grassy yard of a two-story yellow house. She had a rumpled look and wore no makeup, as if she'd just woken up.

"Yes." Dominic nodded. "We're a bit early."

"Much better than being late and holding up the entire group—which happens too often. I'm Francesca Stodder. My husband and I run this spread." We exchanged introductions and shook hands. She added, apologetically, that they were running late this morning. "A new foal got sick and we've been up with the little guy all night."

"Is he going to be okay?" Dominic asked, instantly concerned.

"Yes. The vet just left and the foal is resting. We'll have to watch him for a while, but he's a sturdy little fellow. He'll make it." She smiled for the first time, which made her look much younger than I'd originally assumed. "Thanks for asking."

"Dominic knows lots about horses," I told her. "He's studying to be a farrier."

"I've still got a lot to learn," Dominic said with a shrug.

"Been riding long?"

Dominic nodded. "Long enough. Horses and I understand each other."

"Then I'll make sure Simon gets you a spirited horse, either Skye or Lightning." Mrs. Stodder glanced over her shoulder at the yellow house. "I better hurry back and get things going. Go on over to the stables and check out the horses until the rest of your group arrives."

Dominic didn't hesitate, hurrying off so I had to run to keep up with him. I didn't care which horse I was assigned. I'd learned long ago that you were either a horse person or you weren't. And I wasn't. Sure, I enjoyed riding and was comfortable riding any trained horse. But I could go months without riding and not miss it. Dominic, on the other hand, had a passion for horses.

It didn't take long for Dominic to find an appaloosa named Lightning. He also hit it off with Simon, the tall, forty-something ranch hand Mrs. Stodder had mentioned. Simon had rubbery, weathered skin and was thin except for a middle paunch. He rubbed his goatee as he and Dominic discussed topics like temperaments of different horse breeds, the latest vaccinations, and training techniques.

Not interested, I wandered from stall to stall, petting horses. A friendly Palomino whinnied at me and once I started to scratch behind her ears, she didn't want me to stop. I was a sucker for a pushy mare and asked Simon if she could be assigned to me. Simon nodded, adding that her name was Goldie, short for Golden Nugget.

Soon others from our group arrived.

The three "Ts," Tiana, Tiffany, and Tanya, were mentors and best friends. Tiana explained how they signed up for a worthwhile activity each year as a way to have fun together and do something good for the community. They styled their hair alike in French braids and wore shocking pink cowboy boots with rhinestones. Despite their appalling taste in boots, I immediately liked them.

Cars started arriving, spilling out young campers. Several were siblings, like Evie and her brother Joshua, and Mikayla and her sister Rayanna. Alicia, Vonda, and Tabi looked around ten years old, and they all jumped excitedly, asking a zillion questions about the horses. As more kids gathered, it was hard to remember all their names.

But I recognized Lindsay right away from Josh's description and was delighted we were going to be partners. Her black curls bounced as she showed me her scrapbook of horse pictures and a photo of herself from a few years ago on a carnival pony. I laughed when she made a horse's whinny sound, falling immediately in love with this fun little girl. I really owed Josh big-time for matching us up.

The other kids were great—well, except for Rocky, who wore baggy, ripped jeans and swaggered with a "gangsta" attitude. He was the oldest kid, about twelve, I'd guess, and nothing was good enough for him. He complained that the air stunk, the stables were too dusty, and the horses were boring.

While Simon, with some help from Dominic, matched the kids with horses and showed them where to stow their gear, I kept watching the road for Josh. What was keeping him? I knew he liked to sleep in late, but when it came to his commitments, he was always early. So why the delay?

I turned back to help with the kids. I was assuring Rocky that no one had ever died from the odor of manure when another car pulled up.

I'd never seen the brown Toyota before, but the little girl and her older brother getting out of the car were dear friends.

"K.C.! Zoey!" I whooped joyfully and rushed forward. "I didn't know you were coming!"

"Sabine!" Zoey cried out as she reached me first and gave me a big hug.

She was taller than I last remembered and mature for a first grader. Had it been only a month since our last meeting? K.C. looked as average as ever, I thought fondly. He had a way of blending in and not being noticed. When I first met him at school, he'd been homeless, living out of his car and working in the evenings so he could send extra money to Zoey, who was in foster care with her aunt. He wasn't any older than me but already had huge adult responsibilities.

"It's great to see you!" I hugged K.C. "Are you still living with Thorn's family?"

"Yeah."

"How's that working out?"

"Cool." He grinned. "Although yesterday was weird—serving food in a food kitchen that I used to eat at. I saw some dudes who used to hang on the streets with me. The perks of living with a minister's family."

"Sounds like things are working out for you."

"Well, sleeping on a bed instead of in my car is good."

"So what brings you here, where you'll have to sleep on the ground?"

"Zoey, of course." He ruffled the curly dark head of his little sister. "She signed up for this ride months ago, and that's all I've heard whenever I visit her. When she found out there weren't enough teen mentors, she conned me into coming."

"You ridden before?"

"No." He groaned. "I must be insane."

"You're the best brother ever." Zoey hugged him. "Come on, let's pick a horse!"

K.C. gave a helpless shrug, then allowed Zoey to drag him over to the stables. Having them along would be fun. K.C. was easygoing and hardworking. He had such a quiet manner, people didn't usually notice him—although I suspected he wished Thorn would notice him. Not that I saw that happening. K.C. was like an earnest puppy, while Thorn was more like a piranha.

I heard another car and looked up to see Josh's sports car churning dust and gravel. At last Josh was here. I hadn't wanted to admit, even to myself, that his delay worried me. I had a flash of him blindfolded as he balanced on a high wire over a sea of sharks and felt like I should warn him about something, but my feeling was vague. Besides, he didn't believe in psychics. Maybe I was just projecting my own guilt for planning to break up with him. Was I one of the sharks in his treacherous sea? Still, just because we were breaking up didn't mean I would stop caring about him. We'd always be friends…I hoped.

The sports car jerked to a stop and the driver's door flung open.

"Sorry I'm late," Josh said in a rush. "But Evan and I had to pick up a last-minute mentor."

At the mention of Evan's name, I frowned. He stepped out of the passenger seat, walking in that macho "I'm an athlete" way, and shot me a sour look. I glared back just so he'd know I wasn't any happier to see him. We'd long established our animosity. Josh had warned me Evan was coming, and I planned to keep my distance.

"Sabine, you look great." Josh came over and brushed a kiss across my lips. "I owe you a huge thanks."

"Huh?" I glanced over my shoulder, hoping Dominic hadn't seen the kiss.

"She told me you'd be surprised."

"She? Who?" Now he had my full attention.

He pointed to his car, where a girl stepped out of the back seat.

What the hell was Jade doing here?

# 26

Jade was smiling.

I wasn't.

Once again, my half-sister suckered me into lies and there was nothing I could do without causing an ugly scene. Josh was so happy to have another teen mentor that he practically danced in his boots. And to hear Jade talk about her horse experience, you'd think she'd been born in a stable and teethed on rawhide.

How had this happened? I'd left Jade sleeping and hadn't told her about the ride, yet here she was in Josh's car. Unbelievable!

"Your boyfriend is just the sweetest guy," Jade said with a giggle. "He made a special trip just to pick me up."

"Glad to." Josh smiled at her with this dopey expression.

"I just *loooove* horses and kids. Being here is a lucky accident." She flashed this flirty look at Josh and then at Evan. Both guys were hanging on her every gesture.

"Lucky for us," Josh said. "Now we have almost as many mentors as kids."

"How did you meet Jade?" I asked.

"I overslept and was running late," Josh told me. "I wanted to let you know, only when I called your cell phone, your cousin answered. Soon we were talking horses and she told me about her riding lessons and the blue ribbon she won for barrel racing. When she mentioned her volunteer work teaching handicapped kids to ride, I asked her to be a mentor. I don't know why you didn't think of it, Sabine."

"Yeah, cuz," Jade said sweetly. "Why didn't you ask me?"

"I didn't want to you to feel obligated because of

our...um...relationship," I said through clenched teeth. "It'll be rough sleeping outside. I didn't think you'd like camping."

"You thought wrong."

"Obviously."

I glared, outraged that she'd answered my cell phone and was invading yet another part of my life. I was even more furious when I recognized the embroidered jeans, yellow Western-styled shirt, and brown half-boots she was wearing. My clothes! I seethed inside, especially remembering her snotty comment about not wanting my castoffs. She didn't want them when I offered, but stealing them—now that didn't faze her a bit.

I was tempted to call her something crude, but there were kids around.

A shrill whistled blasted.

"Come on over, everyone!" The ranch hand Simon whistled again from a high perch atop the back of a wagon.

Abruptly, I turned from Jade and stomped over to the assembling riders.

"Now that everyone's here," Simon declared, rubbing his fuzzy goatee, "let's get this ride started. But first we need to cover some basics. No running or sudden moves because you'll spook the horses.

Do not go behind the horses, you'll get kicked. Always mount from the left side. And though it may sound cliché, do exactly as Simon says."

A few kids chuckled while the older riders groaned.

Then we were taken over to the horses and shown some basic techniques; mounting, proper reining, and how to flow with the horse's motion.

Afterwards, Josh read off a list that matched mentors with riders. Naturally K.C. was paired with his sister Zoey. Evan was matched with a shaven-head boy named Mario. And Josh took two kids: his namesake Joshua and Joshua's younger sister Evie.

Josh paired up Dominic to Rocky, the gangsta grouch, and I wondered if this was because of Dominic's ability to handle difficult kids or revenge. Had Josh guessed something was going on between me and Dominic? But how could Josh know? I was still getting used to it myself. And I'd been careful not to give our secret away. If anything, I went out of my way not to be alone with Dominic.

More pairs were announced. I already knew who I was matched with, so I didn't pay much attention. When Josh said Lindsay's name, I started toward her.

But the next name he said wasn't mine.

"Jade will be Lindsay's mentor," Josh stated.

Lindsay skipped over to Jade, waving her horse scrapbook.

"Sabine, you're with Melina," Josh said as if nothing was wrong. Then he continued on with his list and turned away from me.

I stood there stunned until Melina tapped me on the back and shyly introducing herself. She was waif-like with light-brown pigtails, olive skin, and round thick glasses.

"I'm eleven," she said shyly. "Well, almost eleven. I never ever rode a horse, at least not a real one. Do they bite?"

I glanced over at Lindsay, who was smiling with Jade, and felt mad enough to bite. Lindsay had no fear of horses. But Melina was so rattled with fears, she didn't even want to pet her horse. I tried to calm her—not that it worked.

Melina was a squealer, I soon found out. She squealed when her horse snorted. She squealed when the horse swatted at flies with its tail. And she let out a shrill scream when I hoisted her up on her horse—which spooked several other horses. It took all my strength—and Dominic's soothing talent—to settle the horses down.

By noon we were finally ready to hit the trail, with Simon in the lead and another ranch hand, a sturdy-looking brunette named Wendi, holding up the rear.

Our pace was so slow a lame turtle could have passed us going backwards. When the trail was wide enough we rode in pairs, so I was able to talk to Melina. I don't know how many times I told her to relax and loosen her grip on the reins. Her nervousness made me nervous.

We rode for a few hours, pausing whenever someone had a problem. Rocky fell (jumped?) off twice. Melina had to go to the bathroom—which meant ducking behind a thick bush. Then there were the wild-animal sightings, which usually turned out to be rabbits.

By the time we took our first break, I was exhausted.

We tethered the horses to trees and stretched our legs. Snacks were handed out to the kids and a few more kids had bathroom breaks. There was some grumbling about that, but it wasn't like the pack horse could cart along a Port-O-Potty. Josh told the kids that they were getting the authentic outdoor experience.

I watched Dominic from across the clearing,

brushing down his horse and giving him a snack, too. Carrots, it looked like. I considered joining him, but Josh came over to me with his two kids: Joshua (now dubbed Little Josh) and his sister Evie. They seemed like great kids, not at all nervous with the horses, and surprisingly polite. Every other word from their mouths was please or thank-you.

Melina wandered over to talk to some other girls, so I took the opportunity to ask Josh why he'd matched Lindsay with Jade. "You said I would get Lindsay. Why did you change your mind?" I asked, hands on hips.

"I didn't." He furrowed his brow. "You did."

"No way!"

"You think Lindsay's a brat and didn't want to be with her."

"I never said that!"

"That's what I heard."

"That's an outright lie. Did Evan tell you that? You know better to believe him—he'd do anything to cause me trouble."

"It wasn't Evan."

"Then who?" I demanded.

"Jade." Josh frowned. "But why would your cousin lie?"

Because she wants anything—and anyone—that's mine.

But I couldn't admit this to Josh. If he knew war was brewing between me and my "cousin" it would cause too many questions.

I shrugged it off. "Jade's idea of a joke," I said.

"I don't see you laughing. Want me to talk with her and—"

"No!" I shook my head. "I'm happy riding with Melina. She's a sweetheart."

"Really?" He glanced across the clearing. "Wasn't that her squealing?"

"She's exited about riding. But just so you know, Lindsay is great too, definitely not a brat. I would never say that."

Then Simon whistled, our cue that the break was over.

Ironically, it took longer to get all the kids back on their horses than it took for the entire break. But finally we resumed riding, and I relaxed in the rhythm of Goldie's stride. She was a good mount, not too rough or in a hurry.

Tree branches swayed overhead, some so low I had to duck. The weather cooperated by not raining, only steel gray clouds that blocked any chance of sun. Climbing up curving hillsides in a slow straggling line took a while. For about an hour the riders laughed and talked a lot, until the trail grew steeper and everyone had to pay close attention to the trail, avoiding bushes, rocks, and holes.

At first it was just an uneasy feeling—a prickly sense of eyes watching me.

I shifted in my saddle to look around, but saw nothing unusual; only the other riders and none of them were staring at me. Must be my imagination, I decided. Then I settled back into the ride.

The feeling hit me again as we crossed through a grassy meadow. Stronger, piercing like a laser beam—so intense I couldn't shake it as my imagination. Trusting my horse to follow in line, I closed my eyes and looked for answers.

Immediately I got a vision of a dark-brown horse mounted by a shadowy rider. An older man wearing a cowboy hat. He sat comfortable in his saddle, controlling his horse with only one hand on the reins. A yellow ring flashed from his hand and there was a pulsing, crimson-black aura. I sensed he was looking at me.

Was this vision real or my imagination?

I tensed in my saddle, peering out at trees and wild brush. It would be easy for a skilled rider to follow our slow-moving group without being seen.

Shivers rose on my skin. I sensed he was out there, invisible among dense foliage.

Who was the rider? I wondered, adding a footnote of "if he really exists."

I mentally called out for Opal. At first there was no reply then I heard static with fuzzy mind shapes, like an out-of-focus TV. Then the shape sharpened into tawny skin under a white jeweled turban.

*Keep vigilant,* I heard her say.

"Is someone really following me?" I asked wordlessly.

*There is a presence of danger close by.*

"I had a vision of a rider on a brown horse."

*When someone has forsaken their humanity, they are no longer alive in spirit and have nothing to gain or lose.*

"What are you trying to tell me?"

*The rider with blood on his hands will not stop until there is more death.*

"More death? Do you mean this rider killed someone?"

*Remember the details that ring true to your vision.*

Details that ring true? Did she mean "ring" literally? I thought back to Jade's house and the glint of a gold ring on the killer's hand. "In my vision of the rider, he was wearing a ring, too. Is it the same man?"

*There is no need to ask questions when the answers resonate inside you. Even when you travel without your body, there is a heavy weight of responsibility. You cannot live between two worlds without risking self.*

"I don't know what you mean!" I shouted in my head. "Who is the stalker and what does he want? There are innocent kids here, and I want to keep them safe."

*Danger follows the soul witness.*

Her words sunk in, terrifying. There was a static sound in my head and I felt her pull away. I opened my eyes to the bright shock of daylight.

My horse plodded steadily beneath me, but shook her mane as if sensing my fear.

I tried to make sense of Opal's message. She'd hinted that my astral experience was real and that someone was dead. Jade's mother? Then why wasn't Jade upset? If it had been my mother, I'd be hysterical with grief. I would definitely not be on a campout with a bunch of people I didn't even know.

If Crystal had been murdered, that meant both Jade and my father had lied. Lies from Jade weren't anything new, but why would Dad lie to me? The only reason I could think of was that he might be protecting someone.

Did that mean he knew the killer?

Could my own father be an accomplice to murder?

I didn't want to believe this, but suspicion was a germ that grew and spread poison. I tried to remember details of my astral experience. I'd been spying on Jade, then slipped into the next room where I saw Crystal and her killer. She'd trusted him and he'd seemed to care about her, too. The flowers and candy hinted at a budding romance— until he took the ribbon off the candy box…

I wished it had been a dream—but I was afraid it was real.

And somehow the killer had found out about me.

I was the "soul witness."

# 27

I could tell by Goldie's sudden increase of pace that we were near the lunch stop. And minutes later, I saw the clearing. The ranch crew had driven ahead and set out a table with cold cuts, salads, French rolls, and cookies. There was an ice-filled tub with drinks. We were scheduled to rest here a full hour before heading out again.

After I fixed a plate, I looked around for a place to sit. There were several fold-up tables with chairs. Josh sat with some mentors and kids at a center table, while Dominic wandered over to a log and sat alone. Everything in me wanted to go to Dominic, and when he gestured for me to join him, I started forward. Then Josh called my name and waved me over to his table. I stopped, feeling like a wishbone being pulled in two directions.

Josh or Dominic?

My heart chose Dominic, especially since I needed to tell him about my vision of a rider following us. He wouldn't think I was crazy. But what if I was wrong about the vision? I hated to warn Dominic about something that wasn't true. Even if it was true, it could have been a warning of the future. Until I knew there was really someone out there, I didn't want to alarm anyone.

So I hesitated, unsure where to sit. Having lunch with Dominic might give away our relationship. Josh thought I was his girl, and until I could let him down gently, I'd have to pretend we were together. Still, choosing Josh might hurt Dominic.

So I sat with K.C.

When I glanced over at Josh's table, Jade was squeezing in between Josh and Evan. Figures. I rolled my eyes and bit into my sandwich.

K.C. helped his sister Zoey cut her sandwich in half, while Zoey talked excitedly about seeing a deer. I listened a little before my gaze drifted over to Jade. I couldn't figure her out. Studying her like this, she didn't seem so terrible. The kids and other mentors liked her, and she was friendly to everyone except me. This shouldn't bother me—but it did. I mean, the "half" part of our sisterhood should count for something. Instead it was the dividing line separating us. I didn't expect friendship but resented what I classified as her "bitchitude." Would it kill her to be civil to me? I thought, watching her fold two paper plates into a cowboy hat for Lindsay. Other kids begged for a hat, too. But it was Evan she folded the next hat for, fluttering her lashes as she leaned close to place it on his head.

We were so different, yet alike, too.

Differences: Jade laughed too loud, preferred bottled water to soda, and flirted like a slut.

Similarities: No cheese on her sandwich, mustard instead of ketchup, and she idly twirled a strand of her hair around her finger.

I caught myself twirling a curl of my hair and stopped.

It was freaky to realize we shared half of the same genes. But the half she shared didn't include a psychic ability. That came from Mom's side. I tried to use this now, concentrating to pick up any visions about her future or past. But I got nothing, as if her aura concealed her secrets.

There were so many questions I wanted to ask. "What's really going on with you? What are you doing here? Why did you sound scared by that phone call last night?"

She had been scared; I'd picked up on that emotion. But scared of what or who? Did she know her mother was dead? She sure wasn't acting like a daughter in mourning. If I'd lost one of my parents, I'd be a wreck. But Jade was having fun flirting with the guys.

I just didn't get it.

The other confusing thing was Jade's friendship with Lindsay. Jade showed genuine warmth toward Lindsay. I'd seen her hugging the little girl—like she actually possessed a heart. But it could all have been an act.

I had a gut feeling that whatever was going on with Jade was somehow tied in with my vision of murder. It was time to get some answers. Whether Jade liked it or not, we were going to have a "sisterly" chat.

But getting her alone proved difficult.

She and Evan were suddenly inseparable. Evan Marshall's nickname at school was "Moving-on Marsh" because he went through girls like they were recyclable. It was only one of his despicable traits. With Evan hanging around Jade, I couldn't get near her. I'd have a better chance once we set up camp tonight into girls' and guys' tents.

The next part of the ride seemed to drag on for days, although in actuality it was only a few hours. We journeyed deeper into the woods, climbing curving rugged hills that seemed to go on forever. The kids grew cranky and tired, complaining about sore legs, sore arms, and achy butts. There wasn't much talking, only groans over the clomp-clomp of horse hooves.

The kids literally cheered when we reached our campsite.

Like the lunch spot, a truck had come in advance and the crew had set up. There were a dozen khaki-colored tents, an outhouse, several fold-up tables, benches, a fire pit, and a grill where a ranch hand was flipping burgers. Almost all the comforts of home, minus electricity and running water.

"Hamburgers!" someone shouted.

"Hot dogs!" another kid rang out.

"A bathroom!" one of the "Three T" mentors rejoiced as she made a mad dash for the Port-O-Potty.

There was a flurry of voices and activity as everyone dismounted and then led their horses to a portable corral where they'd rest for the night. Simon shouted out orders and I worked with the other mentors to keep the kids under control.

The kids lined up for burgers, hot dogs, chips, and drinks. Melina took her plate to a table with other girls her age. Glad to be free of responsibility, I looked around for Jade, hoping to finally corner her and get some answers.

Only she wasn't anywhere in sight.

I asked Lindsay and she pointed to a tent. "She went in there," she said.

The tent was on the girls' side of the camp and was next to the tent I'd be sharing with Melina and some of her girlfriends.

"Jade?" Bending over, I strained to see through the netting.

There wasn't an answer, so I unzipped the opening flap and peeked inside. Piles of rolled sleeping bags and backpacks—but no Jade. Discouraged, I started to leave until I noticed a cloth doll perched on one of the sleeping bags.

I sucked in a sharp breath—it was the same

Raggedy Ann doll I'd spied in Jade's bedroom while astral traveling. If the doll was real, then everything else must have been, too. Memories came back in a rush—the shouting, terrified cries, and brutal twisting of ribbon around Crystal's slim neck. It really happened. I couldn't pretend it was a dream, not anymore—especially if my vision about the stalker was true.

Ohmygod, Crystal was dead.

I started shaking and felt tears in eyes.

Wiping my cheek, I glanced sadly at the doll's painted smile.

I couldn't keep this to myself now that I had proof it wasn't a dream. I spotted Dominic at the end of the food line, bending over to say something to Rocky. I came beside Dominic and gestured that we had to talk. He nodded, then spoke to Rocky for a moment before following me out of camp.

When I explained about the doll and my vision of a shadowy rider, he listened intently. When I finished, he asked, "You think the killer is following you?"

"I don't know…probably…someone is out there. I can feel it."

"If you believe it, that's good enough for me. I'll take care of it."

"How?" I asked, biting my lip. "Are you going to do something dumb?"

"Would I ever?" he joked.

"Are you going after him?" When he didn't answer, I had my answer and I felt scared inside. "Don't go out there alone. The guy could be a murderer."

"If it's the same guy. But how could he find out about you? Your body wasn't there, so there's no way he could have seen you."

"Unless he's psychic, too," I guessed.

Dominic shook his head. "Too much of a co-incidence."

"Nona says there are no coincidences, only moments of destiny."

"If someone is following us, I'll show him his destiny." Dominic tightened his fists, his expression grim.

"Don't go after him," I begged.

"Not my first choice. There are other ways of getting information." Dominic gestured to the woods around us. "I have friends who can find out for me."

"Your animal posse?" I guessed.

He chuckled. "Not what I'd call it, but you have the right idea."

"Tell me if you find out anything."

"I will," he promised.

I moved closer to him, reaching out to grasp his hands. It was so natural to blend together, leaning against his hard chest and feeling his rough fingers brush softly against my hair. He murmured that everything would be okay, and I believed him.

The next few minutes included some serious kissing. Enough said.

Then I waited for Dominic to leave first so we wouldn't be seen together and headed back to camp.

\*     \*     \*

I hadn't been to a camp since I was little, and had almost forgotten the lighthearted fun that happened around a campfire. The air was chilly and the night dark, only lit by the blazing fire. We huddled close to the fire, a few kids dangling wires with marshmallows.

Simon strummed a guitar and started a singalong that began "I'm being swallowed by a boa constrictor" and urged everyone to repeat "a boa constrictor, a boa constrictor." When he got to the line "Oh, no, he swallowed my toe," he hammed it up by taking off his shoe and sock and wiggling his toe. By the time he was up to "Oh, heck, he swallowed my neck," everyone was laughing.

I was laughing, too. So I didn't notice Josh had come over and scooted behind me on a bench, until he slipped his arm around my shoulder.

"Want to take a walk?" he whispered.

"Now?" I looked around to see if Dominic was watching.

Josh's warm breath tickled my neck. "Sure. No one will miss us."

Wrong, I thought, looking across the fire at Dominic. He'd been laughing a moment ago, but now he was scowling. I searched my mind for a good excuse to refuse Josh.

"I shouldn't leave Melina."

"She's not even sitting near you. She's over with her friends."

"But I'm in charge of her and I take that really seriously."

"You think I don't? But my kids are fine here with the other mentors. Come on, Sabine. We haven't been together in ages."

"That's your fault. You've been busy with secret magician stuff and your friend Grey."

"Don't blame Grey. He's been cool and helped me through the initiation process, but that's over now. I'm a full member."

"Of what?" I pointed to his arm where a long-sleeved shirt covered the tattoo.

"I can't talk about it. I'd rather talk about us." His voice softened. "I've missed you."

"You're with me now," I said evasively.

"Not alone. Let me make things up to you…privately."

"That's not a good idea."

"Why? Don't you want to be alone with me?"

"Of course," I lied. "It's just that…"

"What?" He wrinkled his forehead. "Is something going on, Sabine?"

I couldn't tell him, not with so many people around. He'd be both hurt and humiliated. Still, not telling him was hard, too. How was I going to get out of this?

Ironically, it was Jade who saved me.

Jade jumped and waved to get everyone's attention. The perky way she sprang into the air made me wonder if she really was a cheerleader. She offered to tell ghost stories.

Excited kids raised their hands and shouted, "Yes!"

"Have you ever heard about the Scavenger Bride?" Jade asked with an evil cackle.

"No!" the kids shouted. "Tell us!"

"I can't go now," I told Josh. "I want to hear my sis...cousin's story."

He seemed to accept this, and I breathed a relieved sigh.

Then we sat together and listened to a spooky story about a girl on a scavenger hunt who ends up in a haunted attic and is chased by the ghost of a skeletal bride. Jade's tone held just the right mix of dramatic horror, causing shivers and squeals. When she was finished, there was hushed silence. Then everyone erupted in clapping.

This started others telling spooky stories.

Evie, the small girl Josh was mentoring, came over yawning and told Josh she wanted to go to sleep. She was in my tent, so I offered to take her. Relieved to get away from Josh, I walked over to my tent. Once Evie was settled, I stepped out of my tent just in time to see Jade slipping into hers.

Finally—a chance to talk with her. I hurried over to her tent and peeked inside.

Jade was not happy to see me. "What do you want?" she asked coolly.

"To talk about...about something serious." I

ached with sympathy for her loss. "I have to warn you."

"I'm warning you to get out."

"She's dead, isn't she?" I said softly.

"What! How did you…?" Jade's face paled. "Get the hell out of here!"

"No, Jade." I dug my heels in and refused to budge. "I know what happened…and I want to help. Please listen to me."

"I don't want to hear anything you have to say."

"Jade, I was there…I saw him. How can you pretend everything is okay?"

She faced me defiantly. "You don't know anything about me."

"But you know a lot about me," I said quickly. "That's why you pretended to do everything that I did; cheerleading, the school newspaper, fencing. It's all a lie, isn't it? You've never done any of those things."

"You're full of crap!"

"I only just found out about you, but you've known about my family for four years. Is that how long you've been spying on my life?"

"Get out!" She reached out forcefully and shoved.

I reeled back, catching the edge of the tent flap to stop from falling over.

"Wait, Jade! If you know about me, then you know I see things sometimes. That's what I have to tell you—"

But she'd zipped up the tent, shutting me out.

Real slick, Sabine, I told myself in disgust. Instead of gaining her trust, I'd pissed her off. No way would she listen to me now.

A short while later, Melina and the other girls sharing my tent showed up. There was giggling and pillow tossing and trips to the Port-O-Potty, but finally the kids settled down.

My body throbbed with weariness as I sank into my sleeping bag. I didn't even bother to change my clothes. I'd thought riding a few times on Stormy would prepare me for this trip—wrong! I hadn't been on a ride like this since I was a little kid, and my muscles ached painfully. I closed my eyes and sank quickly into sleep.

*Wake up!*

I heard the shout and wasn't sure if it was from outside or inside my head.

But I was instantly awake, fumbling for my flashlight and running out of the tent. Confused, I expected other people to be running around, too.

But in the fading light of the dying fire, I saw no one else.

Then I heard footsteps—coming from the tent next to mine.

Odd—the tent flap was wide open. Why wasn't it zipped shut?

I ran over to the other tent and shone my flashlight inside. A man! Bending over Jade's sleeping figure. His hands reached out—and I screamed.

Everything happened at once.

Jade jumped up, girls started screaming, and the intruder scrambled backwards, knocking me over as he burst out of the tent and fled.

In that moment when I fell back, my flashlight had shone directly in his face.

My worst fears were realized when I recognized him.

The man who strangled Crystal.

# 28

Jade told everyone it was a bear.

"But you saw him—" I started to argue.

"I know, and it was horrible!" she cried to the excited crowd around us. "The bear would have attacked me if Sabine hadn't chased him away. Thank you so much, Sabine! You saved my life."

What was I supposed to say to that?

Simon came over to thank me, adding how strange it was to have a bear sighting this low in

343

elevation. Others gathered around to praise me, too. I was completely tongue-tied—and terrified because of what almost happened.

Maybe I owed Jade her lie about a bear, because I'd led the killer to our camp, putting everyone in danger. And Jade had nearly been killed. I had no doubt that the killer had mistaken Jade for me. Everyone said we looked alike, and with her hair pulled back in a ponytail like it was now, we looked more like sisters than ever.

"We'll talk in the morning," I whispered to Jade before I returned to my tent.

She didn't argue.

Dominic found me early the next morning, not at all fooled by the "bear" story.

"The horses would have let me know if there was a bear," he said simply.

So I told him the truth. I thought he'd be angry about Jade blaming it on a bear, but he surprised me by praising Jade for her quick thinking. If the others found out there was a murderer following us, the ride would end abruptly and the kids would be sent home disappointed.

"I should have gone after him when you first told me," Dominic said. "I'll make sure this doesn't happen again. Keep an eye on Rocky while I'm gone."

"You can't just go off alone. He's too dangerous," I argued.

"I can be dangerous, too."

There was no reasoning with him, and then he was gone. I was too anxious to eat my pancakes and bacon. I noticed Jade, looking pale, didn't have an appetite either.

I caught her eye across the table and mouthed, "Talk. Now."

She nodded with the weariness of someone surrendering in a war.

Moments later we were alone in my tent.

Jade sank cross-legged on the vinyl floor and covered her face with her hands. "I'm so tired of all of this."

"Me, too. Talking will help."

"I never planned to tell you anything but after last night…" Her voice cracked. "You saved my life."

Shaking my head, I knelt beside her. "You saved my life. He was after me but went to you by mistake."

"Not a mistake. He tried to kill me because of what I saw."

"You were asleep, you didn't see what happened. But I did."

"Impossible." Her eyes widened. "You weren't there."

"I was," I insisted keeping my voice low so no one outside could hear. "I saw you sleeping with your rag doll. Then I went into the next room. They argued and he grabbed the ribbon off the candy and…" I couldn't say it. Poor Jade…her own mother.

She was staring at me with disbelief. "I don't understand…how could you have seen anything? Were you hiding in a closet or peeping through windows?"

"No. My body wasn't there—just my soul," I said. "I was astral traveling."

"No, really. How did you know?"

"I just told you. I'm psychic, like my grandmother."

"Psychic?" she echoed. "No shit. Dad never told me."

"He wouldn't," I said wryly. Then the horror of this situation hit me and I added softly, "I'm so sorry about your mother."

"My mother? What about her? And why are you looking at me like that?"

"Don't make me say it," I whispered hoarsely.

"Say what? There's nothing going on with Mom. She's fine."

"No, she isn't." I started shaking. "I watched him…take the ribbon…and strangle…"

"Ohmygod!" Jade grabbed my hand and clawed my skin. "The ribbon? I found a ribbon on the carpet right afterwards but I had no idea what happened…ohmygod!"

"It was so fast…your poor mother—"

"NO! Not her!" Jade shook her head furiously. "I talked with Mom on the phone two nights ago."

"But she was in the room next to yours. It was dark but I recognized her dark red hair."

"The hair was a wig and the room was rented to my mom's friend. My mother is okay—but Darlene isn't."

"I don't understand. Who's Darlene?"

"I better start from the beginning," Jade said, pushing out a deep sigh. "That night I went to bed early after cheerleading practice—I was not lying about being a cheerleader…well, maybe not head cheerleader."

Then she explained how her mom had this "little problem" with gambling and was off on a casino binge. Sometimes she stayed for weeks. And to help pay bills, she rented out rooms to some "independent business women."

Jade didn't say it, but from her disapproving tone I had a feeling these women did more than sleep in their rooms. I remembered the first time I'd spied on Jade's house and saw the man coming out early in the morning with handcuffs in his back pocket. I bet the handcuffs weren't used in any official way and the guy was a "customer," not a cop. That would explain why so many cars were parked in Jade's driveway.

Deep in sleep, Jade had no idea what was happening in the next room until she heard someone shout for her to get up. She opened her door as a figure ran past carrying something bulky. She followed and heard the front door close. Curious, she opened it and saw a man slam his car trunk. He turned and saw her, illuminated in the porch light.

"I didn't get a good look at him, but I thought he was going to come after me, only he panicked when a car drove by and he drove away," Jade added. "I wasn't waiting around for him to come back and toss me in a trunk, too. So I grabbed some stuff and stayed with a friend. I watched the news, hoping to hear the guy was arrested. But nothing. Mom came home a few days later, and when I told her about Darlene, she freaked and said I had to hide somewhere far away."

"Why Nona's house?" I asked.

"What could be safer? No one knows about my bio dad, and it wasn't like I'd be welcome at his house anyway. Your uppity mother would have kicked my ass out in a minute. But your grandmother was cool, welcoming me like real family, and I felt safe—until Mom called. She told me our house had been broken into while she was shopping. The only thing missing was a note on the fridge with my name and your grandmother's address. I knew the bad dude was after me, so I jumped at the chance to hide out on horseback. But he must have followed me."

So Jade was right—the killer was after her. When he saw her in the porch light, he assumed she was the only witness. But she hadn't even seen his face.

I had.

And I'd seen it again last night.

Now it was my turn to explain, which was embarrassing because I had to confess to spying on Jade.

"I was curious about you," I told her, reddening. "But I only drove to your house once. The other times—going there out of my body—were an accident. When I fell asleep, this whole astral travel thing happened, and I ended up in your room."

"While you were sleeping? Impossible!"

"It sounds weird, but I was there in spirit. I saw you sleeping with your rag doll."

Jade blushed. "My stepdad gave me Annie."

"Was his name Douglas?" I asked.

"Yeah, how did you know?"

"I saw him at a séance. He looked like a hippie, wearing love beads and a tie-dyed shirt. He was worried about you and asked for my help."

"He did?" she asked softly. Like she was starting to believe me.

"He loves you very much," I told her. "It takes a lot of energy for a spirit to pass on a message, and he did it to help you."

The tough edge around her crumbled and real emotion shone on her face. "Is he okay? Can I talk to him now? Is he with us?"

"I'm a psychic, not a medium," I tried to explain. "I see ghosts sometimes, but it's not something I can make happen. Still, I know he's fine. Everyone is on the other side. It's our world that has ugly stuff…like killers."

We stopped talking for a moment, sitting

in the tent across from each other. I couldn't tell what she was thinking, but I sensed we were a little closer. When she wasn't spewing bitchitude, she was okay. Maybe not someone I'd want for a best friend, but someone I could grow to like.

"So what do we do now?" Jade finally asked, shifting away from a glint of sun coming through a tent window.

I shook my head. "I don't know. Maybe we should tell Simon."

"No. He'd report it to the cops."

"At least the kids wouldn't be in danger."

"But my mom would be. You probably guessed she doesn't exactly play by legal rules, although don't you tell Dad. He'd cut off our money if he knew half of the schemes Mom gets involved in. Promise you won't tell him."

"Like I promised him not to tell anyone about you?" I countered. "Look where that lie has led us."

"I know," she said sadly. "I hate lying, too. It wasn't like this when Daddy was alive. He worked hard and was always there for us. He even got Mom to go into a gambler's anonymous program. I thought he was my real dad until he died—then Mom dropped that bombshell. I hated my bio dad at first. But then he was so sweet that I started to care about him."

"And hated me instead," I guessed.

"Not just you—your sisters, too." She laughed wryly. "But mostly you."

"Thanks," I said half-teasing.

"Well, you looked a little like me yet had this great life. I wanted what you had—so I asked Dad for riding and fencing classes. I joined the school newspaper. It's a small school and nobody else wanted to be editor anyway," she added. "I even dyed my hair blond for a few weeks, but my friends hated it so I went natural. Weird how we can have similar faces but I suck as a blond and it looks great on you."

"Wow, was that a compliment?"

She laughed. "Okay, I'll admit I've been a little hard on you."

"Only a little?" I offered a smile of truce. Then I sobered again, remembering why we were having this private talk. "We still need to figure out what to do. I think we have to tell Simon and the others in charge."

"That won't be necessary," a male voice interrupted. There was a swish of netting pulled aside and Dominic stepped in the tent. "That dude is gone."

# 29

Dominic quickly explained to us what he'd found out. He'd followed the guy's tracks to a tree where there were hoof prints and other signs of a horse being tethered. "I'm sure it was the guy who tried to attack you," he told Jade. "There were more hoof prints and I found the trail he'd left when he rode away. I followed for about a mile, until it was obvious he was long gone. He must be miles from here by now."

"Thank goodness!" I cried.

"But what if he comes back?" Jade asked nervously.

"He wouldn't try anything that dumb. Still, I'll keep watch."

Jade nodded, looking relieved. But I felt a sick sense of dread and knew it wasn't over. Since I was the only real witness, I had some hard decisions ahead. If I didn't go to the police with the truth about that night, the murderer would go free and might kill again. But I'd be humiliated and embarrass my family if I reported a murder I witnessed while out of my body. No one would believe me.

After the campout I'd figure out what to do.

Simon's piercing whistle split the air, and we all headed back to mentor duty. Only this time the ride took on a new, improved personality for me. Jade wasn't my enemy anymore. It's strange how seeing her smile at me lifted my spirits. I guess deep down my half-sister mattered to me all along. Maybe that's why I'd spied on her, not out of anger, but because I wanted to know her.

She seemed to want to know me too.

At the next break, she excused herself from the group of guys hanging on her and came over to sit on a log next to me.

"That day we met wasn't the first time I saw you," she admitted. "I was at the Santa Clara County Fair and you were part of a fencing group. You wore this cool silver costume."

"I remember that. It was nearly two years ago and I was so nervous. It was my first performance with Foils and I was afraid I'd fall or drop my saber."

"But you didn't. You were amazing! That's when I decided to be just like you. I took fencing lessons, only I never really got the hang of it."

"No award-winning competitions?" I teased.

"Okay, so I may have exaggerated a little. I'm more into gymnastics."

We talked like this for a while, comparing likes and dislikes. There were still a lot of rough topics we avoided. It was easiest talking about Dad, especially when it came to his terrible lawyer jokes.

"What's wrong with lawyer jokes?" Jade quipped.

I knew this one. "Lawyers don't think they're funny and—

"—nobody else thinks they're jokes." Jade finished.

We laughed, switching to some "how many lawyers does it take to screw in a light bulb" jokes. When Melina and Lindsay, who were eating granola bars near us, asked what was so funny about light bulbs, we laughed harder.

Simon's whistle blasted and we hustled to help the kids back on their horses.

The next few hours were peaceful, with no warning visions of shadowy riders. Aside from some minor complaints from the kids, they were doing great—better than some of the mentors. Even Melina was more confident on a saddle and hadn't squealed all day. With brief splashes of sunshine and crisp mountain air, it was hard to believe there was any danger. Tomorrow, I'd deal with issues like killers and breaking up with my boyfriend. But for now, on this beautiful Saturday afternoon, I was enjoying myself.

We made it to the lunch spot ahead of schedule.

Jade waved me over to her table, but Evan was glued to her side so I shook my head and sat with K.C. again. After we were done eating, Jade came over and hooked her arm through mine. "Come on, we have to talk private," she whispered.

Once we were confident Melina and Lindsay were safe with other mentors, we found a trail that led down to a bubbling stream. It was a steep climb down, with large boulders to climb over and slippery ribbons of water trickling off the hillside into the stream. Once we reached the bottom, there was a large granite plateau reaching over the stream. It made a great place to stretch out and enjoy the sun.

"So what did you want to talk about?" I asked her.

"I've been thinking about your being psychic and having that séance and astral traveling." She pushed red bangs from her eyes. "Can you teach me?"

"Being psychic is just something I am. I have no idea how to teach anyone else. Most of the time I can't figure out my own abilities."

"Could your grandmother teach me?"

"I don't know…maybe. Why are you so interested?"

She glanced down, her feet dangling over the edge of the slab and a few inches over the rushing water. Then she looked back at me with moist eyes. "I want to see my dad once more—I guess he's technically my stepdad—just so I know he's okay."

My heart ached for her, and I assured her that her stepfather was fine. But she wasn't satisfied and kept after me to show her how to contact the other side. I told her I didn't know to explain anything. But she was persistent. Finally I promised that after the ride, I'd talk to Velvet and arrange a séance for

Jade. I thought that would satisfy her, but no—she wanted me to demonstrate astral traveling.

"It's not like a circus trick. You'd only see me lying down like I was asleep."

"Please, you can check in on Darlene's murderer to make sure he's far away," she wheedled, clearly used to getting what she wanted. "I'd feel so much safer if I knew he wasn't after me."

"It won't work in the daylight," I argued.

"Can't hurt to try."

Exasperated, I threw up my hands and gave in. I doubted anything would happen anyway. I told her I needed complete silence while I meditated. She nodded eagerly, even finding a thick pine branch and sweeping off pebbles from the rock so I wouldn't get poked in the back. I cleared my mind, took cleansing breaths, and called on my spirit guide for assistance. I didn't see Opal, but I sensed her comforting support.

I lay back on the rock, closing my eyes. Then I shut away all thoughts and focused on leaving my body. It felt good to relax with the sound of bubbling water and sun warming my skin. I hadn't slept well last night, so I was tired. Tension flowed away.

I was surprised to feel myself lifting. Through closed eyes I watched as I floated above myself. I looked down on a large granite rock and two girls far below. It was so surreal; I didn't quite believe it was happening. But a part of my brain urged me to go on, to complete the task, so I surrendered myself to the light.

That same buzzing echoed in my head as I hurtled forward, colors and shapes flashing by at a speed beyond human sight. Only I didn't get the same sense of traveling to a far distance as I had before. It was almost like I was circling in the same place, waving through treetops and zooming down into a dark fog. As I neared the darkness, the shapes clarified and I saw a man. He crept through prickly bushes like a cougar creeping up on his unknowing prey.

Gold flashed on his finger and there was a dark emptiness in his eyes.

The killer.

Only instead of riding away as Dominic told us, he must have circled back and spied on Jade and I. He followed us out of camp—and was now sneaking up on us.

Panic was like lightning jabbing my essence. I fluttered like a bird with damaged wings spinning out of control. My emotions were a cyclone, tossing me with fear. I couldn't reach out to stop him. Like before, I was wretchedly helpless. And he was stealthily creeping closer, around the corner of the streambed, hidden by boulders. He reached into his pocket and pulled out a sharp knife.

"Jade!" I tried to shout. "Run!"

That didn't work, so I swept back toward my body, looking around desperately. What could I do? There had to be something. If I returned to my body, I might be able to run, but he was closer to Jade and she wouldn't have a chance. Seconds ticked by and I couldn't think of any way out.

Two girls against a murderer with a knife—not very good odds.

I hadn't been able to save Darlene—what could I do now?

*Pay attention*, a voice ordered in my head.

I looked back at Jade, who was bending over my "sleeping" body. She wasn't paying any attention to the subtle footsteps behind her. I scanned the area for a weapon—anything! There were a few river rocks within reach and the branch Jade used to sweep the rock. There wasn't a quick escape route either. We'd have to go back the way we came. I didn't see an easy way across the rushing stream other than swimming through icy water or leaping high to grab a low-hanging branch that stretched across the water from an ancient oak on the other side.

The killer kept moving, slowly, holding the knife between his teeth as he pulled himself up a boulder several yards down from the plateau below Jade.

There was no more time. I made a quick decision—slamming back into my body just as the killer slipped the knife back in his hand and reached out—

"Move, Jade!" I shouted, and this time I had a voice.

Jumping up with such force that I pushed Jade out of the way, I grabbed the pine branch and flung it at him. He cried out. His knife fell from his fingers, clattering down rocks and splashing in the water.

He swore and lurched forward, but I was already grabbing one of the rocks I'd spotted earlier. I flung it at him. I missed, but when he ducked I scrambled out of his reach.

Jade had done as I'd hoped and jumped for the low-hanging oak branch in a springy gymnastic move, swinging up and mounting the heavy branch like a gymnastic bar. She scooted across the branch, then down the tree and took off running. She was out of the killer's range—but I wasn't.

"Who the hell are you?" he demanded, reaching down for his knife, which had only landed in shallow water.

I didn't wait around to answer, scrambling to climb up the steep bank. My hands grabbed onto roots and I inched upward. But I wasn't fast enough. He was closing in and I could feel the wind from his knife as he swiped at me.

So close! Too close!

I climbed faster, higher, but he was coming up behind me with his knife—

There was a sickening thud and a hoarse cry.

I looked down as the man crumpled to the ground, his head spilling blood.

Jade held a long stick as thick as a baseball bat; the tip dripped blood.

"Ohmygod…is he dead?" Jade's face was ashen. She tossed aside the bat and met me halfway. She pointed to the unconscious man. "I know that face! I've seen him before—with Darlene."

"You said you didn't know him."

"I didn't get a good look that night, but now I remember. I don't know his real name, just that she called him Prince Charming because he was the most romantic guy she...um...dated. He came to the house a few times and gave her candy, flowers, and wrote romantic poems. But she said he was kind of strange and overly possessive."

"So he made sure no one could have her," I said sadly.

As we clung to each other, shaking and crying, there were shouts and suddenly Dominic was there. He explained that he noticed we were gone and had been searching for us when he heard a cry.

Dominic checked the man's vital signs and said he was alive, but there was no compassion in his tone.

Catching a dangerous attacker caused a lot of excitement at camp. We tried to shield the kids, but they knew something serious was happening when a ranger arrived. He ran a quick check on the attacker's ID and told us his name was Mick Hatha and there was a warrant out for him; apparently he had a long record of violence against women. His injuries weren't bad and he was starting to wake up when he was handcuffed and led away by the ranger. Jade and I had to go along, too, to give our statements.

We urged Simon to continue on with the ride and not spoil the kids' fun. Although Josh, Dominic, and Evan wanted to come along with us, Jade and I insisted they stay for the kids. The ride must go on.

Josh followed us to the ranger's pickup. "Are you sure you'll be fine?"

"Yeah. Don't worry."

"I'm sorry we didn't get to spend more time together."

"Me, too," I said for completely different reasons.

He bent over to kiss me and I moved so it was only the faintest brush against my lips.

"Bye, Josh," I said sadly. "Make sure the kids have the best trip ever."

"I will. You and your cousin take it easy."

"We will." I paused, glancing over at Jade who was waiting for me in the pickup. "By the way, Jade isn't my cousin. We're sisters."

# 30

I'll never forget the stunned look on Dad's face when he came into the sheriff's station and saw Jade and I together. But he quickly recovered and slipped into lawyer mode. He sorted through facts and accusations, insisting we be truthful. Jade agreed. Then, before I could tell my side of the story, she announced that Mick Hatha was a murderer and that she'd witnessed him killing Darlene.

I was grateful to be off the hook. Only a few people would ever know who the real witness was.

When the sheriff checked Mick's car (parked by Manzanita Stables where he'd left it after he'd stolen a horse), they found bloody evidence, which eventually led to a confession and the location of Darlene's body.

It was early Sunday morning by the time Dad dropped off his two eldest daughters at Nona's. "Let's not tell your mother about this," he said as I stepped out of his car.

But I shook my head. "No more secrets," I insisted.

"Sabine, be reasonable."

"If you don't tell Mom, I will. Jade is my sister and I'm not going to hide it."

Jade came over, her expression close to tears, and hugged me like a sister.

Dad wasn't quite so appreciative, but he didn't argue as he drove away alone. While I watched his car lights fade down the driveway, I knew things would be okay. This was part prediction and part knowing my mother wouldn't throw away her home and family so easily. It would be rough for a few months, but my parents would work things out.

On Sunday I slept in until noon—luxuriating in my own bed without any wayward astral trips. Jade, who was staying a few more days with us, was still asleep.

After making me my favorite hot breakfast of powdered-sugar French toast, fresh fruit, and orange juice, Nona invited me to tell her about my weekend. That took a while.

When I finished, she wrapped her arms around me. "You did good, honey," she said.

"You think? I made a lot of dumb moves."

"Not telling anyone about the killer wasn't smart, but I understand your reasons. You were very brave and I'm proud of you."

"Thanks. And you're looking really good. What's with the new hairstyle?"

She patted her head. "I had my hair cut and colored. I need to look good for client meetings. Business has picked up so much now that I'm better, I may promote Penny-Love to Executive Love Assistant."

I laughed. "She'll love that."

"Now I think it's time to attend to that other matter."

"What?"

"Giving Jade her séance. It's the least I can do for her saving your life."

Then Nona hustled off to call Velvet.

\*     \*     \*

It was another moonlit night and a small group was gathered in Dominic's loft over the barn: Nona, Jade, Dominic, and myself. Candles flickered around the darkened room and a scent of sandalwood incense swirled in the air. It was a small séance, but Velvet assured us there was enough energy with two psychics in the room to easily open the door to the other side.

We sat quietly in a circle reverently while Velvet said a prayer and called forth a protective white light. I was keenly aware of Dominic sitting beside me and tried to shut out my feelings for him and concentrate on the séance. There was a peaceful calm in the room, a receptive energy as if the spirits were eager for us.

Then Velvet called out for Douglas.

And just like that, with no flashes or drama, he was there.

Jade cried out joyfully as he sent her messages through Velvet. I watched in awe, so happy for Jade. I was a little surprised when another spirit arrived, and instead of talking to Velvet, the woman appeared to me. I'd seen her once before—Dominic's mother. So I relayed her message to Dominic, calling him "Nicky" and urging him to continue taking classes and studying hard.

I was so absorbed in these wonderful reunions, I didn't notice any change in the aura. I didn't hear the footsteps that climbed up the steps. I didn't notice a shift in the air as the door opened. And I had no clue someone stood beside the door, spying on us.

Until he stomped into the room.

"Josh!" I gasped.

"What the hell is this?" He stared at the candles, incense, and crystals. His eyes widened, then narrowed. "A séance? Sabine, how could you?"

"What…What are you doing here?" My heart thudded with dread as I faced him,

"I asked Grey to stop here so I could give you this card." He held up a pink envelope. "I missed you and couldn't wait to see you. Ha! What a jerk I was."

"I'm sorry. I meant to tell you—"

"Liar! You've been lying to me since we met."

"Don't shout at her." Dominic came beside me protectively.

"I'll shout if I want because I'm furious. You're all sick! Deluding yourself and everyone who believes you. This is exactly what's wrong with the world." He pointed around the room. "Charlatans!"

"Josh, calm down." I had no idea what he was ranting about and saw he was upsetting my grandmother. I reached for his arm to lead him outside, but he shook me off.

"I suspected things were shaky with us, but I always trusted you. I admired so many things about you. Only you lied to me. You're into the occult, the work of the devil. You practice the very things I detest. And I can never forgive that."

Then he ripped the pink card to shreds and stormed out of the room.

Stunned, I stood there until Dominic pushed me forward. "Go. Talk to him."

So I ran down the stairs and grabbed Josh's arm just before he reached the blue Mustang convertible where a blond guy waited.

"You have to listen to me," I told Josh. "I know it's over with me but I want you to understand. We weren't doing anything wrong."

"Give it up, Sabine," he practically spat out. "Just leave me alone!"

"Need some help, Josh?" The blond guy in the car stood and turned toward us.

"No, Grey, I can handle this," Josh was saying but I hardly heard him.

I was too busy staring at Grey. Ohmygod! I'd seen him before, only he'd been wearing a long jacket and fleeing the scene of a crime.

"Hang on, Grey," Josh called out. "I won't be long."

"Your friend!" I whispered to Josh. "He's the one who vandalized Trick or Treats!"

"What? No way! He'd never go to that wicked shop."

"He trashed the shop. I saw him."

"You can't prove anything. You're only accusing him because he's my friend. I can't believe you'd sink that low, Sabine."

"That's not it…" My words trailed off. What was the use? It was my word against Grey's, and Josh would never believe me. I couldn't change his mind any more than he could change mine. We'd grown apart and there was no going back. The best I could do was end it all with dignity. "Josh, I'm sorry. It was wrong to hide my real self from you."

His expression changed, the anger fading in an instant to regret. "You can change, Sabine. I'll forgive you if you stay away from séances and voo-doo magic."

"Goodbye, Josh," I said quietly.

"Come on, Sabine! Be logical. It's all wrong; you have to see that. You can't honestly believe psychics are real."

"Yes, I can," I said simply. "I am one."

When he walked away, this time I didn't stop him.

Watching the car blur down the driveway, it hit me that it was really over with Josh. Instead of being sad, I felt uplifted and free. I had a vision of Josh with a dark-haired girl wearing a sparkly magician's assistant outfit and knew he'd be fine.

As for me? I was already fine.

I had a new sister, a great family, a healthy grandmother, good friends, and a special guy who understood me and loved me just the way I was. What more could a girl ask for?

I turned around, my heart soaring as I hurried back to the loft.

To Dominic.

*The End*

# Don't Die, Dragonfly
## LINDA JOY SINGLETON

After getting kicked out of school and sent to live with her grandmother, Sabine Rose is determined to become a "normal" teenage girl. She hides her psychic powers from everyone, even from her grandmother Nona, who also has "the gift." Having a job at the school newspaper and friends like Penny-Love, a popular cheerleader, have helped Sabine fit in at her new school. She has even managed to catch the eye of the adorable Josh DeMarco.

Yet, Sabine can't seem to get the bossy voice of Opal, her spirit guide, out of her head . . . or the disturbing images of a girl with a dragonfly tattoo. Suspected of a crime she didn't commit, Sabine must find the strength to defend herself and later save a friend from certain danger.

978-0-7387-0526-2
288 pp., 4 ³⁄₁₆ x 6 ⁷⁄₈                                                    $6.99

## Last Dance
### LINDA JOY SINGLETON

Sabine can't wait to show off her new boyfriend at the upcoming school dance, but she's also worried about her grandmother, Nona, who's suffering from a fatal hereditary illness. The only cure lies within a remedy book, lost long ago.

Determined to save Nona, Sabine goes to Pine City to visit a distant relative who may have clues. But there's someone else clamoring for Sabine's attention: a fifty-year-old ghost named Chloe who's been appearing in her dreams. Celebrated by Pine City every year on the anniversary of her tragic death, Chloe has become a town legend. Despite death threats and missing the school dance, Sabine must use her psychic skills to solve the mystery surrounding Chloe's untimely demise . . . and lay her soul to rest.

978-0-7387-0638-2
312 pp., 4 ³⁄₁₆ x 6 ⁷⁄₈                                    $6.99

# Witch Ball
## LINDA JOY SINGLETON

Sabine is finally starting to feel accepted at her new high school. She's friends with the popular girls and even has a cute boyfriend. But Sabine also has a dark secret—she's psychic, and was forced to leave her old school after she accurately predicted the death of a football player.

Volunteering with her friends to help run the psychic booth at their school's fundraising carnival, Sabine discovers too late that the fake crystal ball she meant to bring has been mysteriously switched. In its place is the strange "witch ball" she locked away after her grandmother refused to have it in the house. Now the haunted witch ball's predictions are coming true, and Sabine must solve the mystery before its final prediction—her own death—becomes a deadly reality.

978-0-7387-0821-8
264 pp., 4 ³⁄₁₆ x 6 ⅞                                    $6.99

## Sword Play
### LINDA JOY SINGLETON

"Help her," insists the spirit of Kip, the jock from her old school who died in a car accident. But his cryptic message is the last thing on Sabine's mind as she packs up to move back home. She's not happy about leaving her friends, her boyfriend, and Nona who's gravely ill, but won't dare challenge her mother's orders. Besides, Sabine's also harboring hope that she can become close to her family again.

Reuniting with her fencing club brings back painful memories of getting kicked out of school and betrayed by her former best friend Brianne, now too entangled with her boyfriend to notice Sabine . . . unlike Kip's ghost who continues to nag her about someone in trouble. But Kip died alone, so who needs her help? As Sabine researches the events of that tragic night, she pieces together a shocking revelation—knowledge that leads to a dangerous duel with a surprising foe.

978-0-7387-0880-5
264 pp., 4 ³⁄₁₆ x 6 ⅞                                    $6.99